Seeking Salamanca Mitchell

A NOVEL

Kenji Jasper

HARLEM MOON
Broadway Books / New York

Published by Harlem Moon, an imprint of Broadway Books,
a division of Random House, Inc.

SEEKING SALAMANCA MITCHELL. Copyright © 2004 by Kenji Jasper.
All rights reserved. No part of this book may be reproduced or
transmitted in any form or by any means, electronic or mechanical,
including photocopying, recording, or by any information storage and
retrieval system, without written permission from the publisher. For
information, address Broadway Books,
a division of Random House, Inc.

This book is a work of fiction. Names, characters, businesses,
organizations, places, events, and incidents either are the product of the
author's imagination or are used fictitiously. Any resemblance to actual
perons, living or dead, events, or locales is entirely coincidental.

PRINTED IN THE UNITED STATES OF AMERICA

HARLEM MOON, BROADWAY BOOKS, and the HARLEM MOON logo,
depicting a moon and a woman, are trademarks of Random House, Inc.
The figure in the Harlem Moon logo is inspired by a graphic design by
Aaron Douglas (1899–1979).

Visit our website at www.harlemmoon.com

First edition published 2004

Book design by Jennifer Ann Daddio

Library of Congress Cataloging-in-Publication Data
Jasper, Kenji.
Seeking Salamanca Mitchell : a novel / Kenji Jasper. — 1st ed.
p. cm.
1. African American men — Fiction. 2. Adult child abuse victims —
Fiction. 3. Washington (D.C.) — Fiction. 4. Single mothers — Fiction.
5. Ex-convicts — Fiction. 6. Criminals — Fiction. I. Title.

PS3560.A67S44 2004
813'.6 — dc22
2003069704

ISBN 0-7679-1675-1

For my Mom and Grandma Sally,

for my Dad, his father, and The

Lone Ranger, for J-Thrill and

Rob J, Millery Polyné and my

biggest sister Kendra, those

who've taught me the realest

lessons in love and loyalty

AND FOR DEBORAH COWELL

She who found paradise

through rugged lands,

Her entrance paid with shards

from a broken promise.

I decided to live.

That is the ever-elusive

point: the point that eludes us all

too often until the grave.

—NICK TOSCHES

Part One

1.

If the soul of our neighborhood were the sun, then I would have been on the planet Neptune, close enough to circle its comings and goings, but never in range of its true warmth. My face, a younger version of my father's, was as familiar to people as a grade school classmate's, remembered more from repetition than from any real noteworthiness.

I received only casual nods and flippant waves as I passed by the dudes that mattered, the ones who had their names and streets silk-screened onto summer shirts so that everyone would know where they hailed from. Keith McEwan and his cousin Monty owned the hoops and backboards outside of the Greenleaf Projects. Phaedra Sanders and her little brother, Justin, were two of the founding members of a crew called the Capers, who in 1991 had turned a private party into a bucket of blood at the Southwest Navy Yard, just because the host wouldn't let them in. And I can't forget Tremayne Jackson, who'd robbed the local Safeway supermarket at gunpoint a record five consecutive times in the same year without getting caught. Then he got hit with a case for boosting bras for his girlfriend out of the Pentagon City Victoria's Secret.

But I was not like them. Because I was my father's child. I was never allowed to wander the night, never permitted to forge bonds with those whose parents let them play unsupervised until the early morning. Most of my sanctioned outings were to my best friend Stevie's house, over on the safe side of the Waterfront's solar system.

I knew nothing of risk, nothing of true danger, other than the echoes of screams and gunfire that came to my window while I slept like a baby. I was neither the hero of a rap lyric nor one who had been schooled in the code of the streets. But I wanted to be. And the desire to obtain something is often all that one needs for its acquisition.

"And now he don't even know where she is," Kevin said with a chuckle to his audience, the twelve or thirteen impatiently waiting regulars planted in the chairs that stretched along the length of the barbershop and salon.

It was a Saturday afternoon, the last of the four in August 1995. The heat that summer had been so insufferable that one city garbage truck had gone up in flames after its fuel tank spontaneously exploded.

"Ain't that some shit, Junior?" he asked, turning his pug nose in my direction.

"Yeah," I mumbled, less focused on his words than on the melody crawling through my skull. I needed to write it down. But it'd have to wait. There was too much going on.

"Goes to show you how little folks care about marriage nowadays," I replied. "That shit is supposed to be sacred."

The smell of oil sheen lingered heavy in the air as the signal came in clear on Kevin's stereo. D'Angelo's "Brown Sugar" made me think of my lady as I let out a yawn. I knew everything Kevin was about to say.

"I remember back when I was a young buck," he began, as if on cue. Roger and Edward, his co-owners and partners in crime, went completely quiet.

Roger, a burly brown-skinned man with a thin line of a goatee, busied himself putting the finishing touches on a high-top fade his customer was in desperate need of losing. And Edward, a peanut-colored kid with a huge Afro, kept to shaving an older man with a glob of cream and a pearl-handled straight razor. Barely five six, he leaned on the balls of his feet for the best positioning.

The other barbers' silence had less to do with the heads and necks before them and more with the hope that Kevin's rambling might end more quickly without their encouragement. But like love, that hope was a blind one.

"See, I was shackin' up with this Indian girl down in Georgia. And I had just got out the marines. And you know one day the girl come out at the dinner table, with her two kids sittin' there eatin' a bucket a chicken I done bought wit' my check, and the bitch tell me that she got a husband in jail for murder. I been feeding and clothing her yellow ass and some other nigga's got the keys to the house I'm payin' the note on? Hell, naw! And so you know what I had to do—"

It wasn't that we didn't like the story. We loved it. The first time I'd heard it, at ten, I'd laughed so hard that I had almost torn a belly muscle. The second time, two months later, it had been equally entertaining. But as the years went on, its frequency rose like waves when the tide was in, from the age of the Afro to the low-taper era, through the temple-taper dynasty, and finally down to the current, even Steven present.

As my eyes watched Kevin's lips flap like wings—his once buckshot-nappy hair relaxed into an S-Curl greasier than Aaron Hall's—my mind was still locked on the message on my voice mail, with that melody humming just behind it. What the hell could Salamanca Mitchell have been talking about on that voice message?

"Ben," the recording of her voice began, "call me as soon as you can. I've got something I *have* to tell you."

I hated when people did that, leaving open-ended messages instead of getting to the point in the space provided. Why not say it there and then, instead of leaving me with one more thing to obsess about? I was already a balloon swelling with nerves. Her words were the pin that could have popped it.

But I couldn't complain for too long when it came to Salamanca Mitchell. She had been my guiding light through six months of post–high school existence. I loved her more than anyone and anything. Anything, that is, except for my piano, Cinnamon.

There had been a time in boyhood when all I wanted in the world was to be in love. At eleven, it seemed as if love, romantic love, that kissy-touchy-feely New Edition/Bobby

Brown/Boyz II Men–inspired love, was everywhere I looked. Or perhaps it wasn't really love, but the objects and providers of that love: the girls, those alluring and omnipresent beings that seemed to reside in every square inch of my shoebox of a world. But the young ladies I craved were far beyond my years, far more mature than the prissy barrette-headed things that were still wearing training bras and learning about their periods. My fantasies didn't wear those frilly dresses with the ruffles at the shoulders, nor did they have to run all the errands with their mothers because they couldn't be left home alone.

My obsessions could be found wandering the halls of high school, that ultimate edifice of cool and acceptability that I would not enter for nearly half a decade. Every other thought was a longing for what they possessed: full, buoyant breasts; plump asses; the scent of oil sheen on freshly pressed and permed manes; the gleam of gold door knocker earrings bearing various names and pseudonyms alike. But all the while I knew I couldn't have them, even when one of three legs argued otherwise.

So I had observed them from afar, hawking them from the second story of the house my parents nearly broke their backs to make the mortgage on. They were always out there, chattering among themselves at dusk before dinner, pecking their nice-guy male friends on the cheek before heading over to rub up against their crack-dealing, gold chain–sporting, designer-nylon-sweatsuit-in-the-middle-of-the-winter-wearing boyfriends, most of whom worked the corners around K Street and 3rd SW.

But alas, the closest I had gotten to my high school Mrs. Robinson was the upright piano on the eastern side of our living room. It took years for me to even look at that heavy wood box on wheels, which had arrived just before my eighth birthday. She had sat lonely and neglected until I was ten and three-quarters, until the night when I dreamed of myself seated before her, attempting to play back the first melody my mind had ever created.

I woke up after three in the morning on a Thursday and started pressing down on keys, getting to know the silent stranger with whom I'd never shared a word, before my grumbling parents sent me back to bed with a warning. Soon after, she, my Cinnamon, became the closest thing to femininity I could get my fingers on. And pretty soon it felt like she was all I'd ever need.

I gave her a good stroking whenever she needed it, bearing down on her keys and pedals until they were slick with perspiration. We took midnight strolls, through sound, on the printed pages before me. We made love, in melody, each time I took a seat on the antique bench that was her companion. She gave me erections, hard and stiff, just to undoubtedly prove that those tramps I'd lusted after were nothing but paper dolls in comparison.

So, at eleven, I had begun my first serious relationship. And I worshipped her even more than I had those sophomore and junior hoochie mamas who had once tickled my fancy. And she *was* enough, for a long time.

But then I kissed grape Bubble Yum–flavored lips in the parking lot of the Capper Projects. Lakiah Murphy's breasts were fleshy balloons filled with warm water, the warmest things in the world on that February night in 1993, when the cold from the freshly fallen snow was hydrochloric acid, eating through the steel toes of my snow boots.

It was spring of the same year when Carmen Matthews

(aka the Catwoman) took me into her mouth at her boyfriend's apartment during fourth-period physical science. Carmen was the finest they came: brown feline eyes, almond-colored skin, and hair done up in Shirley Temple curls. But it was her sculpted apple of an ass that was the true bait for suitors like myself.

Her man at the time was thirty years old, and white. She was sixteen, which made him a pedophile and her in need of someone to fill that father figure void. The role of daddy had been vacated after an undetected cancer took the man to the other side just before she turned seven.

"We need to get out of here," she had scribbled on a pink party flyer, before folding and passing it to me underneath her desk. My right knee sank into the phatness of her behind as it protruded from the seat in front of me. An hour later she gave me my first nonmanual orgasm in less than forty-five seconds. My virginity went about ninety seconds later.

I liked Carmen. But I was still in love with Cinnamon. There was nothing better than pumping her with long and thick thrusts of notes and rests, sharps, naturals, and the best crescendos she'd seen since we'd inherited her from that dying cousin whose name I never quite caught. Cinnamon had shown me how to put my dreams on paper and how to tune my developing voice into an instrument all its own. I could never have loved anyone more than her, until I met Salamanca.

She had that tiny Z-shaped scar between her lower lip and chin, the geometrically perfect eyes bubbling over with a rich ebony, the taut and slender thighs that had earned her an anchor position on the Holy Cross track team. She was beyond beauty, beyond any woman I'd ever known.

And she made me smile at a time when I'd forgotten how to make my lips curl.

From then on, Cinnamon had to learn her time and place. She was still loved and cherished. But she couldn't hold me. She had no hands to touch my face, no lips to plant against flesh that shuddered from the touch.

I needed Sala in my soul. I needed Cinnamon to breathe. So they ended up having to share.

Now, there were a lot of boys my age who wouldn't have admitted to the kind of love I had for either. Nineteen was that age when you felt like you could stop bullets, that nothing could alter the course in life that you, the all-important *you*, chose. But I knew what I felt and would deny it to no man, living or dead.

2.

Alfonse Mitchell, Salamanca's father, was one of the city's movers and shakers, a man who always dressed his success. His suits were accessorized with matching hats, coats, and sometimes canes. He always had the latest-model car the earliest, and he carried an inch-thick knot of hundreds and fifties at all times, just to prove that the car wasn't all he could pay for.

He bought and grilled burgers and ribs for everyone at his annual Fourth of July cookout. He coached the Boys Club basketball and football teams on the weekends before he went in to work. And because his restaurant, Sally

Helen's, was *the* soul and seafood spot on U Street, he had access to people and resources the other local powermongers could only dream about.

Everyone stopped in for a meal at Sally's: city councilmen, CEOs, cops, robbers, muckraking reporters, rappers, singers, and anyone else that could afford the prices. His spot was the den of all dens, the lair of a lion who knew how to pack his place every night of the week. He even ran a carryout on the rear quarter of the place that stayed open until two every day except Sundays, when the place was closed altogether. Because, as he had told me once while swigging scotch straight from the bottle, "Sunday is always the Lord's day."

The Old Man always hired kids from the neighborhood, giving them priority over the hundreds of others who filled out applications each season. And when Dad died Mr. Mitchell asked me to be one of those kids, though I wasn't exactly sure why.

"I always liked your father," he had told me in his office on the first day we'd met. "He gave me a pass once. Caught me speedin' a week after my license expired and he let me go. I know it was against the rules. And I told him I knew he had to write me up. But he just smiled and tore up the ticket. Didn't even say a word. It's a shame that the Lord took him home."

That had been my father. Dad gave everyone a chance, no matter who they were or what they'd done. But if you made the same mistake, he was always there to catch you on your second turn.

It's ironic that Dad made the same mistake twice himself, flashing lights without a siren during rush hour, hoping to catch a group of bad guys with speed and stealth instead of a blaring noise. He and his partner, a bowlegged, freckle-faced half Irish/half Italian named Tony Flynn, both bought the farm when they collided with a city bus. Speed and stealth had brought them nothing but a free ride to the pearly gates and an at-large collar for the still living cops to apprehend.

I learned a lot about Alfonse Mitchell during that first meeting as my eyes rolled leisurely about his office. The desk was cluttered with yellowed receipts and pink phone messages. The eggshell-colored walls sported plaques and citations from *Dossier*, the *Washingtonian*, the *Times*, and the *Post*. A gleaming metal frame held the image of a young girl with braided hair. This was Salamanca, his only daughter.

He had learned the restaurant business at a joint called Suburban Seafood in Southfield, Michigan, not long after an honorable discharge from the marines in 1973. There were ten years between when he began busting suds in the back to running the front office. But during that decade there wasn't a thing he didn't commit to memory in crystal-clear detail.

But steering someone else's ship wasn't where he'd wanted to be, particularly not after he learned that his pretty twenty-something wife would be giving him a child in nine months' time. And he had wanted that child, his first child ever, to have everything. Thus, Salamanca Mitchell, as an idea, had sparked the kindling that would become his inferno of an empire.

"We miss him a lot, sir," I said, responding to the mention of my father's passing. "But I guess I'm going to get to the point because I know you're a busy man. You said on the phone to come see you if I needed a job. And I need a job."

His black-brown eyes took on a supernatural quality as they put me, all of me, under their microscope. He saw all there was to see: flesh, bones, blood, and the soul he needed a shard of if I was going to serve him.

It was simple for me. Good pay, free meals, and the warm feeling of bringing something home to my mother, who was working every hour possible at the Department of Energy downtown so that there wouldn't be time to miss the man who had lain next to her. With a job, I would be the man of the house, the provider, something more than the surviving offspring of a man so noble that his only error had been dying too soon.

Mitchell let out a sigh of contemplation, then leaned forward in his burgundy leather chair to offer his answer.

"I think I can do that," he said.

He'd started me out on the cleanup crew, his own starting position at Suburban Seafood a generation earlier. I washed the dishes, cleaned the counters, and handled the garbage for $6 an hour. I ground myself to nothing for every penny, remembering what Dad had told me about first impressions and letting the boss know that you were serious about what you did, even if you weren't.

I got my first promotion a month later and joined the server staff, hustling drinks, appetizers, and entrées to finicky folks who were almost always a little too impressed with themselves for being able to afford a $50 meal. Yet I still did my best to charm them, flashing the Aquafresh smile the Old Man chiseled onto every employee's lips before he was allowed to work the floor.

It was hard work for me. Flat feet and hard shoes were a one-two punch for a kid who always had school in the morning. The starched shirts buttoned to the neck didn't help matters, either. But the tips were more than worth it. And after thirty days I got another leg up. That was when I got the feeling the Old Man had bigger plans for Benjamin Baker. It didn't take long to prove me right.

The Old Man summoned me to his office late on a Saturday night, right after my shift ended. I thought it was because I'd broken three plates and a glass on a dare, having tried to carry a washtub across the restaurant floor with a single hand. The gate had been $10, and I'd lost it a quarter of the way across the room. Everybody on staff thought I was in for a pink slip. Sally Helen's had a strict reputation for order and perfect service, a reputation that I had foolishly put in jeopardy for the sake of a ten-spot.

I too was pretty sure the ax was going to fall. And I was a little scared. But when he called me to his office I went in like a man, just the way Dad would have wanted me to.

"You doin' a real good job, Ben," he remarked, reclining against that tacky leather chair. He wore a navy vest and pants with a black-collared dress shirt and a matching-patterned tie. His bald Hershey's Kiss of a head had been shaved clean. He was sixty with few wrinkles, having had his first child just past the big four-oh.

"Thank you, sir," I'd said.

I needed the job. Sure, Dad's benefits and Mom's salary made ends meet. But I was the new man of the house. And I had to act like it. Getting fired over a $10 bet was a disgrace not only to myself, but also to the man who had shown me how to be a man.

"I overheard you talkin' to Maurice about money," he said without a trace of the expected disdain. "He told me you said you wanted to see about working some overtime?"

At the time all I wanted was a DAT recording deck so that Stevie and I could professionally record all of the songs we'd been working on. But they were too expensive, the better part of $1,000, far beyond the C-note in savings I had in the bank. But it would have been a big thing for our music to have a real studio-quality sound.

Plus, I wanted something to call my own. All of the equipment was Stevie's: *his* instruments, *his* headphones, *his* blank tapes. If I could get this piece, this final piece in our technical puzzle, I'd have that much more of a stake in our musical partnership. And I wouldn't feel like Stevie's charity case from the wrong side of Waterside Towers.

Maurice's girlfriend, Shana, lived a few blocks from me. So every once in a while Maurice and I rode home together. He seemed like a good guy, about my height and build, with a nose like a bird's beak. He was usually quiet, even passive. But the keloided bullet scar on his shoulder told me he hadn't grown up picking daisies.

I'd mentioned the recorder to him once or twice, dreaming of how great it would be for Stevie and me to be able to make good tapes to give out to the managers and promoters we'd met at shows. I'd told Maurice that I really wished something would drop out of the sky and make it so. And now the manna had fallen from Sally Helen's heaven.

"Yes, sir," I said in response to the Old Man's question. "Things are a little tight right now."

"Ain't they always?" he said with a matter-of-fact sneer.

"I'm from Rocky Mount, North Carolina, Ben. And down there times is always tight for niggas like us."

I nodded, unsure of why I was getting the history lesson or why he'd slipped into Ebonics with me when he usually spoke the king's English.

"So how many hours you need?" he asked.

"As many as I can get, sir," I replied eagerly, knowing that if he said yes, he'd work me to the bone and hoping that the money would be enough to make it worth it.

"Hmm," he began. "Well, I could give you an extra two hundred for the week if you help with something off-site."

"Yeah," I said excitedly. "What is it you need me to do?" His answer didn't matter. I was in.

"You know my house, right?" he asked, putting a flame to the Lucky Strike hanging from his lips. I nodded. "Come by tomorrow at three and we'll talk about it."

"You got it," I said. I would've hugged him if he were the hugging type. Instead I shook his hand, enduring a grip that could have crushed stone. Then I danced my way toward the time clock, anxious to encounter the opportunity that was only a day away.

3.

"Hello," the girl said, speaking more articulately than anyone I'd heard on our side of M Street. She opened the door and took a step toward the screen, less than a foot away from my anxious face. "May I help you?"

It was three in the afternoon. A family of blue jays was nesting in the elm tree at the corner of Half and M streets. Rare Essence's "Six in the Morning" played from a parked car down the block. And I had finally laid eyes on the legend.

Monte Burrough from Greenleaf had been calling Salamanca Mitchell his own for years, dropping her name in lists of the finest things alive, right below Vanessa Williams and Halle Berry. But the windows in Monte's wallets were without her image, providing no hard evidence that she was more than just a name he happened to know.

Monte had played the clarinet with Stevie and me in advanced band. So the three of us often shot the breeze on the way back to the neighborhood. And Salamanca almost always made her way into the discussion.

"I was hittin' it from the back before her moms came home," Monte had boasted, though later he would be exposed as a fraud by his own drunken cousin Larry at a Labor Day barbecue.

Salamanca had fans among the knuckleheads as well. Miguel Vides alleged that he had been the girl's junior prom date, though she was barely a freshman at the time. Even Stevie had once implied that the fruit had been within his grasp. The number one star of their moist dreams.

"Uh . . . yeah," I stammered, my first words at our first meeting. "I'm here to see Mr. Mitchell. I'm Ben."

"Oh," she replied pleasantly. "How are you?" She opened the screen door and extended a graceful hand, and I shook it, impressed that the Old Man had schooled her in proper social etiquette. Most of the girls I knew would have stepped away from the door and assumed you knew how to walk through it. "I'm Salamanca."

"Sala-what?" I asked, coating jittery nerves with false confidence.

"Sa-la-manca," she enunciated, slightly irritated. She had obviously encountered the confusion one time too many. "It's a part of Spain. Daddy visited there when he was in the marines." I nodded, having run out of small talk to stretch the moment.

"Well, come on in. He just called to say he was on his way," she informed me. I took a seat on the rust-colored couch, and she eased into the matching chair across from it. "Would you like to have some tea with me?"

Tea? I was from southwest D.C. I knew Kool-Aid, Rock Creek grape soda, and juice in plastic bottles sealed with foil. But I didn't know anything about tea. Yet I couldn't resist that smile.

So I sat. She went into the kitchen to microwave, stir, and pour, returning with two steaming cups, each fitted with the perfect amount of sugar and milk. I took a look at the images scattered around the room.

The pictures were all of her, at various stages in her seventeen years, save for the gigantic family portrait suspended above the soot-heavy fireplace. The other woman in that image, Mrs. Mitchell, I later learned, had reverted to her maiden name of Green and remained in Detroit after father and daughter's departure nine years before.

All of the furniture was close to the same honey brown: the sofa and chairs, the rectangular glass table, the set of wooden cases filled with all kinds of books and old magazines. The walls were olive green. The carpet was chestnut. And there were figurines, plaques, and trophies all over, all bearing the Old Man's name: marksmanship, football, basketball, swimming, kendo. Mitchell was a Renaissance man underneath his countrified demeanor. This was *his* place. His daughter just lived there.

"You know they have tea three times a day in London?" she said, as if it should have amazed me.

"Yeah, you see 'em drinkin' it all the time in those English movies."

"What do you know about English movies?" she asked.

I knew almost as much about movies as I did about music. It was all that Dad and I used to do on the Saturdays he had off. He'd take my little brother, Henry, and me down to Union Station or to the Uptown, at the top of the city, and we'd catch whatever was playing that week, armed only with tubs of artery-bursting popcorn and tumblers of drink that should have come with their own urinals.

So I knew about the kinds of films she was probably into: *Sense and Sensibility* and *The Remains of the Day,* the kinds of flicks any respected man in the neighborhood should not have known about, or at least not spoken of openly.

"I know a little bit," I replied. "I ain't have to go to private school to get *culture.*"

She laughed at my fake white-boy accent. "Don't believe the hype," she said. "The only thing I learn at my school is that being white is the biggest thing most of the people up there have going for them."

"Then why you there?" I asked.

"Daddy says it's the best school in the city," she replied after taking a sip from her cup. I took a sip from mine and almost burned my lips raw. "And I want the best education I can get."

"But do you like it?" I asked. I wanted to know what she was about. I wanted to know everything there was to know. And I wanted to see the upper thighs shadowed by the denim fabric of that knee-length skirt.

"Yes," she said. "I do. It's hard being the fly in the buttermilk, though, if you know what I mean. But I wouldn't be there if I didn't want to be."

She smiled, and I smiled back.

"Then do your thing," I said. "Goin' to Holy Cross should get you in a good college."

"Are *you* in college yet?" she asked, turning the tables before I could make a first move. She'd assumed, like my mother before her, that a "higher" education was the obvious next step on my road to responsible adulthood. But I could've cared less about hitting the books again. I didn't need them. What I needed was a record contract and my group, the Waterfront, backing me up. Such a deal would give me all the money I needed and more life experience than a million course credits could provide. And it was all right around the corner, all just one performance away.

"Not yet," I chose as an answer. "I'm takin' some time off."

"Any particular reason why?" she asked.

"I'm tryin' to do my music."

"Music?"

"I'm a singer," I continued. "Me and my boy Stevie, we write songs. And we got a singin' group. We're called the Waterfront. You know, after the neighborhood. We won the ACT-SO competition last year. It's like a talent show for the NAACP." An inquisitive nod said that she was impressed.

"So what do you sing?"

"Whatever's on my mind," I said. "But I really write more than I sing. Sometimes I get up in the middle of the night and the lines just come to me, you know?" She gave the same nod, this time adding a piercing stare.

"What?" I asked.

"I'm waiting to hear what you sound like," she said. I could tell she was used to getting her way, an only child who'd been handed the world as her personal oyster.

I looked to my left and right, flanked by the ghosts of my own insecurities, then back into the pull of her ebony eyes.

"Nah," I said. "I can't sing here."

"Why not?"

I needed a reason, something, anything to curb me from putting myself at the mercy of her judgment. I'd sung in church, in the school choruses, even to little girls whose digits I wanted to obtain. I knew I had something that most did not, a sound I was destined to share with my world. But she, Salamanca Mitchell, was a different thing altogether.

" 'Cause I'm here about some business," I said decidedly. "And I don't mix business with pleasure."

"You've got *business* with my father," she retorted, patting a palm against her firm thigh. "Until he gets here your only job is to keep me satisfied."

"Oh, is that right?" I challenged.

"Right that is," she fired back, daring me to continue my resistance, knowing that my gates were already rattling at the hinges.

I wanted her, in every way, in every time, space, and dimension. And as I parted my lips, I was determined to utter the predestined words that would make her mine. Then the front door opened, and in came the Old Man, who by presence alone forced our stalemate into a mutual forfeit. My "overtime" meeting was now in session. Salamanca Mitchell would have to wait.

"It was nice meeting you," I said to her after my meeting with Mr. Mitchell was adjourned.

"Likewise," she said as I started toward the front door.

The Old Man's climb made the staircase creak with strain on the way to his bedroom. She was on the couch, reading a paperback copy of *Tar Baby*, a legal pad and pen next to her in case she needed to take notes. "I'm sure I'll see you again."

"I hope so," I said, slightly worried that the Old Man might still be within earshot. My future queen raised her chin with regal recognition and smiled the smile of all smiles.

"Me too," she said.

4.

Overtime began when I met the Old Man at the corner
of Half and M streets just after
ten that night. Ahmad's Liquors
was alive with heavy traffic
from the local drunks and
sorrow suppressors alike.
Others might have been there
for lottery tickets, particularly
since somebody's grandma had
scored a cool million from a
scratch game card bought
there just a few weeks before.

The Old Man was dressed
in a black short-sleeved button-
up with brown linen pants and
matching shoes. A leather
bomber covered it all. The car
was not his Cadillac, but a 1995
Volvo with an open moon roof
and Nancy Wilson on the

stereo. He was already seated at shotgun. A single key was in the ignition as I took the wheel.

I turned the engine over, assuming he'd want to leave right away. But he didn't even look at me. The Old Man kept his eyes looking straight ahead, toward a group of boys about my age on the corner shooting C-Lo.

"You can't end up like them," he remarked, the closest thing to a greeting I would get that night. I looked over at the quintuplets he spoke of, boys who knew me more by sight than in mind. They stood there swaddled in baggy jeans and gray sweatpants. Some wore matching baseball caps and others construction boots instead of sneakers.

"What do you mean?" I asked. "It's just a bunch of dudes killin' time on the corner."

"Exactly," he replied with disdain. "Time ain't somethin' you kill. It's somethin' you use. If you don't use it, every last bit that God gives you, then you lose out. And I don't want you to lose nuthin'."

The words were tailor-made for my ears. He knew me, a boy chasing a dream well within his grasp. But he also knew I was growing up between Greenleaf and South Capitol Street, in a wasteland often forgotten by those who called themselves Washingtonians.

Where we lived was a place almost always ignored, unless you made a wrong turn on the way to the Suitland Parkway or were headed for a nice night of seafood down by the Wharf. In that place, our place, opportunity reared its head only a flash at a time. And if you didn't bite, there were ten or twenty others ready to tear it off the line.

"I ain't goin' lose," I said defiantly, entranced by the boys in front of us. One stooped to scoop up a pile of singles and fives, his big score for the evening.

"I know you ain't," he said with a sly grin, turning to me. There was Scotch on his breath. "That's why you here."

His approval was an electric blanket over shoulders frosted with absence, the absence of my father, the absence of certainty about the boundaries I could and could not cross, the absence of focus, when it came to anything that didn't have to do with matters of melody and harmony.

"You been through a hard year, Ben," he continued. "But your work don't show it. I been watching you close enough to know that you the best one I got."

Pride pulled my cheeks into a humble grin. "Thanks," I said, reveling in the moment. "Now where we headed, boss?"

"Uptown," he said, straightening his spine in the upholstered seat. "Uptown."

So we drove, from U Street to Florida Avenue, from Florida to Connecticut Avenue, into Uptown, that ethereal den of the white and unfamiliar. Up there pale faces ran the whole show. They ruled their green lawns, clean coffee shops, and wealth-friendly merchants with a titanium grip. Broadcast towers for two of the four local TV stations could be seen within its skyline. And Armand's Pizza on Wisconsin had the best Sicilian slices I'd ever tasted.

Our destination was one of those many streets where blacks folks often worked but never lived, deep in the residential grids beyond the major avenues. If you grew up there, you had nothing to do but enjoy life: ride bikes on smooth strips of concrete, play in private pools and landscaped yards. My house didn't even have a yard, only a patch of grass that never turned green, even after Dad seeded and fertilized it every other spring.

We parked in front of a three-story colonial, an estate by our neighborhood's standards. Two levels and a basement with three huge windows along the front and sides. The padded swing Tarzaned back and forth in the spring breeze. The house was on the corner of 39th and Garrison. The mailbox was marked in raw iron lettering: "The Nevitts."

I had too many questions, but not enough courage to pose them to my employer. Besides, I was there just for the extra money.

"This ain't gonna take too long," the Old Man said as he pulled the exit lever on his door. "Just sit tight and keep the radio down."

A moment later he had dissolved into the foliage that separated one privileged property from the next. I knew the minute he vanished into the shadows, though I told myself it couldn't possibly be as it appeared. Sure, the man had slithered around the back of a house with no lights on and no car in the driveway. But there had to be some rational and perfectly legal explanation.

There had to be some light on in the rear, one that I couldn't see. And that light was burning because the basement tenant had some legitimate business with my employer. Mr. Mitchell needed a driver because there was . . . limited parking. Or maybe he was just . . . tired of driving and wanted to pay me because he . . . he liked me. Yeah, that was it. He liked me.

But there wasn't enough soap for that wash, particularly after I had a full thirty minutes to think it through. Teena Marie's "Portuguese Love" invaded the sound system. Garrison Street was mute and motionless: no car horns, no loud voices, no echoes of breaking bottles or balls bouncing off rusty rims in the distance.

Then "Between the Sheets" massaged its way through the speakers, reminding me that I had willfully climbed onto the mattress of the situation, removing my undergarments and agreeing to take the fucking of my young life, for the paltry sum of $200.

I knew what he was doing in there. Anyone entering into an unlit house was doing so without an invitation. He'd gone in to rob the Nevitts blind, and I was posted out front as his getaway man.

All the blurs about my time at Sally Helen's came into instant focus. The meetings with men carrying gym bags into the Old Man's office. Those kids my age who handed him thick brown envelopes at the delivery entrance. The prominent seating of loud and tacky people who wouldn't have met the dress code in a million years.

There was a world beneath the surface of Sally Helen's, and I had been brought to its gates. I could feel the flames rushing up toward me from shadows below. Yet I did not turn away.

I should have, though, especially since I had already suffered through one near criminal lapse in judgment that year. Stevie and I had climbed into a stolen Acura that Scoonie and Frosty, whom we'd known since our days at Bowen Elementary, had boosted in front of the Folger Library on Capitol Hill. The young thugs wanted to take on as many accomplices as the car could hold, daring us to "have some fuckin' nuts." I went because it was the first time I'd ever been asked, while Stevie, sheltered, middle-class, and still pining to lose his virginity, wanted to be a bad boy and do something "gangsta."

We were riding along fine until three bullets shattered the car's front window at a stoplight less than four blocks from where we had hopped in. Ralph Cooper and his boy Bonesy had mistaken us for some dude he had a beef with and let loose with a Glock he was holding for just the proper occasion.

Miraculously, the lead went through the roof and windows instead of us. We all scattered like rats, leaving the car to fend for itself in the middle of the busiest intersection in the area.

I remembered the wheezing in Stevie's asthmatic lungs as we tracked down L Street, looking for a place to hide just in case some unseen enemy gave chase, hoping to eliminate any potential witnesses.

Running, I had a head full of images of my dad halting our path in his squad car, of him demanding that my best friend and I climb in the back and keep our mouths shut until he figured out what to do with us. But Dad wasn't going to save me. Because he was dead, his vacant shell and casket buried in ground miles from where I laid my still living head.

But if there was one thing I had learned from Dad, it was to be observant. And as I observed myself in a potentially dangerous situation, posted as a lookout and getaway man in the white part of town, I knew that I was in too deep. My boss, the prominent restaurateur, entrepreneur, and community figure, was inside pursuing a career as an amateur burglar and running the risk of getting us both full rides to the doo-rag hotel.

I remembered when they lowered the casket. An ocean of fellow officers stood erect, mourning the loss of one of their own. The crowd encapsulated a lifetime: childhood friends, cousins, and even a high school sweetheart or two.

I was on the front row, my arm around a grandmother sobbing in soprano. My little brother, Henry, held Mom close as the lacquered coffin dropped out of sight. And when it was gone she turned and looked at me, at the same time I was looking at her, both of us wondering what the hell it was we were supposed to do in a life without our Superman.

Mom and I rarely spoke in the months that followed, communicating through notes on the kitchen counter and money in designated envelopes. We weren't angry with each other. We were both angry with him, for not being there, for not activating that goddamn siren, for leaving a hole where his daily love had once resided.

Neither of us admitted to feeling the way we did. We didn't want to be the bad guys for not buying into that bullshit about him dying a hero. Heroes were supposed to save the day. But for us, each day had become a lost cause.

But there was something else there for me around that time: a thirst. I wanted to explore all of the things that having a cop as a father had protected me from, the things that had kept me so far away from the center of things.

Dealers and thieves and men who pimped their sisters out of project living rooms had never asked me to run "packages" down the street for them. No one knew my number. No one invited me to the house parties that spilled into the alleys and project hallways on Friday and Saturday nights. And it was all because I carried my father's name. Fuck my father's name!

Songs on the radio soared and landed like jets on an airstrip. My nerves waltzed to the rhythm of fear. I needed a cigarette, and I didn't even smoke. My eyes plotted all possible escape routes.

But what would leaving achieve other than my downfall? Deserting the boss meant no more job, no more money, and a possible bludgeoning from any one of the Old Man's fans, those boys around the way waiting patiently for a reason to take a bat to my head, because I was among them but not of them. So, keeping my wits about me, I could only wait and pray that Alfonse Mitchell got what he was looking for and got the fuck out.

He reboarded moments later, his brow speckled with sweat, lungs snatching for all the air they could hold. In his lap sat a bloodred child's backpack, filled to capacity with items unknown.

"Just had to pick up somethin' real quick," he remarked as I turned the car over and pulled us away from the scene of the crime.

At a stoplight I noticed the twinkling dust of broken glass on his jacket sleeve, the smoking gun indicative of unlawful entry. He waited for me to ask, and I waited for him to answer. But neither of us would yield to the other's will for the half-hour drive back home.

We parked back at the corner of Half and M, where he peeled off four hundreds and laid them into my open palm before pressing his own digits on top.

"Business here is business here," he said, pointing at the car floor with his index finger. "And business there is business there." The message was clear. This was between us. This was a partnership. We pressed our hands into a sandwich of four crisp hundred-dollar bills. And the deal was sealed.

"I might have some more overtime for you next week, then," he said, putting a flame to another Lucky Strike.

Then I exited the stolen vehicle.

I knew that from then on things would be different. One little ride had moved us far beyond the border of employer/employee relations. A message fired from ear to mind at the speed of light, indicating excitement, pleasure, an endorphin rush not unlike that at the moment of ejaculation.

I was no longer clean, no longer quarantined by a father's badge and the reputation that stuck out in front of it like a battering ram. The Old Man had fully inducted me into the daily grind of the streets, and with four yards to show for my efforts. For that I loved him like a father. And in three weeks my new father made it so that I got a top-of-the-line DAT recorder from Paulie's on F Street for the sale price of $989.99.

Everything changed after that. Dudes around the way pulled me into the half-hugs I'd desired for most of my life. Salamanca and I bumped and ground to tapes of go-go music at an invitation-only joint in the Greenleaf rec room, held by Monte and his cousin Dwayne. I was offered the latest in bootleg movies and stolen designer clothes and the chance to get involved with other types of "overtime." But I turned them all down. I worked for Alfonse Mitchell, and Alfonse Mitchell only.

5.

The Old Man was always at the top of his game,
always one step ahead of any
individual who might have
been on his trail. So he varied
the intervals between our visits
to Uptown's treasure troves.
Sometimes we'd hit only once
in a month. Other times it was
two days back to back. He had
a system, one he never strayed
from, a blueprint hidden from
us all in the safety of his own
devious mind.

Three other dudes came in
on the deal. Maurice, who was
going to Georgetown Prep on
athletic scholarship, had been
playing "Most Likely Negro to
Bring Home to Dinner" with a
few of his classmates. And

those dinners had yielded some very interesting acquisition prospects for the Old Man.

Frank, Sally Helen's weekend bartender, was a Jewish kid from up on Capitol Hill who had an uncle who was a fence up in Montgomery County. And there was Ronnie, our most recently hired busboy, who staked out the houses before the Old Man made his moves, informing him of anything and everything that might lead to potential snags and opportunities alike.

We played our parts as individual pieces. Everything was need-to-know or nothing. The boss assembled the larger puzzle. All we needed to remember was that business inside and outside of Sally Helen's were two entirely different things and that a slip of the tongue could lead to its loss.

We eased into the white-hot bath of the undertaking. But the soothing sensation of quick paydays numbed all concerns. Our nocturnal expeditions became nothing more than fleeting daydreams as our machine ran for months without a hitch. But when the snag finally came, it pulled our whole sweater apart.

I hated singing in bathrooms. There, a voice's imperfections bounced off the porcelain walls at acute angles and screamed right back in your face. But it was what she wanted. And as we both lay submerged in the amber-colored water, H_2O scented with olive oil and peppermint, I had to give her what she'd asked for. I massaged her inundated calves as I cleared my throat, examining the end result of my first-ever attempt at giving her lovely legs a shave.

Sharon Stone had said that every man should shave a woman's legs before he dies. I'd read that in a magazine at the dentist's office a few weeks before. So I figured my razor skills would have been more than enough to get me over on a Friday night. According to Sharon, the feel of steady hands gliding sharp blades over flesh would be better than a trip to the downtown between her thighs.

We were both naked, our bodies slipping and sliding in the absence of friction. My third leg stiffened as I performed the task, combining caution with precision. Her breathing was seductive, tickling a sexual funny bone I hadn't previously known to exist.

I looked down through the transparent liquid to see dessert glistening in the candlelight. I offered my lips to her sacred shrine, and the goddess accepted. I took my time as tongue circled the pearl that would bring her to the throes.

Her legs trembled. Her face went flush. Manicured hands gripped the back of my skull with enough force to crush it. An index finger explored her depths. I put a hand behind her head to keep it from banging against the edge of the tub.

She came, harder than either of us could ever have expected, her spine arching as bliss shot through her. Then she relaxed, sucking in oxygen as if she'd just broken tape in a hundred-meter dash. Her smile was a little girl's on Christmas Day. I had given her something precious, something Santa could not supply. And for that, she loved me even more than she did already. It was the closest we'd come to doing it, and the first time I'd been with a woman since Dad passed away.

"Sing for me," she said again in her sexy little whine.

"What you wanna hear?" I asked.

"I don't care," she said, "as long as it's something you wrote."

I chose "River's Edge," two verses and a hook I'd scribbled about a "first time" on the edge of the Anacostia River. I wondered if she'd figure I was throwing out a hint. But I sang it to her anyway, singing as if I would never sing it again.

"Oh, my God," she said afterward, leaving a gap between her upper and lower rows of teeth. "I've never heard anything like it."

She pulled her lips to mine, a flash of surprise stamped on her sharp features. I blushed, not knowing what else to do, and then we kissed again. I tried to enter, but she stopped me.

"Not yet," she said. "Not yet."

It was after midnight on a Friday. We dried off and then took cover between the blanket and sheets. A lotioned heel ground against my shin beneath the rich red fabric. The scent of vanilla wax crept in from the bathroom a yard or two away as Sade's *Love Deluxe* played on random. Her wet hair dangled over the edge of the mattress in one thick clump.

It was my night off, which just happened to be the same weeknight the Old Man stayed at Sally Helen's until closing. We had the house all to ourselves. And the house knew how to keep a secret.

Her father wasn't supposed to know about us. I never came over when he was there, and I never brought her up in conversation. But in any neighborhood there's always a rat waiting to bare its teeth.

Our rodent came in the form of a Bible-toting neighbor named Mrs. Lutenbacher across the way. She was the only white woman on a black block, and her German accent was still as thick as it had been when she'd moved into the house on Half not long after World War II. Thinking she was saving Sala's soul, she apparently mentioned to the Old Man that some "hoodlum" from around the corner had been making visits to the house when he wasn't home.

That night was the only time we ever slept together until daybreak. We'd drifted off after one and came alive just as the Old Man was coming through the door at seven the next morning. Luckily he didn't check her room or hear me easing out through the basement. I called her minutes later and we talked for three whole hours as dawn became day. Then she told me she loved me. And I told her that my heart held the same feeling. And that was when our love truly began.

"I'm about to tell you the secret to your success," the Old Man had said in his office as he lined an empty cigar with a dime of the greenest weed I'd ever laid eyes on. I wasn't a smoker. But my swallow of the Teacher's Scotch he downed like water had given me more than enough of a buzz.

"You the only one that's gonna take care of you," he said after his first puff. A towel plugged the space beneath his office door to contain the smell of illegal smoke. "Cuz ain't nobody else gonna do it for you."

I leaned against the hard back of the wooden chair across from his. Another night. Another score. Another wad of bills to add to my five-figure stash. Five months and I had more money than I'd ever even touched.

I took Sala shopping at Pentagon City at least once a month. I had multiple pairs of sneakers and designer jeans.

I even hooked up my little brother every now and again. It was the kind of money that turned fear into something foolish. It was the American dream. The Old Man and I were beating the system, and we didn't have to hurt our own people doing it.

There was not even the slightest trace of regret. I no longer tensed up at the sight of a cop cruiser. I no longer subjected myself to long, drawn-out rationalizations on why I, a cop's son, was the head wheelman for a vicious pack of thieves. I was who I was, and was loving every minute of it.

"When it all goes down, somebody always gets left holdin' the bag," he continued, taking another puff, then a sip from his half-emptied glass. "And you don't never want for it to be you."

"You ever get caught out there like that?" I asked. Intimidation surrounded his words. But *I* didn't have anything to worry about. *We* were partners in crime, men of like minds who always had the other's back.

"No sir, Ben Baker," he continued. "And you wanna know why?"

"Why?" I asked, reclining tipsily in the painfully straight chair.

"Cuz I always kept my eyes open. No matter what was goin' on, I always kept one eye on what I was doin' and the other one on everybody else. When I saw a chance I took it. I took it and used it, and then I covered my ass so I could do it again if I needed to." He chuckled. "See, ain't nuthin' but a thing to close up shop. It ain't nuthin' to walk away when you have to." He took a final sip and then another puff, then retired the glass for the spliff, pouring me another.

"Always watch where you goin'," he concluded. "It keeps you from runnin' into shit."

I should've paid more attention to what he'd said. I should've heeded his advice. But I'd just turned nineteen, and I had $12,000 stashed between two different houses and three different bank accounts. So what could I possibly have to worry about?

By that July, Frank had bought out his uncle and was running the fencing end from his house in Hyattsville. He started working full shifts at Sally Helen's instead of weekends. But that was only to make the payments for his new Beemer look legit. And Maurice, ever the pretty boy, could've gone two months without doing laundry because of all the new clothes he'd bought.

Ronnie, however, wasn't big on flash. He had a mother dying of AIDS to take care of. And I was just me, spending but saving, too, waiting for the right move to come along so that I could make it.

"You my main man, Ben," Alfonse Mitchell had said on our way to what was to be the last job. His breath reeked of the usual Scotch, and his eyes were the color of a gaping wound. Our car for the night was a fuchsia Honda Civic. "You're down wit' me for as long as I'm here on this earth."

It took a few weeks for the yarn to unravel. A scorching August followed the hottest July on record. And it was on the first of that month that Ronnie decided to hit a house on his own, a gigantic three-story off Military Road. The place wasn't on the Old Man's list, nor was it in the realm of our usual operations. Ronnie had allegedly given the place a good once-over, checking for signs of life, security systems, and so on, and then just decided to go in.

He didn't pay any mind to the fact that the basement windows were tinted, blinding him to what that level might have to hide. In his mind, it shouldn't have been a concern. After all, who kept any valuables in their basement, anyway? This kind of thinking was what made Ronnie good as a lookout but not for much else.

Young Ronnie made his way into the residence by using a glass cutter to remove a pane from the kitchen door. He'd barely had a chance to grab the $2,000 stereo in the living room before the twelve arena football–playing white boys in that tinted-windowed basement got wise to the intruder upstairs. Those corn-fed fellows beat poor Ronnie an inch away from death. And then they called the cops.

But Ronnie passed the loyalty test in the interrogation room.

"I got this, Mr. Mitchell," Ronnie had told the Old Man during his first visit.

"That's a little nigga after my own heart," the Old Man recounted to me later, grinning.

I knew that Mitchell had plenty of lawyers. He also had the money to get Ronnie out of the clink and even out of the state if need be. But springing him made him a potential accomplice to watchful eyes, eyes that might put question marks where there had been only periods. And that would not have been acceptable.

"What you gonna do?" I asked.

"About what?" he replied, sipping a glass of the house Merlot while he did his weekly review of the ledger.

"About Ronnie," I said.

The glance he gave me said I was being a nuisance. And I was breaking the rule. Restaurant business in the restaurant. Overtime business during overtime.

"Don't you need to be back on the floor?" he asked, returning to his work and draining his glass.

His perfect soldier, I did an about-face as ordered and returned to my post, navigating past the five perspiring blue black men that made Sally Helen's cuisine what it was. Peeled and deveined shrimp plunged into a pot of boiling gumbo. Catfish sizzled in scalding safflower oil flavored with garlic and lemon juice. Three hens did circles around a stainless-steel spit. Collard greens were chopped and lowered into boiling water seasoned with salt and vinegar.

Those men, in their satin button-up uniforms, believed in the Old Man's way, in his standard of culinary quality, in his pride in the physical appearance of all things except for his office. They were as entranced by the spirit of his vision as I was.

So I did what I was asked. I went out and worked my shift. City council chairman David Clarke ordered the fried-clam-and-oyster combo with a side of collard greens. Sugar Bear, from the long since defunct group E.U., sat in a corner booth rubbing his hand on the velvet-panted leg of one of the light-skinned girls from that teen show on BET.

The faces of the patrons were indistinguishable, one melding easily into the next. I provided matches for cigarettes in the smoking section. I pulled out chairs and carried coats to the check area. I reminded Trevor, a Trinidadian with light eyes and a slight limp, of the day's specials before he walked onto the playing field.

Then I looked over all that I'd become a part of in that little bistro, all that had been my life for my first few months of manhood. And then something strange happened. A shudder coursed through me and I felt a disconnection, as if in one instant I'd been unplugged from the Alfonse Mitchell machinery.

Having taken too many cues about criminal loyalty from rap hits, Ronnie signed on the thick black confession line. Since he was under eighteen, the judge sent him to the Oak Hill Youth Facility instead of Lorton. He'd always been one for a lot of mouth, claiming that he'd had a hand in every speck of dirt done up in 640, his native 'hood just above the reservoir. Yet the people we knew from there had never heard of him.

Nevertheless, it was that mouth that brought about his end on the inside. A fight between him and a larger, stronger opponent ended with him being choked to death. His mother, without a son to care for her, died several months later of pneumonia.

Things only worsened the week after Ronnie's demise. Maurice didn't show up for work three days straight. Frank found himself on the sharp end of an anonymous tip about the "holdings" in his basement and was raided and charged with three counts of grand larceny. And then the cops came to Sally Helen's that Friday, with a search warrant and a DA in a teal suit.

The closed-door meeting in the middle of happy hour was more than unsettling for our well-to-do clientele. The flashed badges and shoulder holsters silenced the usual roar in the waiting area. I, however, had made my way into the supply closet, which was right next to the Old Man's office.

I put a water glass to the wall and listened, hoping the sound would be streamlined, the way it was in the movies. Yet all I could make out was Frank's name and something about the Old Man making a deal before they had enough evidence to charge him.

The Old Man used his nonthreatening Negro voice to assure them that he had played no part in any wrongdoing. And then the three of them left as empty-handed as they'd come in.

Up until then, our thing, this "overtime," had been nothing but a six-month-long game of pickup sticks, an endless exercise in getting other people's goods out through jimmied doors and opened windows. The money had seemed endless to our narrow minds. But now the DA had come and gone, and that stylishly stoic look on the Old Man's face had turned to one of concern and concentration, complete with beads of sweat on his bald brow.

"You think Frank said something?" I asked after closing, when it was just the two of us, smoking Luckies on the steps of the kitchen entrance. " 'Cause we know it wasn't Ronnie."

"Even if he did, it's his word against ours," the Old Man replied, looking back into the dark emptiness of the closed kitchen. The sound of scurrying mice could be heard down the alleyway.

"Worse come to worst, we could try to buy off the judge," he suggested, more to himself than to me. "It's a local case. They can't be all that expensive."

He took a drag deeper than the Potomac and ground the butt out against the concrete stairwell. The underarms of his mustard-colored shirt were damp.

"So what we gonna do?" I asked my mentor. He didn't answer.

"I don't know, though," I continued, determined to get a rise out of him. "I don't think Frank woulda gone to the cops. He was makin' too much cake for that. Why blow the whistle on the mouth that was feeding him, his mama, and his little girl?"

He ground the statement through his skull, weighing the possible and probable in the time it took to breathe in and out.

"You right about that," he murmured, his eyes still glued to the empty space just beyond me. "But I was thinkin' Maurice mighta talked. I mean, the boy ain't shown his head around here for four days."

"That's a problem," I said with the timing of a comedy sidekick. "I seen him drink a cup of piss in the break room just to win a ten-dollar bet."

My mentor seemed surprised. "No bullshit?"

"No bullshit," I answered, watching him twist his face into a pucker.

"That's nasty," he said.

"Tell me about it. So what the DA got?"

He didn't answer. He didn't even lift his eyes to meet mine. Instead he gave them a roll, sucked the space between his gapped front teeth, and waved me away.

"Enough," he muttered. Both sets of fingers began their tap against creased slacks. "They got enough."

It wasn't the elaborate answer I'd expected, not what should have come from a partner, or from a mentor, or from a father. But it had been an answer nonetheless. And I once again rationalized it into making sense. I hadn't been fully in the loop before, so why would anything change now?

But my better sense could feel something wicked on its way, bad karma's curved blade coming for my head. And I was determined to duck long before my beheading. So I had to tell the truth, to the one person who mattered.

"I gotta tell you something," I said to Sala, my words all but drowned out by the roar of gushing water behind us. It was just after dusk, and the courtyard of the DOT building bustled with commuters heading away from their civil servantry. Seated next to each other on a bench of black stone, I showed her eyes filled with fear, transferring the emotion into her before I had even uttered a word.

"What is it?" she asked. I didn't know what to say. I loved her so much that I wanted to tell her everything. But I wasn't sure how much of it she could take. How much could she actually believe? This was her father, her provider of eighteen years. How would she handle knowing what he was up to and what I had been up to? Would it make her love for me morph into hate? Would my theft and greed smother the passion we'd come to share? And most important, could I trust her not to run back to the Old Man and tell him all that I was about to confess?

"I'm in trouble," I said.

"What's going on?" She lightly brushed fingers across my face and neck. It was a child's touch, gentle and curious. Her eyes shone with a reflection of the tungsten bulbs at the bottom of the six-column fountain. Her lips pursed in anticipation of my response.

But I couldn't take a hammer to the perfect jewel of the way things seemed on the surface. I wanted it all to stay the way it was: placid, serene, like a warm breeze on a mild summer day. So I said something sweet, something poetic, something I felt from the depths of my soul that would keep things as pristine as they had been for the long and joyous six months we'd been together.

"I can't stop thinking about you," I said with a nicely placed pause afterward. "You been on my mind all day. So you know I had to see you."

She grinned and then crawled into the safety of my arms, a damsel in distress rescued by her Prince Charming. She pressed her head against my chest. I ran a finger down her face, brushing loose hairs back into the well-oiled bun that managed her mane. Then I brought my lips to hers. And we closed our eyes and held each other for a long time, believing in our love more than the lives we were destined to choose.

6.

Destiny announced itself in the form of an article on the front page of the next day's *Post* "Metro" section. Frank Umansky was found dead behind a club known as the 14th Street Lounge up in Dupont Circle. He'd taken four bullets in his back, and one through the head. Following Jewish tradition, they had him in the ground less than forty-eight hours later. But the still missing Maurice did not show up for the funeral, or to Sally Helen's, ever again.

"I been thinkin' about closin' Sally's up for a while," the Old Man said during the repast at Frank's mother's house. The restaurant's crew had the only dark faces at the mostly Jewish aftergathering.

"Closin' up?" I asked confusedly. "Why?"

"I got a call last night from my brother," he began, tilting his shiny head toward me. "My mama ain't doin' too good. Emphysema and all. So I wanna go down and see her for a few weeks."

"You sure that's what you wanna do?" I asked. "I mean, the DA sees you closin' down, they figure you got somethin' to hide."

"Maybe, but the rest of the world sees a businessman with a dead employee and a sick mama, a man who don't let nobody run his business but him."

"But that ain't practical," I challenged.

"Fuck practical," he turtle-snapped. "That's what I'm gonna do."

It was a good enough plan to him. Closing up for a sick mama *was* perfectly praiseworthy. An act of such selflessness might have even made the "Metro" section on a slow news day. And if the cops hadn't brought him in already, they probably weren't going to. He was home free. And, consequently, so was I.

But the pinprick in my gut still said that something wasn't right. And that prick became a stabbing blade as the Old Man's lie came into frightening focus. Sala had told me that her grandmother, his mother, had died of pneumonia when she was five.

"Sala goin' with you?" I asked him, continuing the normal flow of our convo.

"Nah, she gonna stay here," he replied. "Mama don't wanna be seen like that, you know? So she gonna watch the house while I'm away."

There was a glint of achievement in his eye. He knew that I'd bought his story, that I was still all in. But I wasn't. And I never would be again.

"So when you leavin'?" I asked.

"Next few days, as soon as I can get everybody their checks. I'ma throw in some severance for the time we gonna be closed and all."

"Well, let me know if you need anything," I said. And with that he slapped a bone-crushing palm on my shoulder and squeezed, grinning.

"You done more than enough just bein' my main man," he said, pulling me into a pretentious hug. "You done more for me than you'll ever know. And I ain't gonna forget that."

The truth came to a full boil on the blue line home. I sat in that bright orange cushion of a seat, examining the chronology of my time in the Old Man's employ. I needed to erect a wall of defense against his next action, whatever it might be. Because if he'd lied about his mother, who knew what other untruths might be blowing in the breeze?

A nauseating flutter squirmed through me. I was up against my master, my partner, my father. And that was the tallest order imaginable for any young apprentice. The more I thought, the less I could claim to know about our operation. There were too many holes, too many unanswered questions.

Maurice couldn't have been the only person casing our scores. There had to be someone else feeding the Old Man leads and giving him the needed info about the neighborhoods, target homes, and systems that protected them.

Where was he storing the goods until he met with Frank's people? And where was he putting all of the money to make it look legit? None of us knew. And that had been exactly the way he wanted it.

The tale of the tape gave me gooseflesh. My adversary was a wealthy, connected man of means who knew everything there was to know about me outside of the bulge in my boxers. This was not my seventh-grade bout with Claude Craig in the school cafeteria over an insult to my mother. There would be no crowds of allies and spectators to instigate the dustup. People I knew, people who bound the Old Man and me together, were dead. And I could soon end up among them. So I needed a second opinion, someone who could set me straight on my next move.

"See, now who told you in the fucking beginning," my best friend demanded. One almond-colored hand was on the keyboard in front of him, while the other scratched the dry scalp beneath his red forest of an Afro.

He lit a cigarette and fanned the smoke toward me, away from the ceiling vent on the other side of the room. The slightest trace of tobacco would have surely brought down a parental search party from the upper floors. And since the Turners had always been a little shaky about me, because I was from the "other side" of the neighborhood, the shadow lands on the east end of the Waterside Towers apartments, I didn't want them assuming I'd started their boy on his pack-a-week Salem habit.

Stevie was an *Ebony* man in the making: young, gifted, black, and often oblivious to all that thrived beyond the borders of his daily routine. But he was still my boy. I showed him what I knew of the streets, and he showed me the way I wanted to live when I grew up.

The Turners lived right off 7th, across from Jefferson Junior High and a crowded lot of parked cars that never seemed to empty, just a few blocks down from the U.S. Departments of Transportation and Housing and Urban Development. Mr. Turner was an investment banker at the Douglas Bank on Mass. Avenue. And Mrs. Turner was the executive director of a nonprofit for social change in Dupont Circle. They drove a twin pair of 1993 Honda Accords. And there was a pool table in their basement, along with a big-screen TV and room for all of Stevie's equipment (keyboards, drum machine, a guitar), which he'd acquired via three consecutive Christmases and birthdays.

Mom and Dad had been spoiling Stevie in the more recent years, a passive-aggressive attempt to discourage their baby boy from going the way of their first son, who had just been hit with an uppercut of a sentence for possession of and intent to distribute a sizable amount of heroin to some Kurt Cobain–worshipping white boys up on Capitol Hill. Big brother Malcolm had been a major player on my side of the world. Then he walked into a sting of a trap set for someone else and got a ten-year bid for his misfortune.

"It's one thing to take the money and roll," my best friend continued. He was five feet seven and skinny as a rail, his face the color of pinewood. "It's another thing to stick around and get set up for the fall."

I didn't want to hear him because I'd already heard myself expressing the same sentiments. I wanted to give my undivided attention to the bass line for our latest song, a midtempo something called "Checkmate." So I listened to what I'd just played through one earphone and Stevie through the other. The music, of course, had the greater hold.

"Tell me somethin' I don't know," I murmured, laying down the headphones to scribble notes in my composition book. I had tried to exhale all of my fears when I pushed play, taking in the healing of music for as long as the tape lasted.

It didn't take long to see that clueing Stevie in on the current crisis had been a mistake. I had wanted a friendly set of ears and gotten too much mouth. But he was my best friend. And I trusted him more than anyone.

"I'm the only one left," I said, pressing the phones to my ear once more. "And I ain't gonna lie, I'm kinda scared."

"I know I would be," he replied, far from envious of where I stood. "You got your ass in w-a-a-a-y too deep."

No sympathy at all. I had the urge to backhand him into the bookcase on the other side of the room.

"Why don't you just go to the cops?" he continued. "I mean, some of your dad's boys must still be there." He found his way to the drum machine next to me and began to patter a beat.

"Yeah," I said, having already thought of it long before. "But the cops is gonna ask a lot of questions. And if I give 'em answers, they got me by the nuts. Besides, Pop's main boys are down in the Seventh District. So I don't know if they can do that much for me up here."

"I wish there was something I could do," he said with a helpless look on his face.

I just wanted to finish the song. I just wanted to add one more composition to our catalog. The music was always soothing and cathartic, a tangible thing that transcended tangibility. So just then, with fate's anvil dangling above me, I needed the music more than I needed a plan to survive.

"So what's your plan?!" he demanded, as if words could change what was. He could only see the game from the nosebleeds, his mind distracted by memorable moments from his favorite crime dramas. He assumed that the Old Man and I could just take a seat at some checker-clothed table and have some sort of a sit-down. Or maybe I'd wear a wire and get Alfonse Mitchell pinched before he could harm me. Perhaps he even saw me kneeling to kiss the big black man's pinkie ring and make everything all right. What I saw was a single solution.

"I need some heat," I said.

"A gun? That's the wrong move, Ben," he replied earnestly, as if I hadn't told him about the .38 the Old Man kept under the seat of his Cadillac, as if Frank and Ronnie (and probably Maurice) weren't already taking dirt naps. Stevie knew the Old Man had eyes and arms everywhere, yet he wanted me to turn the other cheek. Fuck that! The warrior's way was my only option.

I had to walk up on the man, wherever he might be, and tell him what was what before it was too late. It wouldn't be that hard. He knew I wasn't a snitch. He knew he could trust me to do the right thing as long as he made sure that the buck stopped on someone else's doorstep.

"That's just gonna get you in more trouble," he argued. "Like you said, he's cool with the city council, Barry, Eleanor Holmes Norton. What good is a gun against all of that?"

"That ain't the way he's comin' this time," I said. "He got Frank in the street. Ain't nobody seen Maurice in weeks, and Ronnie ain't even make it a month in Oak Hill. If I don't make a move, he's gonna make one for me."

"He can only come for you if he knows where to find you," Stevie began. "And he ain't gonna run up in your house. He ain't gonna come here, either. He doesn't even know about here. You just gotta watch where you step and wait. When did he say he was leaving?"

"End of the week," I said, fanning away his words like smoke from the vent. "But that's bullshit. He ain't got no sick mama. That shit is just a fake-out."

"Then don't get faked," he said in conclusion, his lungs taking in a final thick gulp of tobacco-stained air before he stubbed the butt on the sole of his shoe. "Just lay low. Like my uncle Todd used to always say, 'The Invisible Man is the safest man in the world.'"

7.

M Street was a skillet on full flame, toasting all of the usual suspects in the late night humidity. Toothless zombies staggered down South Capitol toward their crack homes of choice. A piercing scream rang out from an apartment terrace in Greenleaf. Two chocolate cops eyed me as their cruiser crawled past, heading back toward the city. I was just a few blocks from home. But I had a stop to make first.

Bebe's was the local arsenal. Housed in a burned-out storefront at Howison and M, the place was a daytime lovers' lane for high schoolers looking for a quick place to get their rocks off. But when the sun went down, Bebe pulled up in her '94 Beemer and opened up shop. Tight clothing still hugged the curves that had inspired Stevie's big brother to give them a son.

Yes, Bebe was Stevie's brother Malcolm's woman and the mother of their little boy, Dante. And even with Daddy gone, she still carried more respect around the way than any other female I knew.

The only light came from a street lamp that shone through the rotting hole in the charred ceiling. Bebe wore shades with lenses so dark that they had to have hindered her vision.

"This shit is all you need, baby," she said to me, flanked on her left by a cinder block of a cousin called Aja, a semi-pro boxer who often worked security at the Bank on F Street.

The gun thing was relatively new for her. But it was the only way to maintain a family presence in the neighborhood after Malcolm got hit with ten years of fed time, which meant no parole, and no conjugals, and no money coming in for the better part of a decade. So, as a high school dropout and all-around ghetto princess, she did what she had to, keeping herself and Dante in a two-bedroom apartment off Capitol Hill, with a cover job as a home attendant for some old white woman out in Chevy Chase.

"I hope you ain't got to use it, though," she said, knowing that I was family and not the usual wannabe gangsta muthafucka who shot in the air at night because the sky was the only place where he had the nuts to point the piece.

"Me neither," I replied. "But I gotta do what I gotta do." She removed her glasses to show me the softest hazel-colored contacts I'd ever seen and put the hunk of metal and lead into my palm, folding my fingers over it with her own.

"I hope you ain't in too deep, baby," she said with her deepest sympathy.

"Me neither," I said, pressing the bills in her opposite hand. I exited fully armed, ready and waiting for whatever the Old Man might have up his sleeve.

And I was still waiting, with the .25 tucked into the back of my pants, on that early Saturday afternoon in August, when D'Angelo was on the radio and Kevin was telling his tattered tale. And I was wondering what it was that Sala could possibly have to tell me.

Two previous tries and the line had been busy. Recalling the urgency in her voice, I thought of the last time I'd heard that kind of concern, back on that late April evening when the scent of her wetness, of her ravenous yet still reluctant desire, had made its way into the bedroom with my name on it.

"I don't know, Ben," she had said, trembling slightly as our hands removed the cranberry panties she'd worn beneath her plaid-skirted uniform. "I don't want it to hurt."

"I'm here, baby," I had said to comfort her.

I unclasped her bra, watching her breasts slide toward freedom. Her nipples came to attention as I traced their circumference with thumbs and digits. My tongue ran the length of her breastbone while another coalition of fingers caressed that pearl between her thighs. I remember the way she breathed, lungs charged with electric thrill.

She unzipped my pants and took hold of the stiff thing hidden within and put me on my back as she brought it to her lips like a precious thing. Her jaws tightened around its circumference, moving up and down until my silence was impossible. Then she rose and mounted the obelisk, easing me into her as far as I would go.

She whimpered with discomfort as her face scrunched into a furrow of pain that eventually found its way to pleasure. We found heaven together, touching down on its gilded streets in that final and explosive burst of Al Green's brand of love and happiness. We had become as one and would remain that way until the end of time. But in the present someone was calling my name.

"You waitin' on me, Junior?" Roger had asked, bringing me back to the present as he brushed the loose hair away from the back of his customer's out-of-date fade. I practically jumped into his chair, the butt of the weapon jutting against my spine as I assumed the position.

"Just gimme a even Steven," I said. I liked to keep my hair short, smooth, and out of the way. The clippers began their hum, and he went to work. I hadn't been in for two weeks, so I knew the job was going to take a while.

The melody in my brain was still there. I'd determined the song to be for Frank, and for Ronnie, and for anyone else who'd become a victim of the Old Man's game. The sounds were waves approaching a beach at tide time, rising and then crashing to the rhythm of the imagined drum line. I gave it some lyrics on the spot, a few words that seemed to chronicle my plight:

Half-past two and I'm on the move,
Turning like a table,
Needle in the groove
Too many shots that miss their mark,
In the dark.

The composition process continued as Roger put things in their proper order: shaving and lining, edging and spray oiling. The centripetal force of the swiveling chair left me woozy as I was turned to view the end result. The cut was fine. The song in my head was even better.

The mustache and beard had been groomed to a perfect balance. The hairline had been made into a perfect arch. I had been made anew, yet I was the same. And the same was not going to get me through what was. Regular old Benjamin Baker Jr. would not survive the conflict ahead. I was a child of Chronos, destined to be devoured in the name of the Old Man's self-preservation.

Roger couldn't wipe me down fast enough. There were so many things to do in the day ahead, even outside of the Old Man. So I gave Roger twice his usual $2 tip, stuffed the change in my pocket, and bolted past the rows of waiting customers toward the entrance/exit. The pay phone was just outside.

8.

"Hey, baby," I said into the receiver. She sounded sluggish, as if she'd been sleeping. "You all right? You don't sound all right."

"I'm pregnant," she said fearfully. The words came into my right ear, went out the left, and came back through both again. I had to have heard her wrong. I had used condoms. I had even checked the packaging of each for any holes or tears, just the way Dad had taught me to. And I had pulled out just in time that one instance a week or two before when the one defective rubber had torn from too much friction. Or had I?

My tongue was pasted to

the roof of my mouth. My blood went still. My intestines wrenched. Everything blurred as my eyes watered in uncertainty.

"Tell me you're still there," she said with the same pleading insecurity I'd heard on the message. "Please tell me you're there, baby."

The earth shook beneath my feet. The sun went supernova. The Rapture was due at any moment. Because I was going to be a daddy, a daddy who kept a pistol in the small of his back while he was worried to death that Granddad was going to kill him or have him sent up for a prison bid meant for his mentor.

But for some reason, underneath all the anarchy, all of the death, and the music in my mind, something at my core was happier than it had ever been.

"Yeah . . . I'm still here. I . . . I'm always here, baby."

Sure, I was too young to be a father. Sure, we weren't married and we didn't know if it made sense for us to be. Sure, I had money, but it wasn't enough to last. And she hadn't even finished high school, much less college. That Waterfront record deal hadn't come fast enough. But I was somehow certain that we were going to make it work.

"You're never ready for it, son," Dad had said to me once, as we sat in the living room watching one of those John Hughes movies on cable. A wife had told her husband about the bun in her oven, and the husband had responded with nothing but a high, shrill scream. So I had asked my dad, the guru of all knowledge and wisdom, about becoming a father. And that had been his answer.

"And when you find out it's your turn, you have a minute when you don't know how you're going to pull it off. For one minute you don't have any idea of how you're gonna make it work."

Dad was right. Every man has that moment, that tiny chip of time in which he has to accept that he's responsible for something other than himself, that one of his millions of sperm has made a life. It was a moment most of the boys I knew had chosen as their exit, the starting point for an endless string of excuses to escape the prison of being present in their unwanted children's lives. But my father hadn't reared that kind of a boy.

"It's so good to hear that, Ben," she said softly, sobbing with tears of joy.

"When'd you find out?" I asked into the receiver as my eyes scanned the street for some familiar face to confide in once the call was over. Aside from Stevie, who was on the other side of town teaching a piano lesson, there was none.

"My period was two weeks late, and Charlene told me to take one of those tests because if I called the doctor, Daddy would find out about it."

And her mother was apparently out of the question, a shell of a memory far beyond her reach.

"I hate talking about her," she always said when I asked. She was the only thing my girl never liked to speak of, though she had told me the story anyway, because she loved me.

Incinerated by the best divorce lawyer in the D.C. metropolitan area, one Nicole Stevens, her mama, Viola Greene, had been said to have taken refuge back in Detroit and remarried, and she was heard from only in the form of biannual calls to the new Mitchell residence. But there were always the birthday and Christmas gifts sent by

FedEx. I knew there was more to the story. But by that point there were always tears, and I could never stand to see my baby crying.

I didn't know what my mother would think of being a grandma, particularly without a grandfather to accompany her. But I was too overwhelmed to delve into it just then. That moment was about us, Salamanca Mitchell and Benjamin Baker Jr., joined by fate, fiber optics, and a forthcoming child who needed to be shown the way.

"I guess we gotta figure out what we gonna name it," I said.

"But what about our—" she began.

"Shhhh," I interrupted, hoping to calm her, hoping that I could find the magic words that would keep us from dying of worry then and there. "But look, we shouldn't talk about this over the phone. I'm about to come over."

"But Daddy's on his way home," she replied. "He just called and I don't want him to—"

I cut her off again, because the Old Man was the last person I wanted to find out, as it might have made the current debacle all the worse. But I did want to know his next move, and she was the only person who could tell me.

"Then meet me over at the waterfront, next to the docks over by the *Spirit of Washington*," I said.

"Okay," she replied. "How soon?"

"I gotta go by the house real quick," I replied, remembering that I needed to call Stevie. "So I'll see you in like thirty minutes."

"I love you, Ben," she said.

"I love you, too, Sala, and our baby," I replied. Then I hung up.

As fatherhood soaked into my soul, I tried to see the future, the future I wanted, the one where our writing and singing would lead Stevie and me and the Waterfront to R&B stardom. We would put our neighborhood on the map and be the stars we'd always dreamed of being. And that future had a chance of being certain. We had a show that night, too, our most important one.

"We openin' for Jodeci!" Stevie had screamed to us after he'd gotten that initial call two weeks before. Our basement-quality demo tape had made it into the hands of the club manager at the Ritz on E Street, where the show was taking place. He needed an opening act, and we needed our big break. So it had all worked out.

"Damn, man," I'd said in a semispeechless stupor. "This is like some shit out of a dream."

"Damn straight," Lonnie had added. "This is our big shot." I had looked around at the young and eager souls surrounding my own, faces I'd known since earliest memory. Even with all that had been going on with the Old Man and "overtime," I still had hope. Nothing was going to stop me from putting a platinum plaque in the blank white space above the couch in Mom's living room.

We'd decided to wear the same outfits we had from the AKA talent show a month before, where we had won first prize. We would sing "Twice in a Lifetime" and "She Ain't No Angel," the first two songs Stevie and I had ever written for the group.

The show at the Ritz seemed like nothing in light of the new day's news, just another thing to get done in a long list of tasks. I strolled down 1st toward the Baker residence, the emerald brick building that was the third on the left side of Half Street. That's when I noticed the three cop cars in front of our home. Mom's Corsica wasn't in the driveway.

I figured they were there for the Washingtons across the street, our neighbors who had inflicted countless injuries upon each other in the name of violent co-dependency. Or perhaps they were saying hello to Damian Spruill, who lived in the beige house next to mine. Perhaps he'd been found with another five-pound brick of weed and was thus due for a second bid out at Lorton. But three cruisers meant more than petty drugs or domestic abuse. Three cruisers meant a major felony.

I noticed that the latest edition of *Fluff* was in my mail-box when I heard them call my name. I turned and answered. Then there was a remark about me looking like my father. The next thing I knew, I was being cuffed up against one of the red, white, and blue batmobiles, the contents of my bag being strewn all over the warm summer cement.

Badge number 2416 dangled what looked like a locker key in my face, as if the item had some hidden meaning. Then he shoved me into the back of the cruiser, my arms locked painfully behind me. The gibberish I'd heard had been my rights being read.

An anonymous tip had led them to me. The informant said that I had stacked more than $25,000 in stolen valu-ables in a public storage unit out in Southeast. I was carry-ing the key to it in my backpack. A simple search would produce ample proof. I didn't know how the key had gotten there, or anything about the storage space. But circumstan-tial evidence was a bitch when there were people to corrob-orate it, namely one Maurice Green, who had reared his head after a monthlong disappearing act just in time to sign his name on an affidavit that identified me as a key conspirator in a $500,000 burglary ring with several of his fellow employees, all of whom just happened to be "unavailable" to corroborate his testimony.

He claimed to have overheard me giving orders in the restaurant break room. He said that I'd been flashing a lot of cash and had cut my hours in half. And he'd followed me one night to a house at 39th and Garrison, where he'd seen me walk around the rear of a dark house and return with a bloodred bag that appeared to be filled with stolen goods. I'd been checkmated in a single move.

Neighbors came outside to witness my demise. Mr. Washington wore an old striped sweat suit with a terry-cloth fisherman's hat. Mrs. Spruill wore a sundress covered in petunias. The car pulled slowly away from the curb, with me in the prisoner's rear. I couldn't believe it.

A few blocks down, I looked past the meaty heads of the pigs in the front seat and saw Salamanca Mitchell. She was crossing M Street on her way toward our rendezvous. That was a meeting I wouldn't make, along with the show of all shows that was to take place close to midnight.

"I can't do this alone," Salamanca had cried, burrowing her face into my chest. I was to return to court the next morning after two weeks out on bail.

I had told her everything, about "overtime," about Frank, and about her father. And she'd taken it all in as if it were nothing. Until I'd told her the maximum hit was ten years. That was when she'd come apart at the seams.

I'd already had to face Mom and my little brother,

Henry. I'd had to look the both of them in the face and say that they might not see me for a full decade. Mom had gone silent for the whole time I was on bail, too deep in disbelief to assemble any sentence that might have made sense. And Henry, at four, just cried his eyes out while I hugged him, hoping the embrace would be a better comfort than grown-up words. It wasn't.

"You gotta do it alone, baby," I had told Sala, the rancid stench of the wharf blowing in our faces. "You're the only one that can."

I never forgot the way she brought her head up out of my torso, or the magical way the moonlight made her eyes glow blue. My words had charged her with duty. The tears stopped falling.

"I know," she'd said as she brought her lips to mine, her tongue forcing its way between startled lips. I pulled her to me, taking in as much of her as I could, hoping to save some for what lay ahead, though it could never have been enough. "And I will."

The DA made me an offer I couldn't refuse. I was charged with twenty-five counts of grand larceny and one count of possession of a firearm. They would let me serve the counts concurrently for a total of seven years of my life without the possibility of parole.

On the bus to prison I sang my last song, something I'd written for Malcolm a year before called "Lockdown." It had been a present from Stevie and me for his twenty-second birthday, the fifth one he'd spent on the inside. I sang as if my voice were on its deathbed, as if all my dreams were wilting in an eternal winter, as if I'd blown it all for nothing and now had to pay my penance.

I was pretty certain that the rest of the bus would protest. I thought the guards would have whacked me with their batons or that the other inmates would smother the sound with threats and curses or at least just tell me to shut the fuck up. But instead they all listened, sailors snared by a siren's song.

A tiny tear zigzagged down the cheek of the skinny Salvadoran across the aisle from me. A white boy with the word *Retribution* tattooed on his neck dropped his face into shackled hands and sobbed. But I wasn't going to cry. I was going to serve my time and make things right. I was going to make them the way they should have been, the way they were supposed to be.

9.

She wished that he had said something. She knew that something was wrong that day at the fountain. She could've helped him. She could have warned him. She could have pulled the one card that might have defused the whole debacle and left Benjamin Baker Jr., her man, the blood missing from her veins, still free.

But Ben didn't have a clue of how deep in the well he was. He had no idea of what it meant to be a cog in the Alfonse Mitchell machine, to be unwittingly snared by the strings of the world's greatest puppet master. She, however, knew all too well.

So now young Benjamin was perched at the defendant's table. All who knew him had attested to the strength of his character, in writing and by their presence in the court-room. But there were so many incriminating words on file, not to mention the fact that he was carrying a loaded pistol at the time of his arrest. The defense didn't have a leg to stand on. And Ben's lawyer, a rotund trustee from his mother's church, knew that Ben's magic bullet theory—that her father, the community leader and entrepreneur, was an archcriminal and bare-bones burglar—was far too expensive for any jury to purchase.

The sixty-something sista in the black robe asked the defendant to rise. And he locked his tan legs at the knees and stood steadfast before his executioner. Salamanca stood with him, as did his mother, and his little brother, Henry, and the short and skinny boy named Stevie, whom Benjamin had always referred to as his best friend. And then the old woman said what Salamanca already knew.

Seven years. They'd be apart for seven years. The judge's gavel collided with the wood block beneath it. Then two bailiffs surrounded the defendant as if he were a menacing threat. And amid the sorrow of family and friends, amid the outcry of pity and dismay, Salamanca Mitchell and Benjamin Baker Jr. shared a stare of epic proportions as they escorted him from the defendant's table through the cherrywood side exit.

And when he was gone she felt a trembling deep within her, in that place where a life had just so recently been conceived. It was as if that unborn child, a secret shared only between its parents, knew all that had just transpired and was doing its best to fight against this flash flood of fate.

She took the Metro home from Judiciary Square. Her

ebony eyes were pools of sadness. But she wasn't crying for
Ben. She was sobbing for her future.

She had seen all the ads about teenage pregnancy, about
how abstinence was the only true safe sex. She knew the sta-
tistics about how most pregnant mothers never finished college and the grandmama wives' tales about how babies born
in sin always came out looking like their absent fathers. Yet
these were not the things that made her cry, either.

Her sorrow stemmed from the conversation that was
only a few blocks away, the face-off between Daddy and
his little girl on the one topic she knew he wouldn't want to
discuss. Yet she *had* to tell him about her child. As its
granddad he had a right to know, even if such knowledge
would bind him to his own treachery forever.

She took a shortcut through the Waterside Towers
apartment complex, a series of brownstone structures with
a huge courtyard in the middle. When she was little she'd
always wanted to live there, to have a shorter walk home
from Amadon Elementary, the better of the neighborhood's
two grade school offerings. The other one, Bowen, was
across the street from her house and had broken glass all
over the playground, with an occasional pair of used
panties or a hypodermic needle thrown in for good measure. And her father wasn't having her in a place like that,
not as long as he had influence, and influence was something Alfonse Mitchell always made sure he had.

A soprano harmonized within the walls of Westminster
Episcopal, her voice leaking through a glass entrance door
left open for ventilation. Salamanca had been there a few
times in her seventeen years, mostly to see the Jefferson
Junior High chorus perform their annual Christmas con-
cert. Her good friend Cheryl Smith was an alto in that par-

ticular group, so Salamanca had always gone to support. It was a shame that she and Cheryl had gone to separate high schools. Since then the bond between her and that dear friend of hers had faded like a sun-bleached photograph. Now, friends were few and far between, having lost their importance in the wake of her all-consuming romance with Benjamin.

"Hey, girl!" Charles Washington called from a stoop as she wandered past. In fourth grade he'd laid claim to her as his girlfriend. And she hadn't minded. After all, he was light skinned and had that pretty curly brown hair her father always told her to look for in a man because it made for "good hair babies." She and Charles had even kissed once in the cafeteria after school, when she thought she had left her backpack there and he had gone to help her look for it. Now he didn't even remember her name. All he saw was firm titties, long hair, and pretty legs strolling down his neck of the neighborhood. At least she knew what a real man was. And at least there was one of them who'd always love her, and the child they'd made together, no matter what.

"So what'd they give him?" her father asked barely a beat after she had crossed the threshold. There was anticipation in his voice, a kind of anxiousness that was uncommon for his usually confident baritone. His stubbly face was half-concealed by the folded pages of the day's *Post*.

"Seven years," she said painfully while securing the door with the dead bolt.

"That's a real shame," he replied, lowering the newsprint to get a look at his only child. "I'll keep him in my prayers. I know a man over at Lorton who I can get to look out for him."

She wished he wouldn't play that game with her, that

oblivious "I don't know shit about anything but God and legitimate business" game that had gotten him too much of what he had. From his native Rocky Mount, North Carolina, to Detroit to D.C., it was always the same. And just then, looking at him sprawled across that couch in red plaid pajama bottoms and a baby blue bathrobe that exposed his swelling sixty-something gut, she wished that for once he'd just give it to her straight, the way he *never* had before.

"I really love him, Daddy," she said.

"I know you do, baby. That's why you gotta pray for the Lord to take care of him in there. 'Cause the Lord is the only thing that's gonna get him through."

She came over and sat in the wicker chair across from him. She crossed her legs, thinking it would make her look more sophisticated when she unveiled her secret, though she was pretty sure how he'd respond.

"Yeah, but there's something I have to tell you," she began.

Calm quickly became concern on the Old Man's face. "What is it?" he asked.

She looked dead into eyes that had seen more in sixty-plus years than she could ever know. They were eyes like her own, which they'd both gotten from her grandmother, whom she knew only through her daddy's stories and photos weathered by time. The words were a bullet in the chamber, cocked and loaded, awaiting her tongue to pull the trigger. She rose.

"I'm pregnant," she said.

She fortified her stance, a quarterback bracing for the blitz. But her father, Alfonse Mitchell, the man who had betrayed the love of her life, remained where he was and merely let out a sigh.

"I figured as much," he said all too casually. "No tampon wrappers in the bathroom this month. It's Ben's, isn't it?"

She nodded, nearly floored by the creepy thought that he knew when her period came, that he checked the trash for the wrappers. But she held her ground.

Her father shook his head, his soul submerged in a dark tank of pensive regret. She watched apathy become concern, which then became frustration. He got to his feet and turned the corner of the brass-framed, glass-topped table he'd lifted from his grandmother's house long ago. Then he looked into eyes that reflected his own. And without warning, the fingers on his right hand formed a fist, and that fist traveled upward, into her abdomen and, subsequently, into her womb.

His only child fell to the floor, doubled over, her manicured hands pressed against the area of impact.

"Mortify therefore your members which are upon the earth," he began from memory, a passage he'd taken from the dictionary-size Bible he kept beneath the shelves of trophies against the wall. It was the only thing he had left from the life of false piety that had been much of Salamanca's first eight years of living.

"Fornication, uncleanness, inordinate affection, evil concupiscence, and covetousness, which is idolatry. For which things' sake the wrath of God cometh on the children of disobedience."

It wasn't the pain alone that kept her down, or the words from the book of Colossians, third chapter, fifth and sixth verses. It was the idea that he had gone beyond the usual contradictions that made him who he was. He had shattered the promise forged years before, as they left the Motor City, forever.

He had promised to never bring violence near her. He had promised to protect her, no matter what. Now that pledge was steam rising into the heavens, lost forever.

She felt an itching on her left cheek, a reaction from the cheap shag carpet beneath her. Now she knew without question that Ben had been nothing but right about the man she'd called her father.

Her father's voice faded into a murmur as he climbed the stairs to his bedroom, where a door slammed shut. She knew what she had to do. And there wasn't much time in which to do it.

"You can't stay there," Ben had said from the other side of the glass, the phone pressed to his ear as the words went into hers. "It ain't safe for you. It ain't safe for the baby."

Everything Ben had said was so strong, so right. Yet the words were beyond the reach of what she deemed practical. After all, she was her father's child. And he had provided for her since the day she was born. She was seven weeks pregnant; he was doing seven years in prison.

Benjamin Baker, her lover, her soulmate, had uttered seven words that spelled the ultimate truth:

"He ain't gonna let you keep it."

It was the last thing he'd uttered before their final good-byes, when the CO tugged on his lanky arm, indicating that their time was up. The scene then ran on mute as she bore witness to her man being pulled into purgatory by the forces of law and order.

Now, lying on the floor, worrying that her own father's assault might have brought about a miscarriage, she knew that her man was right. The place she called home was no longer safe. Yes, leaving home, that familiar womb where she was living rent-free, was not the most practical thing.

But it was crucial for the child, and now the child was all that mattered.

She had bought herself a book for her birthday, something she'd heard about in a chatroom. Doug Richmond's *How to Disappear Completely and Never Be Found* was the book-of-the-month selection for conspiracy.org, a Web site she frequented during the many hours she spent surfing the Net. It was on that site that she'd seen the unedited footage of the Kennedy assassination, the particular cut of the film where Kennedy's driver can be seen firing the poison pellet that killed the president on that Dallas morning. It was there that she'd learned the truth about the U.S. invasion of Panama and about the use of that country as a testing ground for new military weaponry. So when she saw the book there, she figured that it might be of some use, one more edge against the rest of the world.

Ben told her that she was silly when she spoke of things she'd learned on that Web site. From his point of view, the world was just as it appeared. Good and evil balanced each other out in the course of every day, and all that one could do was live a righteous life and hope that the Lord allowed you to see another day.

Salamanca would wince every time she heard him say such rubbish, knowing that the scales on earth were always tipped in favor of the adversary. She knew of men who were filled to the brim with evil, men who could not be redeemed. She knew because one of them had brought her into being.

Salamanca Mitchell climbed to her feet and took in the room around her. A decade in D.C. and the place still looked as if he were the only one who lived there. No plants, no flowers, cheap shades where proper drapes should have hung, and carpet the color of peanut butter. Her daddy had a lot of things, but taste was not one of them.

There was the portrait of a husband, wife, and child in Negro Rockwellian splendor, a relic of the past, another reminder of the sealed lips that held father and daughter together. She loved Alfonse Mitchell not because he was her father, but because it was dangerous not to. But striking her womb had been too much. And Ben, her heart, and her child were all saying that it was time to go.

In a matter of hours she put in a page to Stevie Turner, the friend Benjamin had always referred to as best. He returned the call and suggested that they meet in front of the Safeway supermarket at Waterside Mall. And at seven-thirty, an hour after her father had left the house for Sally Helen's, the two of them stood face-to-face. Stevie handed her an envelope filled with $10,000 in hundreds, all the money Ben had left in his possession. She stuffed the envelope into her backpack of a purse and nodded, intent upon walking away without another word.

"You gonna be all right?" the best friend asked. She turned to the sawn-off boy and studied his dark brown eyes. In them she saw ambition, and fear, and the eeriest anticipation. Then she smiled.

"I don't know," she said. "But this is the best thing. Ben and I agreed on that."

"Are you sure, though?" he asked, overstepping his bounds as delivery boy. "You know, I . . . I mean, we just got this record deal and, well . . . I could look out for you, you know?"

She was puzzled by his words. The stuttering and stammering didn't hide the boy's desire to have his best friend's woman, and maybe even the child inside of her. She had a

fleeting thought about Ben's naïveté again, about him trust-
ing too much and how it undermined his intelligence.
Something had been comforted inside of the boy before her
when the judge passed the sentence. Something positive for
him had come out of her man's demise. And these were not
good things. But she had come for the money, which she
now had. There was a train to catch at Union Station in exactly two hours, and there was no time to waste in words.
She had to act.

"I'm okay, Stevie," she said as she started away, leaving
the boy frozen by his own guilt and confusion. A "yes" to
his proposal meant his hidden fantasy coming true. A "no"
indirectly spelled the end of a best friendship.

Checking the time, she decided to be nice, and delicate,
and jovial, and just move on.

"Take care of yourself," she finished as she started
toward the house where she'd lived since the age of eight,
her back to him until she turned a corner and vanished out
of sight.

"Lemme know if you change your mind," he had yelled
after her shadow. But the words never reached her ears.

Part Two

A postcard-color photo of downtown Charlotte, N.C., on one side and these words on the other:

September 1, 1995

    I went to see the doctor right after I talked to you. She said that everything's OK with the baby. And I'm still due March 24th. I have about $9,500 after the train ticket and a few little things I had to buy. And I've got a place here, a room in a boardinghouse. The landlord, a really nice man (who I'll call Mr. Walker), said he doesn't do leases and he only takes the rent in cash, which is wonderful. Because I don't make any paper trails for Daddy to find me. But I'm fine, baby, and it's your money that gave us a chance to do this. It gave us a chance to have our child and raise her with all the love in the world. But I write big and this card is so small. So I'm running out of room.

    Until . . .

Sala

P.S. I got a Charlotte postcard in the layover, but I'm really somewhere else. I figured that if Daddy has a man there at Lorton he could read your mail and find me. Love—
SSM

1.

On the outside, memories run like a movie, a
continuous stream of
audiovisual enchantment in
fully equalized surround
sound. The colors are vivid,
the resolution crisp. Life
out there is sensory overload.

But on the inside, it's
more of a slide show: cold
repeating stills mechanically
advancing backward and
forward until "lights out."

"I'm still gonna make it,"
I had said on my first night,
my voice directed at the
thin man on the rickety
bunk above mine. I could
see his reflection in the
mirror above the tiny sink,

or at least the circular cigarette glow that marked his position.

"That your dream?" his deep tenor asked.

"Only dream I got," I said with confidence, my ears monitoring the hard-soled steps of an approaching CO.

"Then ju better stop dreamin' it," he said after a sucking of teeth. The words were barely audible through his heavy Panamanian accent. "Before they find it and eat it."

"They who?" I asked.

"Miedo y muerte, chico. Fear and death. The two twins that make *this* world go round."

He was showing me the ropes in a day, seeding the soil in my mind with all he had learned. Because when dawn came he would be a free man, after five whole years of the opposite.

"What do you mean?" I asked again, wishing that he would hop down and look me in the eye. It was his last night, and my first. I needed to see his lips mouthing the words. I needed to know that human beings could make it in and through the animal factory. I needed to see him tell me that I was going to be all right.

"They all afraid of not livin' till *mañana.* But they don't want to die—*ninguno.* I think they call that a pa-ree-docks, *sí?"*

"Sounds like it," I said, a few steps further toward understanding.

"Sí, they're afraid of the dark, but even more scared of the dawn, because it means they gotta do it all over again. And if they fuck up, they die, or they get more time, or they go crazy and never be themselves again. *Miedo y muerte.* You wanna survive, you believe in one or the other. And the one

you choose chooses your path in here. But you can't believe in no dreams. 'Cuz when you dream you can't sleep with one eye open. *¿Comprende?*"

In the light of the new day, Cuchillo Martínez would be revealed as a man of five feet six, fair skinned with hair cut close to his head and a belly that spilled over his waistline. His shirt had been open enough to reveal a piece of the seven-inch scar across his chest, where he had been slashed with a box cutter while fighting to the death in an Adams Morgan alley, over a woman, the other guy's *"esposa."*

But the husband never left the scene, his neck snapped after two slashed nerves rendered his arms useless. Martínez was a surgeon with a blade and had earned his seven for manslaughter because of it. But he was walking in five, strolling into the light I wouldn't get to see for seven more years.

"Yeah, I get it," I said in response. "But I can't let my dream go, man. Lettin' go of it is like lettin' go of me."

There hadn't been a day in eight years when I hadn't written, when I hadn't arranged or rehearsed or criticized some piece of shit a superproducer earned a million bucks for. Cinnamon had been with me through everything, through the arraignment and the plea deal and even on that bus into the depths of the penal system. She had held me in her hot embrace when Salamanca could not. So there was no way for me to put her to sleep. There was no way I could get her to leave me.

"You can let anything go in here," he said, his last words before falling into a snore, his final snooze as a prisoner of the state of Virginia.

He left me to lie sleepless as I reviewed his words. It was one thing to survive. But what was surviving if you were without heart? What was living if there was no soul to live for? Without Cinnamon I knew that I would die.

So I decided to prove him wrong. I wrote lyrics and tracks on notebook paper and then in the blank journals that Mom and Salamanca sent. I read biographies on Marvin and Jimi, Miles and Prince. I gorged myself on music in every way I could. What music and I had was for life. Or at least I thought it was.

But then time began to stretch. It took longer for the days to become weeks, and weeks months. I saw an old man beaten to death over stamps. I watched the COs cut away the underwear that Bobby Randall had used to hang himself in the cell across the aisle. And I saw the letters and calls from Salamanca dwindle as time went on. Then one day there was nothing in my head but brain and blood, nothing in my soul but the will to make it through.

I'm sure that you can see how a dream can die in there. You've heard stories about the life inside. You've seen the Hollywood reenactments of men being stabbed in the chest with unwound bedsprings or the use of a blade in a toothbrush to slash the jugular of an unsuspecting adversary. You've seen actors portray inmates struggling to avoid gang rape from makeshift faggots bent on getting that piece of ass they so desperately wanted for Christmas.

It ain't summer camp. It ain't even boot camp. It's a killing field.

But I knew a few things even before Cuchillo schooled me. I learned how to get letters, or "kites," around undetected. And I knew that you had to let them know who you were the moment you arrived. You had to be proactive. And that was how I made my mark before I even got to Lorton.

I was in the hallway of the holding tank, being processed. It was less than an hour after the judge had sentenced me. I had just told my mother that I loved her when some dude put me in a choke hold and told me that his dick and my ass were going to be really good friends. He was much bigger than me, massive, in fact, with thick biceps and a neck as wide as my torso.

He finished his threat, released me with a victorious grin, and started to walk away, undoubtedly certain he'd have fresh meat on the hook at the end of our bus trip. I knew that I had to react, that doing nothing was worse than dropping my drawers and saying I was "ready for Big Daddy."

So I had nothing to lose as I reached for my weapon. My arms trembled in fear of the outcome. But it was that fear that allowed the deed to be done. It was what I had to do.

I grabbed hold of the rubber-gripped handle close to the floor and bludgeoned my enemy from behind with the janitor's mop wringer. The cleanup man had carelessly left the thing out in the open while rinsing his mop in the sink.

The gash washed his skull in crimson, the blood dribbling onto the previously spic-and-span linoleum. I scarred his brain, leaving him with a limp and weakened sense of feeling in all four limbs. I didn't even get charged, since no one actually saw me deliver the blow. From then on he turned the other way when he saw me coming.

I wasn't a violent person. I wasn't a criminal. I had just gotten a little lost. And I had seven whole years, 364 weeks, 2,555 days, to find my way back. I had only one other incident in my tenure at Lorton. But it was a big one and was thus the reason they transferred me out west.

After two years as a model prisoner, I had the misfor-

tune of having my work detail switched to the kitchen because somebody with more juice wanted to be on laundry.
And the kitchen had been one man short since a recent parole. I was to be his replacement.

Hector Morales ran the show in there, and a little
heroin whenever he got the chance. Since I was new, they
had me and the other newer guy doing all the cooking.
They'd have us washing as many as a dozen pans and pots
at once, just so I'd stay out of their way. I was so busy that I
barely knew where they kept the napkins, much less their
stash of powder.

But somebody else in there did know. And this stranger,
being in some sort of a tight spot himself, ratted Hector out
and got him hit with another ten years on a mandatory
twenty for murder one. Of course, everybody pointed the
finger at me just because I was new. You never trust the
new dude, until he ain't new anymore.

Of course, I didn't know I'd been fingered. I just came
to the kitchen and did my job day in and day out, until
Sanders, one of Hector's boys, tried to push me into a corner and gut me with a shiv. He made his move, and the shiv
hit nothing but brick. I found the room to spin out of the
way, yoked him from behind, and snapped his neck. He hit
the floor before the blade did.

The warden was a Polish asshole with pigeon toes. And
he didn't buy my story. But he couldn't prove I was lying,
especially since Sanders's prints were all over the shiv. So,
both being pissed off that he couldn't nail me and knowing
the beef and its body count would only escalate, he called a
buddy in Arizona and had me shipped out to the middle of
Bumblefuck, Nowhere. And there was nothing I could do
about it.

On the inside, I tried not to think about the outside. I just focused on keeping all of the blood in my body. And that was more than enough to occupy me until day's end. But at night, after the lights went out, when one of my three different cellmates' snoring created a gravelly bass line that lulled me into a meditative trance, I allowed myself the seductively sweet privilege of remembrance. There, on my brick-hard bunk, I went beyond the colorless inside slide show and took in full-fledged films of who I had been, the mistakes I had made, and the way I was suffering, the way *we* were suffering, because of it.

Salamanca was there, but she wasn't. She was freedom too often choked out by the sorrow of the bars and bunk. But her letters were enough to keep me alive. Her words made me feel all that I could never forget: the tang of her wetness, the tickle of her nipples against my own, her hands stroking me as she invited me inside. And her telephone voice was enough to make me come in my drawers in a room full of the hardest niggas I'd ever known.

"She's getting so big," she had said in the eighth month, after the obstetrician had said that everything was all right. I could tell from the pictures that her face had stretched a little, that her hips and thighs had spread, making plump what had once been firm. But I loved it. I truly loved it. I loved everything she said and did and sent because it was hers, because she managed to share so much with me without every laying eyes on the prison that could have made me hate her.

"Until," we would say to each other at the end of every call. It was the neutral word we'd chosen to stand in for all of what we felt. That one word gave us the strength to make it until the next time, and the one after that, until we could see each other face-to-face.

But it was still hard. My cellmates said I called out to her in my sleep, whimpering her name as I stained the sheets with self-induced passion. But I knew the day would come when that life would be a past one, when I could hold her to me until we both felt safe. And then our kid would lie down next to us and spill all the grade school secrets we already knew from having been there.

That was a life to look forward to. And that life was going to be mine.

The postcard is from Montpelier, Vermont. There is an image of Winnie the Pooh standing on a stool, trying to reach a jar of honey on top of a shelf. Through a window we see a lake and trees outside of the cabin.

November 16, 1996

Sweetie:

I went out and bought a calendar today. I went out and bought a whole book of days and dates and times just so I could mark them off. I want to put a slash through each and every second that we spend apart from each other. When this is over, and when we both go home, I want us to sit down and count the time together. And I want us to burn that number into our memories. We'll be able to smile about it. I know we will, because seven years is nothing in the span of a lifetime. It's nothing when you think about the years we'll spend raising our babies, and all the time it will take for you to make your records and go on tour. And I'll have my own engineering firm. And we're going to be happy, my sweetheart. We're going to be full of joy. And this time won't be anything but the distant past. We have to live in the future. I'll write you again soon.

Until . . .

Sala and Sasha

2.

I didn't say a single good-bye when the time came.
There wasn't much of a point. I had parted with my real squad three years, six months, and fifteen days before, when they transferred me out of Lorton for my act of self-defense. Sure, there were a few folks I'd gotten down with in that second place. No one stands alone on the inside. But those who'd stood with me knew who they were, and the bonds we forged didn't need sappy farewells to make them real.

I didn't sleep that last night. There were too many memories of a world fast approaching. There was my mother, my brother, my best friend, my mentor and enemy, my child, and a woman I loved more than life itself. Many miles to travel. Many steps back to what should have been.

Anticipation bounced on my eyelids for hours before it finally retreated just before dawn. I slipped off into a few moments of a doze, and then I had the dream I would always remember.

I was in a white hospital room, wearing a white suit. And it was just the two of us. Me and the Old Man, who was just a few feet in front of me. He looked older than I'd remembered him. His skin was thin and wrinkled. The circles under his eyes looked as if they'd been colored in with a permanent marker. But that goatee of his was shaved clean as a whistle. And his bald head still gleamed in the sunlight forcing its way through the outer window.

He was lying on a reclining bed in front of me, propped up by pillows, his arms a pincushion for numerous tubes. There was even a tube running out of his dick and another one coming out of his other end.

Tears slid down his cheeks as his eyes met mine. He was filled with shame for all that he'd done to me, and to his daughter, and to the innocent little girl who had suffered most from his machinations. Then his mouth gaped as if he wanted to speak, but no sound came out. And then I woke up.

That morning, that first morning of my next life, Steven Marvin Turner sat in his 1978 Corvette convertible puffing on a Parliament and bobbing his head to an audio track I'd never heard before. He was no longer skinny as a rail, as a slight gut could be seen through the cotton blend of his white guayabera shirt.

But everything else looked the same. He was still my best friend. And he had still been there for me, when he could've kept his distance like all of the others.

There was another recurring dream I'd had inside. But it stopped after my first few months, after I buried my musical hopes in a tomb at the bottom of who I was. That dream was my vision of the show at the Ritz the night the cops took me away, the show that was supposed to make me a star. I imagined myself on the edge of that elevated stage, with Stevie and the others backing me as I stole the crowd's hearts and minds.

We wore matching periwinkle suits and shiny patent-leather shoes. Both levels of the long-halled and narrow-walled club were packed tighter than an ass in spandex. The only way to that stage, our stage, was to walk on top of the crowd. And we did. Their hands supported our feet and ankles as we shuffled on air, taking our place in music history at the very beginning of our careers.

In that dream I had no idea of what song we were singing. But a bleach-blonde with a blue black face jumped onto the stage and tried to kiss me before security removed her. Stevie and I traded falsettos, bringing the house down while Lonnie and Andre moved along with the chords and choreography at the rear. And just as we finished, Johnny Dopeness pulled us to the side of the stage and told us he wanted to give us a record deal. It was the greatest moment I'd ever lived, inside my head.

In the real-life version, Stevie *had* brought the house down. And when he and Lonnie and Andre were finished, after they'd sung my words and the music I helped to make,

Johnny Dopeness did appear. And he told them that he wanted to sign them to his new label, Pure Uncut. The only difference was that I, Benjamin Baker Jr., had not been there.

"What you want me to do?" Stevie had been quick to ask when he came to visit me that next day, my first full day in the holding tank after being picked up the afternoon before. Stevie being the only one from the group there said a lot about where I stood with the others. Andre would've had a sex change if it meant singing in a school talent show. So he didn't have a qualm in the world about saying sayonara and turning our quartet into a trio. And Lonnie hadn't really liked me since I'd fattened his lip on the Bowen playground back in sixth grade. But that was what he got for calling my mother a jungle bunny.

"You know what you gotta do," I said to him sadly as I watched my dream sail away. "This is what we wanted, right?"

I didn't let him see the fear churning in my gut. He didn't see my overpowering impulse to beg him to take me with him, to hook a chain to my barred window and tear down the fourth wall that added up to a prison.

Instead I just looked at him, his rectangular lenses resting on the bridge of his nose, his eyes shadowed by the brim of a dark blue baseball cap. He didn't answer. He couldn't answer, not until he weighed the magnitude of what I was saying, not until he understood that I was telling him to move on, to make our dream *his*, and to make me proud. All of that came in one poignant question. When he finally answered it was only in a gesture, in one silent, solemn nod.

"I'm keepin' all the songs," he said. "If you can't sing wit' us, I'ma at least blow you up as the writer!"

"Just do what you can," I said, unfazed by his naive but generous proposition. I didn't care about the credit or the money. I cared only about the music that was still beating warm inside of me, right then.

"Keep everybody together," I ordered, feeling the torch drop from my fist. "And don't let 'em forget where we came from."

"I can't forget that," he fired back. "Too many years for that. Too much time doin' the work."

My name was mentioned in Waterfront interviews and in the album credits and special thanks. The first two records went double platinum worldwide. I was supposed to be there, but by then my Cinnamon was long gone, dismissed, some loose broad I used to fuck.

However, everything crashed after album two. Andre screamed that he wanted more creative control. He wanted the group to be all about guest rap verses and big-name producers, whatever it took to make the next record cross over into the sludge of the mainstream. Lonnie, as his cousin, felt that he had to go along with the new program. The results were rather disastrous.

The Water Won't Run Dry, the Waterfront's third and most likely final album, dropped out of the top two hundred in eight weeks. Andre and Lonnie stormed off for New York in search of solo stardom. And Stevie went to Los Angeles, got married to a B-movie actress, then divorced her, and started working on his own as a producer. He'd worked on a few different records and was working with a new artist, a twenty-two-year-old girl from St. Louis named Seeka.

———

"It's about muthafuckin' time," Stevie shouted as he discharged a round of applause. His right wrist was wrapped in diamonds set in platinum. His overbite had retreated into perfect alignment with his lower teeth. And there was a day's stubble on his face, signs of facial hair I hadn't previously remembered.

"I'm just glad yo' ass wasn't late," I said as I glanced at the imaginary watch on my wrist. Then we hugged as though twice the time had passed. His hairline had crept back a quarter of an inch at the temples. But he kept it cut so low that most wouldn't have noticed. But his eyes held a hint of something unsettling.

"Today only happens once," he said, drawing two squares from the hard box in his shirt pocket. He lit us up with a silver Zippo that gleamed in the rays of Arizona light. "Looks like the clothes fit you all right."

He'd sent me a white button-up shirt, some dark brown khakis, matching socks, and a pair of loafers a week before, since there was absolutely no way I could still fit the suit I came in with. My massive biceps rubbed against the fabric of my sleeves. I looked forward to shrinking back to human size.

I gave Wilson Nance State Penitentiary one last look, an analytical gaze that cased the joint from top to bottom. It was the first time I'd seen the place from the outside since I'd checked in. It looked exactly like what it was: a prison. And one from which I had just been freed. Yet I still had to free myself from it.

"Let's rock," my best friend shouted excitedly. I took a long drag from my cigarette and nodded. Freedom curled through my lungs and came out a thick, cancerous cloud dissolving into the warming desert air. It was time to get back to where I was supposed to be.

"I could leave you here if you want," my best friend said, snatching me out of my trance.

"There's nothing left for you to leave," I said, lowering myself into the pure pleasure of white leather interior. "I'm already down the road headed home."

3.

It made sense that Stevie had been the one to come get me. After all, he had always been the one doing the pickups. He'd wheeled both of us and our dates to the prom in his father's Pathfinder when Mom couldn't afford to rent me a car. He had even driven all the way up to Adams Morgan when my first car (a raggedy 1982 Corolla with a missing window) broke down and I didn't even have the money for a fare card.

I'll never forget the first time our paths crossed. We were both in the sixth grade at Bowen, and it was the day for band tryouts. We were both leaning against the rear wall of

Mr. Russell's music room, watching the rest of the hopefuls chatter like teeth. To them, playing an instrument was no different than playing a sport. But we knew better.

"Once you truly learn your instrument," Mr. Russell, our teacher, had said, his bulblike Afro blowing in a fan-powered breeze, "it will never leave you. And you will never leave it. Because music is like a friendship. All the pieces have to work together to make it sound the way it's supposed to. And that's the way all of you are going to have to work, if you want to learn from me."

There were two music teachers: Mr. Russell and Ms. Swinton, a fifty-something lady with wrinkled light skin and horn-rimmed glasses. Swinton had you playing out of the songbooks. But Russell had you playing songs off the radio. So you know who everyone wanted.

Our first words to each other came in conflict. We both wanted to learn guitar, and there was only one guitar in the school inventory. So one of us was going to be playing something else.

I didn't know the kid. But I knew where he lived, on the *other* side of Waterside Towers, which meant that his family had to be some kind of different to send him to the bad school when the good one was right down the street.

So that made me curious, curious enough to make a little sacrifice to find out more. But I never got the chance. Nakia Thompson got to play the guitar that year. Because we both opted for the piano, in deference to each other.

"Are you sure?" he asked me while sipping coffee in the hundred-plus-degree heat. We were mired in a grease pit called the Serene Café, though there wasn't much serenity in a ten-by-ten shack any health official would have shut down on sight. But we had to go for it, since it was the only spot for thirty miles.

"How many times we gotta go over this?" I asked, feeling a headache coming on. "I'm done, man. The only thing I care about now is finding Sala and Sasha."

"You're acting like you can only have one or the other," Stevie growled. "And it ain't like that."

"You been trying to bully me into playing again for six years, and I ain't never budged. I don't see why you keep tryin'."

" 'Cause I know you, Ben," he argued. "I known you longer than almost anybody. And I know that *you* ain't *you* without music."

"Maybe I just ain't the *me* you remember," I snapped back, hoping my tone would be firm enough to table the subject.

"Whatever," he grumbled, blowing a wisp of smoke at me in semidefeat. "I *know* you."

"So what did Malcolm say?" I interjected.

Stevie's older brother had gotten out just a year before me and started his own bounty-hunting and private eye firm, with a little help from his little brother, of course. I had a little job for him, something I needed to keep all of the bases covered upon my release.

"I didn't talk to him long," Stevie said. "But he told me that he found out something about a house out on the bay with the Old Man's name on it."

"Really?" I asked, not expecting to have snagged such a big fish.

"That's what he said," Stevie replied.

"So what, I can just drive up to his crib, ring the bell, and say hi?"

"Yeah, even though 'hi' ain't what you wanna say. As a matter of fact, I get the feeling you don't want to say nuthin' at all."

"Could be," I said with a shadowy grin.

There'd been a lake full of moments when I wanted to spread the Old Man's brains to the wind, or burn him alive, or separate head from spine with one clean slice. But I had pushed those things away, telling myself that I'd found the tree-lined path to forgiveness.

"But I ain't that dude anymore," I continued. "I just wanna tell him that I'm out, let him know that he failed, cuz I'm still gonna be his son-in-law even after all he did to try and stop me."

Stevie looked at me with worried eyes. He could see the emptiness behind my words, even when I couldn't.

"Just watch your step," he said.

"Don't worry," I answered. "I got one eye on the ground and the other straight ahead. Ain't nuthin' I can't see."

"Except for what's behind you," he replied.

"Here ya go," our waitress twanged in a southwestern dialect. She set down our plates: buttermilk flapjacks and OJ for me, a well-done steak and scrambled eggs for my driver.

"Yo' ass got big in there!" he said, looking me over as he shifted back into "reunited and it feels so good" mode.

"Liftin'll do that to you," I said, glancing down at the paunch that shone beneath his form-fitting shirt. "And yo' ass got a little fat."

He looked down at his gut and then began to smile. "All that time in the studio," he said, slapping the pouch with his palm. "Need to get my ass a treadmill. Do Tae-Bo or something."

"Man, I don't care what you do, but you better do it quick." What started as a shared chuckle snowballed into a bellowing that had both of us practically face first on the tabletop.

"It's good to see you out, Baker," he said.

"It's good to be out," I said, cleaning my plate.

There was an odd silence in the moments that followed, all the warmth and reminiscence having petered out. Stevie ordered more coffee and tapped a finger against the table with no particular rhythm in mind. Then his lips curled into a grin more devilish than usual.

"So how long I got to convince you?" he exploded, now sounding more like a car salesman than an accomplished musician.

"Convince me of what?" I asked, pretending not to understand.

"To convince you that you still got it, that where you need to be is in the studio making records." He was starting to piss me off.

"I'm going home," I said definitively. "And I ain't gonna say it again. If all picking me up was about was—"

"Seven years and you can't give your homeboy one day? One fuckin' day?" His face instantly flushed with anger. But there was fear there as well.

I just looked at him: not fidgeting, not sighing, just looking. The way I had looked at Jimmy Stein during our five years' worth of chess games.

Jimmy and I got together on Tuesdays and Thursdays. Convicts of all colors drew heat and numbers to day room C just to watch us play. Stein, a wiry Jewish dude in his early thirties, had been running crystal meth out of the McDonald's he managed in the suburbia outside of Phoenix. He was probably the only millionaire in the world who went to work in a uniform marked for the minimum wage. And ironically it was one of those five-buck-an-hour earners who turned him in, just because he was tired of not getting the hours he wanted for his weekly shift.

For a whole year Jimmy kicked my ass without much effort. I knew how to take rooks and pawns. But I never saw his full threat to my king until it was far too late. I could only see things in the short term. But losing to him, time and time again, taught me how to form a strategy, how to see all the way to the end, win or lose.

My strategy was to get my ass back to D.C., find my woman and my baby, and start over. So any and every action I took was to be toward that end. Even a day off course was too much to ask. Anything else was the shed skin of a life that no longer mattered.

But then again, he *was* my best friend. And it had been a lifetime since I rode a city's streets with him. That morning had been the first time we could slap hands away from the watchful eyes of contraband cops. I hadn't danced a step or drunk a drink or laughed a free laugh since I was eighteen years old. So at twenty-five, I was kind of overdue for all of the above.

"Two days," I said sternly. Stevie gave me that devilish smile again and flagged our waitress for the check.

"You're a good man, Benjamin Baker," he said. "That's a whole day longer than I thought you'd give me."

December 23, 1996

Hey, baby! Merry Christmas again, just in case the last letter caught you too early or too late. I just finished trimming the tree and putting Sasha down for a nap. My nipples are so sore from feeding her. But they still miss you (smile). I hope you liked our presents. Sasha chose everything. After all, she knows you better than me, because you're a part of her. You brought her into this world, and I'm so thankful for that even though I wonder if I'd give her up if it meant that I could see you right now, if I could hold you in my arms outside of those goddamned walls. But I'm counting the days. I'm making them slide by in my mind. But you gotta help me. You gotta see the end the same way I do, right around the corner and across the street. I know we can do it, baby. And I know you know, too. You still got my heart in your hands.

Until . . .

Sala and Sasha

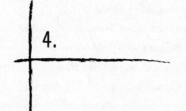

4.

The ultrasound jelly was glacial against her skin. And to make it worse, the good Dr. Gonzalez took her time in spreading it across Salamanca's bloated belly. The mother-to-be was jittery. This was one of the biggest parts in her time as a human pouch. Her hands trembled. A repeated chill shot up and down her back. Her constant phrase to the doctor was, "Am I okay?"

But it was all worth it when her trusted doctor put the magic wand to her womb. Then she looked to that tiny screen and saw the little rugrat that moved and kicked every chance she got, most often when her mother needed it least. But those kicks were important, a telltale sign that her child was going to be a fighter, like her mother and her mother's mother before her.

Salamanca had loved her mother more than anything, until that night she had gone away, forced into the forgotten by the same man who had put a ring on her finger.

"She's looking good," said Dr. Gonzalez, her blond highlights gleaming in the white light overhead. The T-shirt beneath her white coat proclaimed, HAY SIEMPRE ESPERANZA. There is always hope.

The good doctor asked her about the prenatal yoga and sticking to the prescribed vegan diet and all the other things they normally chattered about as alternative doctor and alternative patient and as alternative, earthy, Afrocentric women of color.

It was a cross-generational friendship found where neither would have expected it. Thirty-eight to eighteen. Venezuelan to Washingtonian. Yet to those who saw them in the streets of the West End, one of the poorest and yet most historic sections of southwest Atlanta, they might as well have been sisters, a single mind with a single determination to do things their way.

The good doctor, or Marlene Gonzalez, as she was known outside of the Obstetrics Unbound clinic on Cascade Road, handed Salamanca the first image of her child-to-be, a glossy square of a black void with the centered outline and contours of the evolving fetus. Salamanca cheesed at the sight of the uterine snapshot, instantly seeing Benjamin Baker's profile in what there was of the developing baby's face. But even though it was far too early to know for sure, she had the concrete belief that Sasha Salamanca Baker would have her chocolate eyes—eyes that were destined to make a mark on the world.

Salamanca kept her eyes on the picture through her good-bye hug from Marlene, and her walk down the clinic hallway, and into the parking lot, where her 1990 Cherokee was parked. It was January 1996 and just under fifty degrees. Salamanca loved Atlanta. And she knew that Benjamin, when the time came, would love it too.

It had been six months, two weeks, and three days since she'd said good-bye to the old neighborhood. Sometimes it felt as if she were a lifetime away from who she had been there. Other times it was as if every day were the first day. She would get out of bed barely knowing where she was in that little bungalow surrounded by weeds and shrubs on Richland Road.

But at least she wasn't totally alone. Her two squirrelly roommates were always around the place to keep her company. They were two potbellied characters out of some twisted version of a Disney flick, always wandering the crimson-carpeted halls of the tiny house they all shared, singing gospel hymns in the breakfast nook at daybreak and then getting their afternoon rocks off watching porn compilation tapes. Sala was amazed that they'd made it through three years of classes at the school many knew as the "Black Harvard."

Dean and Jerry were definitely not her cup of tea. But their telephone-pole flyer had announced a vacancy. And she had needed an immediate roof overhead. Plus they wanted the rent in cash. No ID. No credit check, either. It was everything a pregnant girl on the run could ask for.

Sala knew that her father was looking for her. She envisioned hired men combing through electronic records and bank accounts, employment files and credit card computers, all the systems used to keep tabs on the consumer. So she'd had to learn to consume in an undetectable way. That meant that all accounts payable and receivable dealt only in a single color: green.

She'd put $5,000 of the money Ben had given her into a safety-deposit box under the name of Ms. Mariah Carey. The rest was stashed in various corners and crevices: stitched into the center of her goose-down pillow, some in the lining of her only suitcase, and the rest in a plastic sleeve in her half refrigerator that had once held frozen french fries. She'd even taken a base pay cut at Mugs and Slugs, a watering hole in Little Points, the city's crunchy bohemian center, just to keep everything in cash.

She cruised down Cascade Road as if she had all the time in the world. The setting sun painted the sky a rich tangerine as she moved toward the last traces of true community the city had left.

A gathering of old men smoked pipes and squares on a crumbling stoop. Four little girls took turns on the silver sliding board in West End Park. And a crew of workmen gathered around a fallen oak with roots thicker than the men themselves, dismantling it with shears and electric saws.

At every red light she would glance down at the sonogram image, which she'd propped up in the passenger seat as if it were a living thing, imagining the day when that picture would begin to talk to her. That little girl would sit on the backseat and ask her and Ben questions about how the great big world worked. The thought made her smile. But with that smile came concern.

She didn't know enough about the world to teach it to anyone. She was a high school dropout who got a perfect score on her GED exam. She audited engineering classes at Georgia Tech on her off days. Her partner in this parenting venture was doing a seven-year stretch in the clink, living at the mercy of a system designed to take him out as quickly as possible.

The light turned green and she went on through the intersection, bobbing her head to Mary J's "Be Happy." She flipped on her signal to merge into the right lane and got a slight surprise. She *knew* the car that was directly behind her.

It was a black 1986 Toronado, a lot like the one her father had had in Detroit back when she was a little girl. It had been parked in front of the SuperKroger grocery just before noon when she went to get tofu and veggie burgers. There had been another car like it in front of the student center over at Georgia Tech. Now it was right behind her, with the same pear-shaped figure at the wheel.

She pulled a hard right on the first available street, staring at the emptiness behind her for a few seconds before finding relief when the car didn't follow. Tense shoulders relaxed. Heart rate lowered. The changer waved good-bye to Mary and ushered in Marvin's "Soon I'll Be Loving You Again." The child inside of her made a slight shift to the right, causing her last meal to gurgle deep in her belly.

But everything seemed to be all right. She seemed to be safe. She made two lefts and was back on Cascade. The singer's hypnotic soprano made her think of her incarcerated man, of the way he'd put the tip of his tongue to her neck, sparking that tickle that made her smile and moisten below in the same moment.

She held on to the memory, trying to re-create the sensation with a free finger. But it didn't even come close. Richland Road, home, was one more left turn away.

The car made a perfect arc onto the strip of side street. Otis, the neighborhood weedhead, waved a subdued hello from the dirt brown shack on the right. He, like so many others on the block, had blind hopes of filling the space in her heart, or at least the one between her thighs, though both were adamantly reserved for her one and only.

She grinned to herself, once again thinking of Ben. But what she saw ahead wiped that grin away just as quickly. That black '86 Toronado was parked right in front of her humble abode. Her father had already found her.

She could've screeched to the street's end, banged a hard U, and sped back up the street to safety before the driver had even turned his key. But that was some shit off of prime-time TV. And even if that did work, he could still follow her. And no matter where or how long such a chase might stretch, that shadow in the Oldsmobile knew where Salamanca Mitchell would eventually have to come back to. Her clothes, her money, even the passport she'd recently purchased, were in that little hovel of a house.

She could've picked up her cell phone and called the cops to scare him off. But that would take far too much time in that particular neck of the woods. Besides, she knew that cops could never be trusted.

She shuffled a full deck of thoughts as she sat in her ancient Cherokee with the dying muffler, the engine idling in the dead center of that narrow street. Her chocolate eyes zeroed in on that pear-shaped silhouette. That shadow could have been Death itself.

Then the Oldsmobile's door opened, and the mysterious form became a coal-colored man of five feet eight with a bald head and a beard, short legs and long arms, one of which bade the girl to come closer. There was a bulge at the bottom of his right pant cuff, probably a .25 or a .38.

"Now I'm not gonna hurt you," he said, sounding like Mushmouth from *Fat Albert*. "Your daddy sent me because he's worried about you."

Now wasn't this some shit? Daddy was now worried about her. But worry hadn't stopped him from throwing that uppercut to her abdomen or his sadistic attempt to destroy the life that she and Ben had created. The guy in front of her probably had a stun gun, too, or a taser, or chloroform, whatever it might take to get her into that car and on her way back to the fiery hell of her daddy's wrath. But she wasn't going out like that.

"I don't want you to hurt me, either," she said calmly, keeping her hands out of view. She turned her wrist to check the time while the fingers on her right picked up her cell phone and dialed the one number in the neighborhood that could save her and her baby's high yellow asses.

The man started toward the Jeep, his palms wide and visible, the pantomime version of "I come in peace." And she let him come, as she reached for the pepper spray in the plastic bin on the door. She even rolled down the window to make it easy for him.

"You're a pretty girl, Salamanca," he continued. "Your husband will be a very lucky man." She could smell her father on him. She could see his will stained on this unknown man's hands. And it made her afraid, though she'd be damned if she'd ever show it.

He was almost to her when she looked in her side mirror to see exactly what she had hoped for. Tahir was coming up fast from Cascade Road. Right on time.

Until Atlanta, Salamanca hadn't known much about men, aside from her father and Benjamin Baker. The rest had been boys. Little monsters with hands, lips, and ding-a-lings that wanted her for the body they fantasized about before, during, and definitely after class. But she wasn't stupid. She knew how the boy/girl game was played, and she knew how to use what she had, when she needed to.

Tahir lived in the house behind her on the next street over. A part-time student, he made his tuition crafting fake IDs for baby-faced freshmen and sophomores. Just over six feet, slim, and chiseled, with a head full of long, thick locks, he would have been her type if there hadn't been Ben. Thus, his attraction to her was nothing more than a tool she used for her survival.

They hung out from time to time, usually to smoke herb or thumb through whichever books they might have been reading at the given moment. He said he liked her energy, that he was someone she could trust. He'd given her a code of her own to put into his cell phone if she ever needed anything or if anyone gave her trouble.

The man in the Toronado was trouble personified. And Tahir had spent a year or two in juvie for assault. She loved it when a plan came together.

Tahir's walk became a run when he took in the scene. The pear-shaped man lunged just as he saw Tahir approaching. Salamanca, seeing his attention diverted, quickly doused the man's eyes with her fiery spray. Death hit the asphalt, and

Tahir was standing over him a moment later, not even out of breath.

"What's goin' on?" he asked, his Georgia accent making every word into a guitar pluck.

"My father sent him," Salamanca said, watching as Tahir searched him for weapons, discovering a stun gun clipped to the belt beneath his shirt and a .38 in a holster on his right leg.

"What for?" Tahir asked.

"To make me go back home," she replied. Tahir nodded, her words being all the explanation he needed.

"I ain't the only one," the man said, his face still scrunched in pain as involuntary tears streamed down his face.

"What the fuck did you say, nigga?" Tahir demanded, his pectorals flexing beneath his green camouflage coat. Salamanca turned off the car and returned the pepper spray to its compartment.

"He probably sent some other ones," she said.

"I'm just doing my job," the man proclaimed, still blinded by the vicious chemical. "This shit ain't personal."

She put a manicured hand to Tahir's neck and saw the flesh rise on his forearms. It gave her a power she'd never felt before.

"Well, you need to stop doin' it," Tahir said, "particularly if you don't want no problems around this way."

"He's been following me all day," Salamanca said, using the damsel in distress pitch she'd perfected since moving to the Peach State.

"Is that right?" Tahir asked, his eyes never leaving the senior man beneath him.

"Yeah," Salamanca said, knowing that what she wanted was already in motion. "Let me go and park my truck."

"You go on and do that, baby," Tahir replied. Something in his eyes darkened as the woman looked away. Death was bloody before she shifted into drive, and flat-out unconscious by the time she'd parallel-parked between the Oldsmobile and Jerry's Volkswagen Bug in front of her house.

There was a spot of wet blood on Tahir's blond boot as he turned to her.

"You want a drink?" she asked him.

"You know I do," he replied, following her up the walk for a glass of Salamanca's notoriously good raspberry iced tea. Inside she called the cops and reported a drunken man yelling in the street. But minutes later, when she and Tahir looked out of her window to make sure Death was still down, they found nothing but drying blood on the cracked asphalt.

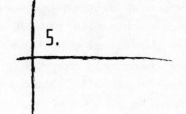

5.

"He's out," Maurice said as he lowered the black cordless into its charger. "He got processed this morning." The young man waited for an answer, but the Old Man did not reply. Instead, he took a moment to remember when Maurice had been a beanpole of a boy, scared of everything outside of his own shadow, a boy who had turned to crime in hopes of changing his neighborhood rep for being as soft as ice cream in summer.

Alfonse Mitchell remembered when Maurice had started waiting tables for him and when he used to wash his car every Saturday for chump change. And then when the time came, he robbed homes for him and helped him to set up Benjamin Baker, the poor soul who had dared to pose a threat to his all-important freedom.

Maurice was like a son. Not a favorite son, but a son nonetheless. He was one of the few he knew he could depend on, whenever and wherever.

"So whatchu wanna do?" Maurice implored, unnerved by the boss's silence.

"Let him come home," he finally replied. "After seven years he needs to come home, see his family, see what's changed."

Maurice's brow wrinkled with emotion as he remembered the face of the man they spoke of, of the smile he could never escape before it was locked away. Benjamin Baker had had him beat at every game there was: every job, every restaurant tip, and every score at every house their employer had targeted. He'd even gotten the girl Maurice had been pining for, that slender, big-tittied redbone who hadn't given him as much as a hug.

"But what if he wants some get-back?" the younger man pleaded, wanting nothing more than for the Old Man to give the order that would have Ben disposed of.

"He can want a million in hundreds, but that don't mean I'm gonna give it to him," he said casually. "Besides, it ain't like we even in the city anymore. We ain't got trails or tracks. We ain't leave nuthin' for him to go on. So he can look for it all he wants. But he ain't gonna be getting it."

Maurice wanted to ask about Ben's other half, the prodigal daughter whom no one had seen for more than seven years. But he had learned long ago that she was never to be spoken of in the Old Man's presence, for reasons that everyone understood. So he kept the question to himself and returned to the larger room, where there was work to do.

Alfonse Mitchell waited for his exit before he let out a deep exhalation, ending his struggle to maintain the cool facade that was his trademark. The pain was a white-hot drill grinding through his abdomen, wrenching through bone, nerve, and tissue all at once. The bright crimson in his bowels had increased in prior months. But while he was a millionaire several times over, he had refused to see a doctor.

It wasn't that he didn't believe in medicine. But he had more faith in the Lord and his own destiny. The Man Upstairs had a swift sense of vengeance, one that Mitchell had become increasingly deserving of as his life moved toward its end.

And he was certain that the boy was coming for him, to exact his revenge for the hand he'd been dealt. So the Old Man had pleaded guilty without trial and left a trail for his foe to find him.

He climbed up from his squeaking leather chair, the one he'd had at Sally Helen's before he sold the place, the one he'd stolen on the night of his final year of running that seafood joint out in sorry-ass Southfield, the only thing left of a past he'd all but erased the minute people started asking questions. He'd thought Ben's arrest and conviction would lower the heat. But instead the whole thing had gone on full flame.

The IRS did an extensive audit of the books he'd cooked to a crisp. There were rumors of a burglary division task force created just for him. And when that kind of heat came down, the only thing to do was get out of Dodge. Sell it all to men who were never in need of silly things like loans and mortgages, men who didn't ask questions, and then disappear.

"You gotta know both worlds, boy," Cortez Mitchell, his father, had said to him nearly half a century before. They were on a dirt road fifty miles from the closest doctor. And the bullet was lodged in the father's belly, making his imminent death insufferably slow. If only they had known that their partners were going to betray them. If only they had known that the man at the wheel had a pistol under his seat.

"You gotta know how to find that respect, that love, that fear, in the face of every man that sees your face."

The words had come out slow and raspy as his lungs strained for oxygen. At fifteen, Alfonse was washing dishes in back of the hole where his father often played cards, making his handful of change one way while Pop did it just the opposite only a few steps away.

All the young man had wanted was to be a businessman, to marry a good woman and have babies and take them all to church every Sunday. But that life didn't seem to be in the cards on his father's side of Rocky Mount, North Carolina. The boy often found himself sleeping among thieves, whores, and thieves who whored, his dreams scored by the sound of some sixteen-year-old getting the shit fucked out of her by men old enough to have called her daughter.

He'd learned to clean guns and play lookout before he'd learned how to read. But worst of all, he had that burn deep in his gut, that drive to get over on all those chumps in the world who only knew how to play it straight, and those pink-skinned mongrels who never seemed to remember that they'd set his people free three generations before.

But then he found God, in a black book left in a train station, and then the marines, and then the life he'd wanted, that all-important straight and narrow. But in the end he couldn't make it stick. Instead, his two sides of a soul got all smooshed together like a cluttered plate of barbecue. And he had to take it all in, no longer able to separate one from the other.

Now he was sixty-seven years old. He had more money than he could count, a daughter he hadn't seen since sixty, and an ever-changing empire that meant less and less as the cancer inside of him grew. He walked over to the two-way mirror overlooking the outer office and saw his only semblance of a future.

The new boys were out there, five of them. Different heights and sizes. But they were all hungry, all struggling to quell that same burn for action he'd inherited from his old man. And Maurice was at the head of them. Mitchell hoped that he could be their leader in his absence, that he wouldn't get himself killed by the first man to cross him or squander the riches and resources he'd inherit with the keys to the Mitchell kingdom.

Those driven young men did their jobs well, scrambling the green and powdered products across the Pennsylvania countryside. The Old Man was a rich man getting richer, though money would mean nothing in the place where he would soon be headed.

6.

The high rocks melted into mounds, and the mounds into flat California plains, all beneath a clear sky of the richest blue. There were palm trees and passing cars and cops hiding out in patches of brush and beneath underpasses. I was glad to see nature in full bloom, to see life at the beginning of a harvest season. All I'd known was desert and death for four years straight. And it had most definitely taken its toll on me.

"So what's L.A. like?" I asked, breaking what had seemed like several hours of silence. Jill Scott's sweet alto breathed tranquility through the fine-tuned system.

"You'll see soon enough," he replied.

Stevie could never give me a straight answer about why he'd moved out west. He wasn't a movie star. His record label was based in New York, as was that actress who had once carried his name. So I figured that there had to be something otherworldly about the place, something vibrant, something far beyond what our Chocolate City had to offer.

"Like nothin' you've ever seen," he said with pride. Dark designer shades covered his pupils, blocking me from any emotion his eyes might have carried.

"Is it like home?" I asked.

"Nah," he said, shaking his head. "It ain't nuthin' like home."

"So what's it like, then?"

"You just gotta see it for yourself. Like I said. We'll be there soon enough."

"Oh, my God!" the woman yelled fifty miles later. Stevie had barely gotten the nozzle in the tank before she was on him like a refrigerator magnet. "I can't believe it's you!"

She was a big, beautiful woman, with almond-shaped eyes and walnut-colored skin that glowed under the harsh lights. Just being in proximity to a woman sparked a fire inside of me. Even with the $5 stretch pants and high-gel hairdo that hadn't been *in* since before I went in, she was still my contender for Ms. Black America. My eyes glued themselves to her pronounced curves, a chunky shape that might have been too wide for most. But not for me. At least not then.

"You know, I was the first one around my way to buy your records, both of 'em!" she boasted.

Stevie painted on a smile, hoping that it would hold for as long as needed. "Thanks for checkin' us out, Ms.," he said, obviously having used the words for the trillionth time.

"We was just on our way from the grocery store, and I told Alvin that we should go ahead and get some gas so we wouldn't have to do it on the way to work tomorrow mornin'."

Alvin was the name of the caramel man a few feet behind her at the cashier's booth sporting a Monchichi Afro and the monster truck radial of a gut that went with it. They were soulmates if I'd ever seen them.

I hadn't seen people, excluding the imprisoned and their imprisoners, in more than a little while. And those two, along with the waitresses and gas station attendants, the good ole boys hacking wads of spit into the sizzling soil, were all so benign, so self-centered, so clueless as to how much they truly had and how they squandered it with every chance they got.

I remembered the life I'd had before, the young and impressionable one filled to the brim with possibility. Before jail, I'd believed I was special, that I carried some divine mark of distinction. I had the golden voice. I had the music in my mind. I had the girl the whole neighborhood wanted, she who never as much as batted an eyelash in any other direction.

But I'd learned what life really was on the inside. I'd learned how precious a breath can be the minute it's controlled by someone else, someone bigger, or smarter, someone with a badge or a gun. Inside I learned that living was being able to do what you wanted when you wanted, and milking that freedom to its absolute fullest.

So it amazed me that this woman was wasting her time kissing up to some guy who'd made a few records she liked. Maybe she'd seen the video and thought that he was cute. Or maybe she'd just liked the director's choice of edits and imagery. Either way, she and Mr. Afro had better things to do than be up Steven Turner's ass.

"Yo, Stevie, we got that thing to do," I interjected, offering him a life ring. The woman then gave me a brief glance, freeing me from my previous invisibility.

"This a friend of yours?" she asked suspiciously.

"Yeah, this my best friend, Ben," he replied.

I reached over and offered a hand. She shook it loosely, silently pegging me as the insignificant homeboy riding shotgun, and not the man who'd helped give birth to the hits she'd been the first in her neighborhood to buy.

"So what you doin' now?" she asked, moving back to Stevie, her arms folded in entitlement. "Y'all ain't put out a record in a while."

Stevie put an index finger to his earlobe, a nervous tic he'd had for as long as I'd known him.

"Well . . . the group broke up about a year ago," he said with a slight stutter. "But I'm a producer now. "We . . . well . . . I got a lot of projects I'm workin' on. So look for my name."

"Okay," the fan said with a nod. "But you need to do a record. Them other two ain't gonna be shit without you." My best friend's sagging jaw tightened with an egocentric grin.

"Don't worry," Stevie replied loudly for all the gas-guzzling patrons to hear. "That's coming, too. Be on the lookout."

And with that, the fan with no name headed back to her man and the bright yellow Ford Explorer on the next island over.

"You gotta love the fans," he said as we pulled away. "That bitch had enough eye shadow for every ho in L.A."

Stevie's house was built on the side of a mountain, overlooking a beach in a place called Malibu. Driving up, I could see the moonlit ocean, its waves crashing against an invisible shore. His palace was actually the smallest on his street, with a two-car garage, four bedrooms, a huge living room, and a recording studio he'd had built into the lower level.

It felt good to stretch my legs as we started up the curved walkway that led to the front entrance. My ass had been glued to his seat for hours.

We climbed a flight of lit stairs to the main level. The inside seemed endless. Two long corridors of unidentified rooms filled with unidentified things I would be sure to explore later. But the only thing I wanted to explore right then were the backs of my own eyelids.

In twenty minutes, I was perched on a fully made mattress in one of the three guest rooms. The cushion beneath me was the softest thing I'd known in a lifetime. The surrounding walls were covered with photographs of Stevie, pictures of men and women I didn't know and six gold and platinum plaques, each with my best friend's name on it. His putting me in that room meant something, even if it was something I didn't want to believe.

"Why you sitting in here in the dark?" he asked with a smile, looking on from the doorway.

"They ain't got no night-lights in jail," I said, faking a grin. "Besides, I'm about ready to crash. Getting out has been the second longest day of my life."

"What was the first?" he asked curiously.

"Going in," I said. He laughed. I didn't.

"I know you gonna sleep good," he said as he started out the doorway. "Enjoy it."

He closed the door and I closed my eyes. The bed felt safe and I felt safe, until I found myself listening for the jingling keys of an approaching CO or the squeak from a shifting mattress overhead. But there was none of that anymore, only the distant sound of a single passing car and the nearby rumble of the ocean.

A postcard with a black background and a photograph of Tupac Shakur, bare-chesting and holding a cigarette, along with the words *Thugs Never Die* in white block letters across the front:

November 22, 1996

I can't believe I'm a mommy, Ben. I mean, it's one thing when she was inside of me, when the only thing I knew about her was the way she moved, or the way she responded to my voice. But now I'm watching her crawl across the floor and I can't believe she's ours. I can't believe we're both responsible for something so beautiful. You can't tell it from the pictures, but she's got my eyes. Matter of fact, when I look at her it's like my face on your body. She's got knobby hands like yours, and the same little bear feet. But sometimes I look at her and all I see is you. Gotta go to class now. But you know I'll send another one soon.

Until . . .

Sala and Sasha

7.

My eyes opened and I thought I was dreaming. Then those plaques brought me back to piercing reality. I looked down to see that I'd slept in my clothes. So I started out into the rest of the house rumpled and wrinkled.

The living room was coated with freshly squeezed sunlight. There were more framed pictures on the tables and mantels, each twinkling in the glow of a new day. One wall held an oversize mirror; the other was a blowup of us, the original Waterfront, on the night we won the NAACP ACT-SO competition freshman year of high school. We wore identical Coogi knockoffs with brown slacks and matching shoes: a stylistic cross between Boyz II Men and Biggie Smalls.

There were other photos, as well: of Mr. and Mrs. Turner with Malcolm and his little boy, Dante, of Stevie, Lonnie, and Andre holding up their American Music Awards, and their Grammys, and the platinum plaques from the first two albums. I took it all in, then turned my back on the memories, dismissing them as my Sodom and Gomorrah.

"How'd you sleep?" Stevie asked, emerging from his own bedroom, which was only a door down from mine. He was wrapped in a green crushed-velvet sweat suit and monogrammed matching slippers. A flock of gulls swooped past the window, undoubtedly heading toward the beach. Then I held up the okay symbol as the aroma of sausage, eggs, and hash browns hit the air.

"What you got cookin'?" I asked with a giddy smile.

"Me?" he replied, poking a finger at his chest. "I'll fuck up cereal. But *she* can cook her ass off."

I followed him two doors down the corridor and got a full view of exactly who "she" was. Her back was to us as she worked at the stove, managing skillets of sausage, eggs, and hash browns all at once. Pink sweatpants clung to her lower half like Saran Wrap. The ass was to die for, as were the long locks of curly black hair flowing just past her shoulders. This was Woman #2 in my new life, and I was once again as stiff as a corpse.

"Marianna," Stevie called. She turned around to prove that the front was even better than the rear. Her skin was an even light brown. She had a small nose and full lips to complement eyes that were a speckled hazel.

"Right here," she said in cool, heavily accented English. Then she flipped equal portions of the three ingredients into soft tortillas. Breakfast was served.

"Good," he replied. "This is my boy Ben. He's gonna be with us for a while."

"Two days," I interrupted, flashing him a scathing look.

"Hello," she said warmly, and then quickly returned to her work.

"Hi," I said. "This looks good."

"We'll eat in a second," Stevie interjected. "But first I gotta show you somethin'."

The recording studio stretched the entire lower level. The soundboards and mixers were in a small separate room, encased by wood and glass. And the booth was a few feet away from it. Beyond them were a grand piano, one electric and one acoustic guitar, and a wine-colored electric bass. Each instrument was hooked up to its own microphoned station.

It was galaxies beyond what we'd had back in the day. The carpet was spanking new, the instruments polished instead of scratched and scraped. And there wasn't that musty smell from the ever-leaking washing machine.

"I ain't done much in a while," he said with embarrassment. "The shit ain't been comin' so easy lately."

"It's nice," I said, looking the place over with a touch of envy. "But why don't you let me get to that breakfast up there." My uninterest knocked the wind out of him, though he tried not to show it.

"Yeah," he said, stunned as he ushered me out of his sanctuary. "Let's do that."

When we returned there were two tumblers of pulpy

OJ to go with the meal. The first bite made me think of home, the second and third of whether Sala could burn like this in a kitchen. Stevie only nibbled while I tore my plate to shreds.

"You didn't use as much cilantro this time," he muttered to the cook, not even offering the kindness of eye contact.

"*Lo siento, señor,*" she said with a frown, her eyes peering through the thin glass over the double sink. "I'll get it right next time."

"You did it right *this* time as far as I'm concerned," I said while still chewing. "This shit is *good.*"

"Thank you, señor," she replied before exiting the kitchen and disappearing down the hallway.

Stevie let out a sigh. "Bitch is probably goin' to smoke another cigarette. I'm startin' to think I'm payin' her too much."

"What are you talkin' about?" I asked with jaws full of food. "She can cook her ass off."

"So can my mama, or any of them other wetbacks past Echo Park. And I ain't gotta pay them two grand a month plus benefits."

"She seems all right to me," I said before another forkful.

He smiled, seeing a subtext that wasn't really there. "You like the ass, huh?" He winked. "Most niggas do. That's the real reason I keep her around here."

I was about to ask the next and most obvious question when Marianna returned to pick up our dishes, the faint smell of tobacco traveling with her. Within five minutes she'd put our plates in the washer, cleaned the stove, and poured us cups of the best coffee I'd had in life. To me she was worth every penny of what Stevie was paying.

"You got it all covered, huh, Marianna?" I asked.

"I try, señor," she said, giving me a thin smile. "I really try."

I found myself alone a dish cycle later. Stevie had a meeting with his manager in North Hollywood, then a studio session with his songbird, Seeka. After that he would return, and we would have lunch somewhere, followed by an evening engagement he didn't specify.

Until then I'd been left to my own devices, encouraged to wander the levels of his hillside estate. And I did just that: inhaling the salt air on the deck, perusing the suits and ties on the motorized rack in his walk-in closet, flipping through the four hundred channels in the living room to see that the world hadn't changed as much as I'd hoped. Jerry Springer was still on the air, and his guests had even less self-respect than I remembered.

I did push-ups and crunches. I shadowboxed for thirty minutes, as I had for most of my time inside. I treated Stevie's big rooms like the little cell I'd made a home of, with Marianna's ass darting across my field of vision as she performed various tasks. Our eyes collided with every pass, and each time I turned away, hoping to erase the beauty she'd sprinkled across my senses.

I went out front and sat on the tiny stoop, my face shielded from the sun rays by the canvas awning up above. Cars passed, one luxury coupé and SUV after another. No muffler trouble or rust problems, no trunks vibrating from the bass of souped-up systems. This was not home. But I hadn't expected it to be. I hadn't expected anything other than giving my best friend what he'd asked for, forty-eight hours of my time, before taking my plane home.

Three hours later, I felt as if I'd exhausted all of the possibilities. There was so much silence. No voices, no yelling, no clanging of metal on metal. Countless changes of clothes and shoes organized and filed. The outside was eclipsing the inside.

Stevie's piano was a Steinway, with a transparent case so you could see all the moving parts inside. I circled the thing like a predator, my ear to its aura like a hound sniffing for scent. But there was nothing.

I took a seat and rubbed callused fingers across the keys, and they started the first tune I could think of. "Lift Every Voice and Sing," the junior high school assembly standard. I didn't miss a note for twelve bars. And then I stopped. I stopped because I didn't *hear* it. I knew how to push the keys, but nothing sang within my soul.

I started again. This time it was Miles, "Blue in Green." Sad and somber, but sweet in its own way. And once again I played like a virtuoso. But there was still nothing.

"I don't know much about music," Marianna said, startling me. I jumped away from the ivories to see her shoulder leaning against the door frame.

"Neither do I," I said. "I was just playing around."

"Don't bullshit a bullshitter," she fired back, struggling to make the phrase sound authentic with her accent. "You know what you're doing."

"Nah," I said. "Not anymore."

"Stevie talks about your gift all the time."

"Well, it's in the past tense now," I said. "I don't sing no more."

"What does singing have to do with playing the piano?" She approached me as a cat on the prowl. Something within me began to tremble.

"A lot more than you think," I answered. The tone of my

voice should have sent her running back to her chores. Yet her only move was toward a seat on the couch against the wall.

"I'm glad you liked your breakfast," she said. "I came down to see if you wanted lunch before I leave?" There was something mischievous in the way she narrowed her eyes in my direction. She was baiting me. But I wasn't sure why.

"That ain't why you came down here," I said.

She grinned as she replied. "You're right," she said. "It's not."

She stood up and twisted toward the far corner of the room, where she lowered a sliding panel in the wall to reveal a fully equipped bar with matching glasses. She filled a glass with ice and a blond liquid and brought it over.

"You like tequila?" she asked.

"No thanks," I replied, waving it away. She shrugged and took a sip, instantly accepting it as her own. "Does your boss know you drink on the job?"

"*Sí,*" she answered after a swallow. "He calls it a fringe benefit. Besides, I'm entertaining his guest." She dug a pack of Spirits from her shirt pocket and offered me a smoke.

I nodded, pinching the square between my fingers as my eyes once again followed the curve of her hips. I envisioned my hands spread across them as I entered from the back, slamming into her until we spilled onto each other. She came closer, violating my personal space to put a flame to the cancer stick. I took a deep first pull and then wondered what she might taste like. It had been too long. But I had a woman, Salamanca Mitchell, the love of my life. And she was all I needed.

"So how'd you end up here?" I asked, pacing the room to loosen the erection. She shrugged her narrow shoulders, causing her B-cups to bounce ever so slightly.

"It was a job," she said plainly. "My babies had to eat. So I had to work."

"You got kids?" I asked, thinking of the little girl I'd brought into the world, the one with her mother's eyes and my everything else.

"Two boys," she said. "Both just like their father, hard-headed as they come. But I love them more than anything."

"More than their father?" I asked. She didn't answer.

We took a moment of silence as she sipped her drink. I walked over to the bar and made one for myself, a rum and Coke, like the one Jimmy Stein had made me once in the back of the library, where he'd stashed a few fifths with the help of our lush of a librarian.

"You're not like him," she said abruptly, returning me to there and then.

"Like who?" I asked.

"Steven," she said. "Friends are usually alike, even if it's just in some little kind of way. But the two of you are like night and day."

Her words were unintentional razors, slashing at something that had yet to come fully into focus. And it made me angry. Stevie was my homeboy, the only one I had left, the one who always had my back. And who was this woman to say we were nothing alike? She hadn't been where we'd been. She hadn't seen what we'd seen.

"Is that a good or a bad thing?" I asked, doing my best to hold back all emotion.

"It's neither," she responded before taking a puff and a sip. "It's just what I see." She glanced down at her watch and then jumped up, almost spilling the last of her glass. "Shit!"

"What?" I asked.

"I've gotta get outta here. It's PTA night at my son's school." Then she started up the stairs without a word. "We'll talk tomorrow," she said. Three minutes later I heard the faint shutting of the garage-side exit. Then I knew that she, too, was gone.

I went up to where I'd slept and opened the backpack that held all I'd owned in the world: a Bible, a Qu'ran, Fama's *Fundamentals of the Yoruba Religion,* my correspondence course certificates in plumbing and bartending, and, most important, my pictures and letters. Seven years of inked paper and glossy prints curling at the corners.

There were 116 of them. Some long, some short, some dirtied by carriers' hands, others as clean as a cloudless day. They were all I had to hold me between calls and care packages. I read each one until my eyes hurt, my free hand holding on to whatever was the most recent image of her and my little girl. I imagined myself squeezing between them, a living teddy bear for them to clutch as hard as they wanted to.

8.

"You got it," Tahir said from behind her in lane six of the SWATS Gun Ranch.

It had taken time for her to get the stance right. Hollywood said that you could shoot with one hand. But that didn't work on a range, or anywhere in the real world, for that matter. She raised the Colt 1911 and fired seven rounds into the black outline. She pulled the trigger until the slide clicked empty and then reeled her target back to her. Her seven bullets had all landed in the torso area, though she'd been aiming for the head.

"You're getting better," her instructor said.

"Thanks," Salamanca

replied, even though she felt patronized. "Let me go one more."

"Nah," Tahir said, taking the gun she offered butt first. "This last clip's for me."

Salamanca backed away as her neighbor reloaded and set up a fresh sheet. The black tank top revealed his muscular arms, defined shoulders achieved by sets of push-ups done three times a day.

They'd stayed with each other since the Angel of Death's appearance, taking turns so that neither of their homes went too neglected. Salamanca, however, had made a habit of keeping the essentials on her. She'd had her money changed into an ankle wallet of traveler's checks, with her passport always in her right rear pocket. All that she might need for the quickest of quick getaways.

Tahir took his time with some shots and rattled off others indifferently, always striking the same pose, his right palm under the pistol butt to support the left's grip, the ball of his right foot behind the left. When he brought his target back there were three holes through the skull and another four straight through the heart.

"Let's get up outta here," he said.

Sala hadn't called or written Ben since the incident. She would go to work and then to school and then to wherever Tahir might be. There was something about him that calmed her. It might have just been the fact that he was present, that he could come to her rescue if she needed him, and though she told herself that he was just a tool to get her through, she was beginning to see lies hanging in the frigid air of her solitude.

There she was: eighteen years old and out in the world with a baby on the way. Sure, Ben had set her up with some money; and sure, she loved him more than anything. But what was that shit with more than six years to go? How was that going to help when she went to bed alone at night? What could Ben do when other predators caught her scent in the wilderness of the outside world? Absolutely nothing.

"It's only gonna be a couple more minutes," Tahir said back at his house. A framed Lion of Judah hung on one wood-paneled wall, a Burning Spear poster on another. Salamanca ran her fingers through the dingy green carpet as Tahir stood over the hot plate with the wok on top of it, stir-frying broccoli, carrots, and pea pods in sesame oil. The rice was already in the pot.

She watched the muscles flex in his calves as he stirred and flipped, his skin glowing with a sweaty shine.

"I'm not timing you," she said with a smile. "After all, this is my last meal."

She'd been dragging her heels about leaving, even though she knew she had to. She'd gotten her ticket from the airport that morning, paying $107 for a one-way to Detroit after using the fake ID Tahir had helped her procure.

"It doesn't have to be," he replied. "I mean, you know I ain't gonna let nuthin' happen to you heah."

He was so cute, so male, believing that the organ between his legs gave him some sort of advantage on the playing field, when it more than likely did the exact opposite.

"Nah," she replied, "I'm six months in. It's bad enough

you got me shootin' guns and shit." He laughed as he added the veggies to the pot of rice and mixed them around.

"Hey, it was yo' idea," he replied, setting a hot bowl of dinner before her across from his own.

"I know," she said, looking away from him, trying to avoid those chinky brown eyes that revealed the Native American in his bloodline.

"I'm gonna miss you," he said. She focused on the bowl beneath her, taking in her first bite only to realize that it was too hot to swallow. She took her bottle of water to the head and smothered the flames just in time.

"Watch yourself," he said. There was a speck of rice on her lips, and he used a napkin to wipe it away. It was the closest a man's hand had come since her father's blow. That touch sparked a warmth in a spot long neglected.

"Thanks," she said, continuing to scarf down the meal, her eyes focused on anything other than him. And he did the same, knowing how much she loved her man and knowing what it had been like when he'd discovered that *his* "she" hadn't been faithful while he was locked away.

An hour went by in near silence, the only sounds coming from the stereo. Stevie Wonder and Donny Hathaway, Main Source and the Wu-Tang Clan. He sliced peaches for their dessert as she explained that she had to get up early in the morning, even though it was barely past nine. He, too, was *tired*.

The bed was a twin mattress without a box spring. The boy owned two sets of sheets, each washed only once during the given semester. But she liked it because they reeked of him, of the frankincense oil he wore compulsively with a little of his funk mixed in.

A night owl by nature, she'd never gone to bed early, not even since she'd gotten pregnant. So this sleeping thing was just plain ludicrous. It was the best excuse she could think of to be close to him one last time before she went away forever.

He knew that this was the last night he'd ever see her. And he knew that Benjamin Baker still had his name stitched where it counted. In their few nights he'd heard her calling to him in her sleep, begging him not to leave her alone. He would get her where she needed to go and go on with his life, bringing her side of the sheets to his face until there was nothing left of Salamanca Mitchell but the choice portraits within his own brain.

The two of them lay there for hours, pretending that they didn't want the same thing, even if they wanted it for two very different reasons. But somewhere within the act they found themselves asleep in a joint embrace, riding out their last moments together without either of them fully knowing it.

9.

"See, you can get away with takin' the train in D.C.," Stevie said as we turned onto what I learned was the infamous Sunset Boulevard. The avenue was a tidal wave of sights and sounds: young people of all colors, ages, and implants in ravenous search for all that was hot and happening. "But in L.A. you gotta roll."

The temperature had dropped after sundown. So I'd borrowed a sweater and some khakis from Stevie's ample closet. I returned what remained of the blunt to his fingers after a very long pull.

"See, I was lucky," he continued. "I came out here with paper. But them dime-a-dozen muthafuckas, the ones that come out here trying to be directors and movie stars and shit. See, they gotta ride the bus. And when you ride the bus you stuck with all the maids and the Mexicans. And from what I hear, sometimes the bus don't even come. You might be on one of them benches for a hour waitin' on some shit that ain't even gonna show up."

I rolled my eyes as he handed the blunt back. He'd obviously forgotten his own bus-riding days.

"God, I love this city," he continued as the high took its effect. "Sometimes I think we shoulda been born here."

"Speak for yourself," I said coolly as my skull started to climb away from my torso. "Where we headed, anyway?"

"To my special place," he said. "And your special place, too."

Harmony was a club built on the edge of a strip mall. It had two levels, a huge sign done in green neon letters, and a line that wrapped three-quarters of the way around the building. Valets in leather jackets parked cars in the fenced-off lot at the back.

"I think we got a little wait," I said as two red-coated men opened our doors for us.

Stevie shook his head and gave me a condescending smile. "Nah," he replied, pointing to the club-going hopefuls before us. "*They* got a little wait."

A Samoan bouncer named Hanif showed us through an opening in the velvet ropes that separated staff from potential patrons. And we were on our way in.

"Sir!" the valet yelled behind us. Knowing the answer, Stevie Hail Mary'd the car keys over his shoulder without looking, for every eye in the waiting line to see. And they landed directly in the Asian boy's hand. Stevie smiled, once again pleased with himself.

"I love doing that," he said, patting me on the shoulder as we headed inside.

There was a Japanese theme to the place, paper lanterns and sliding doors that separated one area from the next. The overhead lighting turned the place into alternating shades of green, purple, and pink. The DJ was on a terrace a story and a half up, flanked by a pair of bikini'd and booted go-go dancers, one black and one white, both their heads filled with weaves more expensive than their costumes.

Stevie was a politician, doling out shakes and hugs like handbills as he moved through the crowd. I followed behind him, watching him work as we parted the sea of bodies and beats, making our way to the sliding door on the west wall.

Somewhere along the way, a Polynesian girl with breasts the size of my head dropped a single white pill into each of our palms. Stevie popped his like candy, and I followed suit, hurling caution to the wind. Why not live it up? I was only in town for two days, and there wasn't a pill in the world that was going to keep me from hopping a plane at the end of my stay.

The passageway was guarded by two bouncers larger than I was, their eyes hidden by identical pairs of wraparound shades. Stevie gave them a nod, and one of them pulled the door open, rolling it away like a stone from a tomb. We were crossing into an entirely different dimension.

The closing door muted the music down to nothing. The flashing green lights were exchanged for a seductive blue. My eyes locked on to a Latina of twenty or less as she hung from the array of polished poles and beams. A sequined thong squeezed between two firm cheeks glazed with oil and stage glitter. Her bare breasts were hardened into shapes formed by scalpel and saline. But as she lifted her entire body into an upside-down letter A, the implants didn't bother me so much.

"See, this is the real party, nigga!" Stevie hollered with glee. Prince's "The Ballad of Dorothy Parker" superseded the Isleys and their "Footsteps." A plump Persian man filled half the leather couch against the south velvet-coated wall, cloud-nining his way through a lap dance from the curvy Filipina straddling his pelvic region. Narrow-rimmed specs rested ever so lightly on the bridge of her nose as she shook her thing close enough for him to taste it.

A wiry white boy with sandy dreadlocks pressed his lips to the nipples of a pasty redhead with hair longer than his. Her knee-length boots were the color of blood. An hourglassed silhouette led a tall and bald brother through one of the several steel doors in the narrow hall at the far end of the room.

Familiar stirrings pressed against my zipper as I took in the sights. But I forgot all about them when lust personified took the stage at the center of the room. Her ample onion was parted by a thin piece of silver. Nippled mangoes swung to the rhythm of the Purple One as he took his first bubble bath with pants on. Her eyes were covered with glow-in-the-dark contact lenses, and a mane of brown weave trailed down her back in a thick but perfect braid.

Safety parameters had been breached. Self-control was on the edge of extinction. I needed someone to touch me. I needed to feel a woman to know that they were still real

and not just the figments of lucid desire that kept all convicts sane. I needed her to make me feel like a free man.

I started away from Stevie, closing the gap between
Lust and me at several feet per second. Someone on the FX
team cued the strobe light, forcing the fluid image into a
million stills popping off at the speed of light. My front
teeth sank into the lower lip beneath them. I salivated. The
bulge swelled into a cramping pain beneath my freshly
creased khakis.

Her curves handled the drum and bass lines with ease.
Then she dropped back on all fours: nipples hardening,
butter fudge quadriceps flexing to bear the load. And her
eyes, the ones behind the glow-in-the-dark gimmick, never
left my own.

She had that gaze often captured in the pages of those
skin mags I'd used to get by on the inside. I remembered
mentally pasting Salamanca's face on the physiques of
those bona fide sluts, fantasizing that upon my release she
might be willing to do what they did: be bodies without
minds, pussies with false names attached.

The song changed again: "Moments in Love." Her man-
icured toes brushed against that bulge of mine. Sexual
Chernobyl was upon me. Her lips mouthed the words:
"You want a dance?"

I nodded, and she immediately slithered off the stage,
tugging me toward the last of those metal doors at the back
of that narrow hallway. I forgot about Stevie. I forgot my
purpose. I even forgot my name when she closed the door
shut behind us and locked it.

Lust removed a condom from between the cushions of
the velvet chaise I reclined against. She straddled me,

spreading naked thighs to release that most savory aroma into the air. Hard male entered moist female, and her climb became a ride. Nails ground into my biceps as perfume filled my lungs and pores.

"Welcome home, baby," she whispered as she nearly doubled her velocity. My pulse climbed to meet hers, and then she put her tongue to my neck, to that delicious little spot that always set my pleasure centers ablaze. I fired a round into the latex barrier and collapsed, telling myself in the last bits of consciousness that I was just dreaming. Then it all faded to black, even before the Art of Noise got to finish.

I opened my eyes into the nothingness of antiafterglow, the blue light above my only welcome. The used rubber still hung from me as awareness brought a grinding churn to my intestines. Lust's scent hung in the air around me, though the woman herself had apparently kept it moving, more than likely off to give her gift to other good little boys, or in search of more dollars back in the velvet-walled room that was her lair.

My life came back to me all at once. I saw my father and my mother, my little brother, Henry, and Stevie, the Old Man and Maurice, and then Salamanca. I wanted to close my eyes, but they were already shut. She was there, standing before me holding our newborn child, horrified at the sight of me, lying there in the blackness of my own desire. I wanted to speak, but she vanished before I could utter a word.

I couldn't believe it. I had blown it all over a piece of ass I'd barely remember once that pill wore off. Salamanca was out there running the world's longest obstacle course, scraped and scarred by all the enemies that might have been giving chase. Yet her letters and calls had still boasted of a woman immune to the temptation, a bulletproof diva running on nothing but love, for me.

And she had been raising *our* child, wiping her nose and changing her diapers and filling her belly with the nectar from her nipples. She had given up her dreams, her comfort, and even her own father, for me. And I had repaid her with a fist, a seething blow to the one thing she could always be certain about: that I, Benjamin Baker Jr., would never stray from her side.

I pulled up my pants and wiped the sweat from my face with a sleeve. Then I left the scene of the crime. Stevie was, of course, right outside the door, massaging the satiny locks of an Asian in six-inch heels and legs for days. His fly was down, but he was up, his eyes narrowed by pleasure and that little white pill. I eased past him without a word, taking refuge in one of the main area's many empty chairs.

A new siren owned the stage, tall, caramel, and built like a brick house. Her red hair was braided into thin, perfect cornrows. My eyes watched as she broke it down to the booming bass of "How Do You Want It?" But she lacked the allure of my partner in the crime, who was still nowhere to be found. Stevie placed a hand on my shoulder a moment later.

"Hungry?" he asked. The slow burn of hunger superseded the prior churning sensation. My head nodded on its own.

"Cool. I know just the spot we can go to."

"So how was it?" Stevie asked after placing our orders. I'd gone for the New York strip and a salad while he had asked for the turkey dinner with cranberry sauce.

I looked away from the question, foolishly hoping that if I played dumb, he might leave it alone. My head had unfortunately cleared in the air-conditioning, reminding me of all that I'd done in the hour before.

"What you mean?"

"The titties, the ass, the fuckin' eye things that glowed in the dark. C'mon, nigga! I know you was geeked to bust a nut, especially after seven whole years of jackin' off."

I couldn't help but revisit the moment after such a description. Guilt stretched minutes into years. But the details hadn't worn down one bit: her hips grinding into my crotch, nipples slapping against my jawline. I felt it all over again, and it felt even more wrong than it had the first time.

"It didn't last too long," I confessed, hoping that the questions would stop then and there. But my words only widened that smug grin on his face.

"Nigga, it was damn near a decade!" he yelled. Heads turned in neighboring booths. And he noticed them, quickly lowering his volume. "All I wanna hear you say is, 'Stevie, that shit was just what I needed.' "

I checked my reflection in the glass, to make sure I wasn't wearing lipstick. I'd been on the inside for seven years. And in there, saying what somebody else wanted you to say was a textbook sign of submission. I had the urge to pop him in the mouth, to reinforce that I wasn't his bitch, that him bringing me to Harmony had brought about the greatest betrayal of all.

But he was my best friend. He had driven through sun and sands to bring me back to civilization. He had fed me, clothed me, given me access to words and sounds and all else beyond the grasp of a prisoner of the state.

And I was no longer on the outside. I no longer had

anything to prove, other than my love for Salamanca, which I had so willingly just forsaken. And for better or for worse, it *had* been just what I needed.

"Stevie," I began with my first smile in a long while, "that shit was just what I needed."

"Now that's what I wanted to hear," he said, extending his hand for me to slap it. I obliged, feeling content that at least one of us was happy about something. "Best grand I ever spent."

I *had* to have heard him wrong.

"What did you say?"

"The broad in there. Around-the-world is rather expensive up in that piece."

I melted into the leather beneath me.

"What? You thought you was Denzel or somethin'? Do some time and the high-card hoes just give it up for free?"

Now I could smell the disgrace rising from my privates.

"Hey, look at it this way. You're always payin' for ass. She was just more up front about it."

"I need a drink," I blurted, unable to say any more.

"I know just the place."

The Whisky was a hole of a bar in the lobby of the Sunset Marquis, a place so chichi that you had to be in the hotel registry just to walk in. Unless you were Stevie. White and yellow faces smiled and sipped, some slamming empty glasses against the glossy bar for emphasis. A hand rested on the bare thigh of a short-skirted blonde, the edge of her garters in plain view. An '80s hairband reject muttered to himself while staring at his own reflection in the bar mirror.

Stevie and I were in the darkest corner of that dim hole,

three drinks in, talking about the old days as if they were really that old.

"You're really throwin' 'em back," he said, more affected by the spirits than I. Proofed liquor's pretty easy after years of jailhouse cocktails.

"It takes the pain away," I muttered. The words brought that feeling to my eyes that comes before crying. But that was as far as I let it go.

"What pain?"

"I played her out."

"Who?"

"The fuck you mean who? Sala."

"What? I don't know why you're trippin' about it. She ain't gonna know unless you tell her."

"Yes, she will."

"What, she's a telepath now?"

"She knows my heart and I know hers."

"Maybe so," Stevie said, smirking cynically. "But seven years is a lotta lonely nights."

"What's that supposed to mean!" I charged, loudly enough to twist several heads off their necks.

"Oh, c'mon, nigga! You way smarter than this. Either way, it is what it is."

Dad had once said that alcohol was the best serum for truth. For once I wish he hadn't been right.

"What is what it is?!" I demanded.

"That the bitch probably fucked twenty other niggas since—"

I didn't feel it when it happened. I just saw his head snap back. A moment later blood flowed from one nostril.

"Don't ever call her that again," I said in a surprisingly

calm tone. He nodded, still unable to push sound through that hole between his cheeks.

It wasn't that I hadn't heard it before. On the inside, every cell had a tale about getting tricked on. And it had only happened because they, we, had fucked up. We'd played into the hands of a system we knew was against us from jump. We snatched ourselves from their warm clutches, leaving them out in the open for other predators to stalk and slay.

But not Sala and me. What we had was different, something above and beyond those boyfriend/girlfriend husband/wife bullshit bonds those others swore were so unbreakable.

But there had been room between Lust's thighs, ample space for me to plunge deep within, and I'd taken it. So why wouldn't it have been the same for her?

She was twenty-four years old wherever she was, and still as fine and freckled as the day I'd met her. Maybe she, too, had given in to another. Maybe someone else was keeping her warm while I was drinking the night away and punching my best friend in the face for being honest with me.

"I'm sorry," Stevie said, a stack of napkins to his nose.

"No, man," I said. "I'm the one who's sorry. It's just that she's the only thing that—"

"I know, man," he interrupted. "I saw her before you, remember?"

Something shifted within my friend and he was seventeen again, standing on that green line train and seeing Salamanca for the first time, that high school spider sense telling him that she was something worth pursuing. So he'd followed but was too shy to follow up. And to make it worse, she didn't even see him. But she had seen me, his best friend, his partner in crime and supposed musical equal, sew it up without much effort. Maybe we weren't as equal as we'd always thought ourselves to be.

We got back to the house a little after one. Stevie went to bed with an ice pack, and I flipped through the same four hundred channels, my eyes and ears on the hunt for something to salve the wounds of betrayal within me. But there was nothing.

10.

The street was silent as Salamanca stood before the door frame, aside from the jittery-engined cab at the curb. She pushed the button into its rusty casing a second time, triggering the high-pitched ringing that echoed through the house. Impending motherhood hung heavy on her lower spine.

The house was just the way she had remembered it: the front lawn cut slightly uneven by the manual mower the family had owned for nearly half a century. Her great-grandfather, Rudolph Nickens, had brought that mower home as a retirement gift from the landscapers who had employed him on the arid plains of Oklahoma.

A gust of wind blew plastic flower petals clockwise. And that wood swing was still in the backyard, dangling from the giant oak by thick ropes older than she was. She'd found everything she'd expected on the corner of Abington and Kendall. Grand River was still to the north. School-craft was still to the south.

When the door finally opened, her aunt Pat, her hair still in natural braids and eyes still behind thick-framed lenses, was as pretty as she'd been the last time Salamanca had seen her.

Patricia Davis looked her niece up and down, noting all the things that had changed: sharpened cheekbones, the more defined dusting of freckles across her cheeks, and most important, the big bubble in her womb that was about to tip her over.

"Sala?" she asked, still unsure of the face before her, or at least of its reality, after far too long.

"It's me, Aunt Pat," her niece replied, already feeling the warmth of like-blood less than a hug away.

"Oh, my God!" she yelled, smiling and grabbing up the girl as if she were a runt loose in a barnyard. Salamanca pressed her big belly against her mother's sister, inhaling the perfume that radiated from the woman's two-piece sweat suit.

"We never thought—" Pat began.

"I know," the girl interjected. "But I got some bags in the car. Let me just go and—"

"Oh, no, you don't!" she commanded. "You ain't car-ryin' nuthin' with that baby in you."

Pat trudged down to the curb and gave the cabbie a twenty and a thank-you, carrying the heavy bags as if they were nothing. Salamanca watched her, noting that Pat's hips hadn't been so wide the last time she'd seen her. And there had been less flab around her waistline. But aside from that, she was the same, still her reliable baby-sitter for the Saturday nights when her parents went down to Legends for drinks and dancing.

Pat had lived in that same house for more than thirty years, through a marriage and a divorce and the birth of a girl and a boy, both of whom had already left the nest, one west and the other south. Camille, at twenty-eight, danced with a ballet company in Houston. Robert, at twenty-five, directed films in Hollywood. And Pat herself was still teaching lead-headed high schoolers at Henry Ford, armed only with a kind heart in a place where a student had once thrown another from a third-floor bathroom window over taking the last towel in the dispenser.

"I was just watchin' some TV," Pat said as the girl waddled behind her through the foyer and into the living room. There was still that same elegant staircase that spiraled up to the second floor. And the walls still held countless pictures of her aunt and cousins. Each room was still a different color: light blue, bright orange, lime green.

Pat set the bags between the sofa and the upholstered recliner and bade the girl to plop down while she made her some food. Ice water and a big bowl of collard greens followed, since they were the only things in the kitchen that went along with the mother-to-be's vegan diet.

"How'd you figure I was here?" Pat asked, finishing off the last of the pork chop before her, licking the grease from her manicured fingers.

"You've always been here," Salamanca said. "And besides, it was the only place I could remember how to get to."

"You spent enough time here," Aunt Pat joked.

"I could never spend enough time here," her niece replied. "You're my favorite aunt in the world."

"I'm your only aunt," Aunt Pat said dismissively.

"So what?" Sala replied with the widest smile she'd given in months. Pat returned the gesture, her mind filled with joy that her little niece had grown into a woman, and one seemingly unscathed by the monster who had taken her away more than a decade before.

To Pat, Alfonse Mitchell was pure evil, a scourge she had told herself for years she needed to seek out and destroy. But amid her work, the kids, and the forces against her, she'd never quite succeeded.

"You still livin' with your father?"

Salamanca hesitated, knowing that an affirmative answer would prompt questions, more probes aimed at discovering the ultimate hows and whys surrounding her older sister's disappearance. And that was ground the girl was in no way ready to cover. Even if she had been, she still didn't know if she could have told the truth.

She had made her daddy a promise all those years before on that cold Friday night. The smell of rain had been in the air, and the music from the house party a few houses down could be clearly heard through her bedroom window. She had made a promise that night. And for Salamanca Mitchell, promises were things not easily broken.

"I need a place to stay for a while," she blurted out nervously. The way she said it hinted at more desperation than there actually was, hoping that it might buy her some time, that Pat wouldn't make her answer *those* questions just yet.

After all, she had just gotten there. She'd just sat down in the living room after fourteen years of being God knew where.

"Of course, baby," Pat began. "For as long as you need. We ain't even talked about whose baby you carryin' and where the daddy is and—"

"I'll tell you everything," Sala interrupted. "You know I never keep anything from you. It's just all been happening so fast."

The next thing Pat knew, she was reliving the night more than twenty years before, the night when her big sister came to her with the secret of the seed recently planted within. Viola had been on the verge of tears as she rubbed her belly, talking about how much she loved Alfonse and how she just knew that he would take care of her. Pat hadn't known what to say, so she'd just held the girl to her and hoped that God would get her through.

By then God had gotten the Davis sisters through so much already. Like Alfonse Mitchell, they had for the most part grown up without parents, without structure, without models for how grown folks were supposed to live. Pat had barely been fifteen when the three of them had done shots of whiskey at Smitty's on the east side, right across the street from the auto repair shop where both sisters worked. Pat, the younger by two years, answered the phone, while her big sister, always a wiz at math, looked after the books.

Pat had always thought that Alfonse was fine. And she was forever grateful that he always let her go out with them and paid the bill with nothing but a smile. She liked the way he dressed and the way his outer ears bent back toward his skull. But there was still something beneath the surface that always bothered her, something behind the man's eyes that told her he was dangerous, even though she never saw him fight, or curse, or not hold his liquor.

But he'd made Viola happy, happier than she'd ever been since they took the $1,000 inheritance their grand-daddy had left for them and put it down on that house on Abington. So she let her be happy, though that choice still tortured her a generation later.

"It'll be all right, girl," Pat replied, glancing at her ma-turing reflection in the oak mirror across the room. She'd said something similar to Viola the last time she was here, during their monthly tradition of Thursday night drinks at her house while the husbands kept the kids.

"I'll tell you how it goes," Viola had said more than eight years after Salamanca had come into the world. She'd run a nervous hand across the curls at the back of her neck, knowing that Alfonse was not going to let her leave, even though he knew he was wrong, even though he'd promised that he'd never do anything to hurt her.

It hadn't been the other women. Their grandma Mabel had told them in childhood that "men are only faithful when their dicks don't work." It was the other things he was hiding, the money that came out of nowhere, the .38 revolver he kept taped beneath their bed, the way those two men who came by the house just happened to end up as death notices a matter of weeks later.

Viola didn't want her daughter growing up around that. And she definitely didn't want the two of them living in fear. The girl was getting old enough to start figuring things out for herself. And that would only make the transition more difficult.

She had hugged Pat longer than usual before she left. The better part of twenty years had passed, and the younger sister could still feel the uncertainty in her embrace. Pat had wanted to say something, but she didn't want to make it any more difficult than it already was. And that was the last time Pat had seen her, the last time she knew for sure that her only sister was still alive.

Salamanca saw the tears now welling in her aunt's eyes and wished that she could comfort her in some way. She wanted to believe that saying the right thing might take the pain away. But she didn't bother. Words and thoughts had done nothing for her own loss, or the jarring understanding that she would never have all the answers, and that the mother she adored was never coming back for her.

Pat pulled away from the past to glance at the future in Sala's womb. The girl was due soon. Her ankles had swollen to three times their normal size. Her fair and freckled face was flushed. Pat remembered being the same way when she was expecting, a little darker and heavier, but still very much the same.

And she remembered the way Michael used to rub her belly at night, whispering their unborn children to sleep with the pied pipe of his own rich baritone. She remembered the way he made love to her at the magic hour, the way he filled the spaces often left empty during the long daily grind. But now he, too, was gone.

"Is he a good man?" Pat asked her niece.

Salamanca smiled, almost as if she'd anticipated the question. She flashed to every image she had of Benjamin Baker and all of the dreams they would share if they could just hold on for a few more years.

"He's the best," she said. "He's the best man in the world for me."

Neither woman spoke for a moment. And another minute had passed before either realized that the other was crying.

"I always knew you'd still be here," Salamanca said, wiping her face with a knit-sweatered sleeve.

"And I always knew you'd come back," Pat replied. They stood and met each other halfway to embrace again, their tears smearing in a sandwich of cheek. "I'm just glad I was here when you did."

Sala took her cousin Robert's old room, which was still painted a boyish blue, its walls still adorned with shelves of board games and sketch drawings, the faintest trace of cigarettes ground into the ash-colored carpet. At night the skylight in the ceiling gave a view of the heavens, of the stars and planets Salamanca would never be tall enough to reach. But she still held on to the childhood dream of doing so, and to all of her other dreams. Through them, anything and everything was possible.

11.

"Checkmate," I said to her dismay. Game three in as many hours, and she had yet to defeat me.

"Did you do anything else in jail besides play chess?" Marianna huffed, rising to replenish our coffee.

It was nine in the morning. I'd been up since five. My soul was still smothered in guilt about the night before. The housekeeper had come in at six and had served me a big breakfast of fresh fruit and a medley of sausage, scrambled eggs, garlic, and green chiles all on one plate. Stevie was still out like a light.

"Don't be a sore loser," I replied to the salt-coated question.

"I almost had you," she grumbled.

"You got beat," I taunted. "It happens. Accept it."

"I'll have my vengeance," she said with a smile.

"Not in this life. How'd the PTA thing go last night?"

Her personality switched from playful player to motherly mother, her face tightening into a prim and pragmatic mask.

"Arturo's having trouble with math," she said. "And Santiago's having trouble with his English. And both their teachers don't want to do anything but send them to summer school. But I guess you have to take what you can get with the public system."

I didn't know a thing about California's public school system, or the state of schools in general. I hadn't held a child in my arms since my brother, Henry, came into the world when I was ten. I'd read about children and childhood and black men not taking care of theirs, even though my dad had done his duty until the end.

"What's it like being a mother?" I asked her as I put the pieces inside of the collapsing board/case. The question caught her pleasantly by surprise. "I mean, I have a little girl. But I haven't seen her since she was born. I been inside the whole seven years since she's been alive."

"¡Dios mío!" she replied, putting a hand to her chest. My words were apparently the stuff of nightmare. "That's hard."

"Tell me about it," I remarked. "She and her mama are out there somewhere. But I don't know exactly where. So as soon as I leave here, I gotta go find them. But when I see them, I don't think I'll know what to say. I mean, it's my fault things ended up like this."

"A father always matters," she said, dropping her soapy rag into the sink. "My boys still love their father, even though they haven't seen him in a long time."

She'd mentioned the man she'd married, a dark-skinned Mexican with a shaved head and a chiseled physique, his flesh covered in markings of *la vida loca* from the deltoids down. They'd tied the knot after a month, the both of them eighteen and certain that they had it all figured out. But a spray of slugs had left his tank top soaked with blood just before their third anniversary and Marianna with a heart to mend and mouths to feed.

She didn't believe in love anymore or in the men who tried to melt the frozen passion deep within her. She was just getting through the day, every day. It was the safest way to live. But deep inside she knew, as I did, that safe wasn't always best.

Our conversation faded as the sun climbed toward the heavens. She had things to do and I wanted to get out, breathe the salt air, and hear the sounds of Malibu one last time, before I left it forever.

I walked down the twisting asphalt to the beach, to an ocean bluer than any I'd ever seen. A lone surfer hung ten on a skimpy wave a few yards out. Gulls hovered in search of Tuesday brunch. Four tanned teens in bikinis and designer shades lay on long towels just a few feet shy of the shoreline, hoping to get just a little darker before dusk. This was life on the outside.

There was so much to do, yet two full days had passed and I had yet to do anything. All I wanted to do was stay still, to reflect, to ask God to forgive me for my sins from the night before. I asked Him to protect us all in the face of what was to come. And then, like an answer handed down from heaven, I heard my father's voice at the beginning of any household chore neither of us wanted to do.

"The sooner we start, the sooner we finish."

I made the call back at Stevie's estate, taking deep breaths as each of the four rings came and went. She answered on the fifth, out of breath. She'd just come through the door.

"Hello?" she said in her usual professionally polite greeting.

"Hey," I said plainly, as if I'd just seen her yesterday.

"Where are you, boy?!" my mother demanded. "You been out two days and this is the first time I hear from you?"

"I'm sorry, Ma," I said, noticing a sailboat far off on the horizon. "I guess I'm still adjusting. Lost track of time."

"It's okay, son," she said, her voice calming. "I was just starting to worry. Where are you?"

"I'm still in L.A. with Stevie," I started. "He picked me up from the jail just like I told you."

"You still should've called us first," she reminded me, just to show that she hadn't fully let the point go.

Ma had been a different kind of lifeline for me during those inside years. She sent walnut brownies and oatmeal raisin cookies, *Daily Bread* prayer books and subscriptions to *Jet* and *Ebony*. She relayed messages for Salamanca and prayed with me over the phone in the tougher moments. She'd been the mother she always was, never judging and never blaming, but always expecting you to do your best.

She'd started to gray in the recent pictures she sent, a thick strip of white in a scalp of dark brown. But there didn't seem to be one more wrinkle, not a single extra pound, as if all but her hair had been dipped in a fountain of youth.

I heard the TV on in the background, *Jeopardy!*, to be exact. She never missed it. She even kept a pocket TV in her purse just to make sure she got her daily dose of Al Trebek and daily doubles.

"I don't know," I responded to her pinch of a complaint. "My head's been all over the place. Plus it's three hours earlier here. And I know that you in bed by like ten."

"I woulda lost the sleep to hear from my firstborn," she said earnestly.

"It's just all been so much, Ma," I said, recalling all the words and sights and feelings since my release. "I'm back in the world, but I'm not in *my* world yet, you know? I still gotta find Sala, and—"

"She called yesterday," she interjected. "She said to tell you that she's on her way back to D.C. She gave me a number for you to call her."

"Where?!" I demanded, feeling robbed that I'd missed the call and, more important, that I'd missed her voice. But if the words were right, she was coming home. I wouldn't have to look for her. I wouldn't have to search. She and my baby were coming right to me. All I had to do was get home to greet them.

"She made me promise not to tell you over the phone. You know how she is about phone lines."

"You know I do," I said, remembering the way she spoke in code during our conversations, referring to her father as "the principal" and our child as "the student," throwing in patches of Spanish for good measure.

"I got it right here, though, son. I'm not gonna lose it."

"I know you won't, Ma."

"Your brother asks about you every two seconds, when he's here, at least."

I hadn't forgotten about Henry. I couldn't have. He'd made sure I knew what he was up to, sending me letter after letter and newspaper clippings of things he thought I might be interested in. He'd sent pictures of the new house he and Mom had moved into out in Hillcrest. And he'd kept a sharp eye on everything that was mine. He put my awards and my plaques on the walls in the guest room and claimed to polish them whenever he got the chance.

I knew about the girls he dated, his current stats on the Dunbar basketball team, where he was enrolled in the preengineering program. He even sent some of the pictures he took as a hobby. Yet none of those things had made me feel any closer to him or any less guilty about the way I'd left him, too, at only ten years old, to be the third "man of the house."

So when you gettin' your skinny behind back to D.C.?" Ma asked.

"It ain't skinny no more," I said. "You seen the pictures."

"Well, get it back here anyway," she said, chuckling.

"I'll be there sooner than you think," I said.

"Keeping an old woman in suspense, huh?"

"You're not old, Ma," I said.

"Maybe not," she said. "But I feel like it. And they say that's what really matters."

"Well, *they* need to shut up," I said.

She chuckled again. "Now get off this phone and get back here. I'll be praying for you."

"And me for you," I said. "I love you, Ma."

"Love you, too. Bye-bye."

"How's your ma?" a voice said, startling me. I balled my fists and spun around, anticipating some unseen enemy. But it was only Stevie, still wearing his clothes from the night before, his breath still reeking of the rum from the Whisky.

"Damn, man," he said in response to my pose. "Ain't nobody gonna kill you in here." There was a dark bruise at the bridge of his nose.

"I guess you don't shower first thing in the morning, huh?"

"Fuck you, nigga," he replied with a smile. "When I woke up first thing I thought about was last night. You know I ain't mean that shit."

"Yeah, I know," I said. "It's cool."

"How's everybody?" he asked.

"Ma's all right. Henry wasn't home."

"I know you can't wait to see 'em," he began. I heard the pitch before it came. "But I need one more favor."

"I gotta go home," I said. "I told you, two days."

"Oh, I know that. I just want you to meet somebody before you do."

"Who?"

"My manager," he said, his lips covered by a fanning of fingers.

"Your manager?"

"Yeah, I told him you were out and he asked me to bring you by."

"What for? I mean, he knows I don't do music no more, right?"

Stevie turned and looked out at the ocean. "Not exactly."

"Why the fuck not?" I asked. "I mean, how many times have I told you? How many times have I said the shit in the last forty-eight hours alone? I don't do it anymore. I let that shit go."

He turned to me with all of his remaining courage and hope. "No, you didn't," he said. "You couldn't have."

"Why are you bringing this shit up now, Stevie?"

"Cuz you're gonna listen to what the fuck I have to say before I buy you the ticket to get your ass home."

I took a moment to breathe. The words could've broken his nose, shattered a rib, crushed his windpipe. But instead they achieved their purpose.

"Then talk," I said.

"All right. All the shit I've done for you since you went in ain't have nothin' to do with the music. Nothing I did. Nothing I sent. Nothing I said. Trying to pimp you is like tryin' to pimp myself. You know that, don't you?"

"Yeah," I said with suspicion. "Yeah, I know that."

"All this money I got. This crib, these tracks I've been doin'. Yeah it's work, but it ain't me. Once every couple weeks I go down to the studio and I put on our old tapes— you know, the ones from the four-track and that bullshit ass mike from Radio Shack—and I hear all the fuck-ups and the static and the off-timed ad libs. And I still think it's the best shit I've ever worked on. Cuz I was workin' with you."

He was trying to sway me, trying to undo all that had been done on the inside. He wanted me to break the lock on Cinnamon's coffin and breathe life back into her lifeless bones. He wanted his basement back and the high school rehearsal room and all the yelling we used to do at Lonnie just so he'd get his parts right.

And I'd wanted those things, too, every once in a while,

when I'd hear the bullshit top forty on contraband Walk-men or the community boombox in the day room. Even Jimmy Stein had said that Puffy Combs needed to get his ass beat for fucking up American music.

But then each time I would remember the Panamanian's words on that first night inside. And I remembered how I'd blown it all for some extra dollars and a surrogate father's approval.

And then things came clearly into focus. And all that was there were Salamanca and my little girl, the two pretti-est things on earth, patiently waiting for their lover and father to make his way home. Everything else was a swarm of gnats easily repelled with a few waves of hand.

"I miss those days, too," I said. "But that was then. You lived that dream for me. And you gotta keep on livin' it."

"But I'm not livin' it," he argued. "I'm just spinnin', givin' 'em what they want so I can change cars every year."

"What are you talkin' about?" I asked, refusing to heed the blatant truth in each and every syllable.

"C'mon, man, you've heard what I've been doin' over the years. Recycled beats and reused hooks. The shit we clowned other niggas for doin' at all those talent shows. I've been goin' through the motions cuz it pays the bills. I got all the drinks and pussy and money I want. But I don't have the one thing I started out with, that thing we both had since the day we were born."

I didn't know what to say at first. After all, this was my best friend. Still brutally honest. Still sensitive as a clit. Among bitches and bullies, the music had been his only safe place, just like it was for me. But he still had it, while I had long since let it go.

"I know what you're askin' me to do," I began, knowing

that whatever I said would not be enough. "And I would if I could. But it's gone, Steve. What you see is what you get. I got a notebook of old pages I scribbled on every now and again, but nuthin' solid, nuthin' that's gonna help you."

He rubbed his neck nervously, the mixture of liquor and morning breath tainting the air all around us.

"I mean, can't you just try?" he begged. "For me? Just go down to the studio and sit down at the piano and—"

"I already did," I interjected. "And it ain't there no more."

It took a moment for the words to sink in. But I knew when they finally did. His eyes darkened, forecasting the storm he was about to unleash.

"I waited seven fuckin' years for you to get out and you play me like this?! I mean, what the fuck? I got you up in my crib like you Nelson Mandela or somebody. Drivin' you around, gettin' you pussy, makin' sure you got the fuck back home from that jail out in the middle of nowhere! And I ask you to help me out with one goddamn thing and you can't do the shit!"

My first impulse was to argue with him, to call him out for contradicting words he'd said only a few moments earlier. I was going to tell him about himself, that it wasn't my fault that he'd sold out, that I didn't have anything to do with the short circuits in his creativity. After all, I had been the one who was on the inside. I was the one who watched him live the life that I was supposed to have, getting hooked on squares and books just to keep the time moving at a normal pace.

And who the fuck was he to be yelling at me? Harping on the fact that he was buying my ticket home. If he didn't want to do it, then he shouldn't have said he was going to do it. I had a future wife. I had a child that didn't know me.

I didn't have time to be standing on a Malibu balcony argu-
ing over the motherfucking inarguable! I had to get home.
And I was willing to do it on foot if I had to, or with raised
thumbs in the backs of pickup trucks. I didn't need this! I
didn't need him!

"I'm sorry, man," I said plainly. "Especially if that's what
you brought me here for. And don't even worry about the
plane ticket or whatever. I'm a grown-ass man, Stevie. And
men get themselves where they need to be. I'll grab my shit
and walk my ass home step for step if that's what it—"

"Nigga, shut the fuck up!" he yelled back.

"What?" I demanded, taking a step toward him. He
shrank away, almost stumbling into the screen door behind
him, a hand to his obviously aching belly.

"Don't talk that stupid shit," he murmured. "I'll get you
home."

"Don't do me no favors, Stevie, especially if all I was
here for was your next hit."

"It wasn't like that. I'm hung over, man. The words ain't
coming out right."

Everything inside me said he was full of shit, that he'd
say whatever it took to keep things cool, just in case I decided to change my mind. I remembered when Salamanca
had told me that I trusted too easily, that my worst enemies
would always be those that "hugged me the tightest." This
man could not be my friend. And yet I knew without a
doubt that he was.

"You know me, Turner. You know I'd take a bullet for
you any day of the week. I'd do anything in my power. But
what you need ain't in my power, at least not anymore."

He turned toward the sea, and we both looked out at
the sun rays bursting through a patch of cloud.

"Anything?" Stevie asked.

"Anything," I said.

"All right, then," he said with a smile.

" 'All right, then,' what?" I asked.

"Let me hop in the shower," he replied, indicating that the conversation was over. "Then we'll get you home."

Marianna offered a kiss on the cheek as she said good-bye, along with a Ziploc bag of butter cookies. I asked her if she'd miss me, and she said that she wouldn't have to, because I'd be back sooner than I thought.

Stevie changed into a bright red button-up that made him look like a tourist. He explained that it had cost him four hundred bucks. And I replied that I couldn't have cared less.

There was a chill in the air on the way to LAX. Using the piece in his ear, he and his travel agent booked me a direct flight home for noon. But it was only nine-thirty.

"We can take the scenic route," he said excitedly. "Show you a little L.A. on your way out. Besides, I gotta make a quick stop."

He was inside the Wells Fargo on Wilshire for more than a half hour, leaving me to bake in the afternoon heat. A Mexican woman my age pushed by with a double stroller, hips wide and thighs thick from the burden of multiple childbirth.

I wondered what Sala looked like. I hadn't gotten a picture in a while, but I didn't think it would matter. She was always the same beauty, with child or not, hair up or down. And Sasha would always look as though her mother had spat her out, except for the eyes she'd gotten from yours truly.

Seven years of life and that little girl and I had never talked beyond "Hi, Daddy" and "I love you, baby." I'd heard her in the background, singing and playing, asking Sala for more juice, or to get a book for her off the shelf, or if she could watch one of her many favorite movies just one more time. But I'd rarely had the courage to talk to her, not from where I was, not so that she could hate me for making it all so complicated.

"You don't know how much she loves you," Sala had assured me. "She prays for you every night and keeps your picture on the little nightstand next to your bed. She even sleeps like you. Always on her stomach with her head to the right."

"For real?" I'd asked excitedly, knowing that the minutes on our call were dwindling.

I'd projected myself into the child's bedroom, wherever it might have been. I'd imagined myself standing over her, watching her sleep the way I once had, a guardrail on one side of the bed frame to keep me from rolling off during the night.

"We're always here for you, baby," Sala had said after that. "That's the easy job. Getting you out of there is the hard one."

It was around then that Stevie dropped something into my lap and snatched me away from reminiscence.

"What's this?" I asked, referring to the thick envelope that now rested on my thigh.

"Open it and find out," he said, daring me to break that manila seal.

"What's in it?" I asked again.

"Just open the goddamn envelope," he said impatiently.

"All right."

I tore open the seal to find an ATM card with my name on it wrapped in a slip of paper with a PIN printed on it. There were six years' worth of annual bank statements and a total of $1,163,000 in active assets, including mutual funds, stock certificates from Wal-Mart and Microsoft, and $1,000 in hundreds and fifties, folded over and clipped with a chiseled piece of silver that bore my initials.

It wasn't meant to be a surprise. He'd told me that his accountants would take care of me, that he'd make sure I got everything coming to me. But somewhere on the inside I'd managed to forget, storing his words away with my deadened dreams and all the other shit I couldn't let show from the wrong side of my cell. But the numbers were a *lot* bigger than I'd imagined them.

"All for you, baby," he said with the biggest smile I'd seen from him since he'd picked me up at prison. "Interest's been running the whole time."

"Damn," I said. "When you said I was taken care of—"

"I meant you was taken care of," he said proudly.

My eyes kept cutting to the statements. So many numbers. More than I'd ever seen before a decimal point.

"Damn, man. I didn't think it was gonna be this much. I . . . I don't know what to say."

"You ain't gotta say nuthin'. You worked hard, and you got paid for it."

I was a millionaire, but for all that, one who didn't have a clue of what to do with his fortune. I couldn't spend it. I couldn't even think about spending it, until I found Sala, until I knew where she was and what she needed. Until then, the $1,000 in my pocket had to be treated as if it were all the money I had on earth. And even that was more than I'd ever imagined during the commissary years, when $50 was all you could have in your cell at any given time.

"Any more surprises you wanna tell me about?" I asked, still mesmerized by the numbers printed on the balance statement.

"No," he said innocently. "At least not yet."

Three hours later I was thirty thousand feet in the air, looking through triple-paned glass at a cloud that was the spitting image of Salamanca's face. It had that hooked curve where her nose would have been and the narrow jaw and even the marbled cheekbones most models would have died for.

"So many things out there," said the elderly woman next to me, equally engrossed in the view.

She was a frail stick with a dark complexion, her head of gray hair cut close to her head.

"I was just thinking the same thing," I said, finishing off the chilled Sprite before me. First class was pretty all right.

"This is a nice flight," she remarked after a pull from her white wine. "You fly first class all the time?"

"No, ma'am," I replied bashfully. "This is the first time I've ever been on a plane."

It was the truth, though I'd sat in a plane once, a fighter jet at Andrews Air Force Base on a fifth-grade school trip. And that was the closest I'd ever come to flying the friendly skies. Stevie had dropped $1,500 for my last-minute ticket, making it the most expensive ride of my life. But with the money I was carrying, that was likely to change.

The woman and I were the only flies in a section full of buttermilk. Yet we'd pretty much ignored each other until the Mississippi River, when the batteries in her headphones died and I'd finished the copy of *Rolling Stone* someone had left in a chair back at the terminal. But even if we hadn't spoken, the Purple Rain tour T-shirt would have etched her in my memory bank forever.

"My daughter gave me this," she explained. "After that big tour when the movie came out. You know, when they was sayin' he was almost as big as Michael Jackson."

I remembered that time, back around the second grade when I got hold of Andre Step's copy of the *Right On* that had the both of them on the cover. Prince had looked so much cooler than Mike. I'd never been a big fan of that glove thing, though everybody knew that Mike was the better dancer.

My dad, however, had perhaps been the Purple One's biggest fan. He'd even gone so far as to play "I Would Die 4 U" at Henry's first birthday party. All the little infants and toddlers looked at him as if he were crazy, while he wrestled with the several parents lunging for the stop button.

"So, you from D.C.?" she asked me.

"Born and raised," I said. "But I been away for a while."

"Me too. I been in L.A. for a month seein' my daughter, you know the one bought me this shirt. Smart, pretty girl. She just had a little boy and the daddy locked up in jail somewhere. I always tell her she needs a good man. I should give you her—"

"Sorry, ma'am," I interrupted shyly, "but I'm taken. As a matter of fact, I'm on the way to see my girlfriend right now. We got a little girl together ourselves."

She chuckled to herself and then killed what was left of

her wine. "Well, bless your heart. You can't blame me for tryin'," she said. "Young men like you don't grow on trees."

A good man. Would I have been less of one if she knew that her son-in-law and I might have been on the same cell block? Or that I'd very recently put my dick in a slit tagged with a FOR SALE sign? I didn't think so. But Jimmy Stein had said it best:

"In the end life is more about what you sell yourself to be than what you actually are."

Our plane thumped onto the runway at National Airport, which I soon learned was now named after Ronald Reagan (though I refused to give that asshole any verbal air play, so it was still National as far as I was concerned). My bag, an overpriced leather duffel I'd picked up in a shop at LAX, had everything I owned in the world, including the few overpriced shirts and pants I'd picked up while I waited for the plane. I didn't want to wear other people's clothes anymore.

I wanted to kiss the ground when I set foot on D.C. soil. Fresh off the jetway, the lilt of local lingo was music to my ears, that "country but don't even think about calling it country" accent I couldn't lose after seven years on the inside. Looking out past the runway, I saw the city skyline exactly where I'd left it.

There was the freeway and Pentagon City in the other direction, Haines Point and East Potomac Park, the Wharf and the Mall, all the little mental postcards I'd mailed to myself, as reminders of who I was and where I came from.

Night had already fallen, but the heat index made it feel as if it were two in the afternoon. Ninety-plus-degree heat and humidity that made it feel like a jungle. Arizona would never know air that thick.

African cabbies ushered anything Caucasian into their backseats. But they wouldn't give me a second look when I tried to signal them. Maybe it was the baggy slacks or the pulled-down cap of khaki. But more than likely it was just the same ole thing, them buying into centuries of lies about their own kidnapped kindred. It was a good thing that I'd actually wanted to take the train.

The ride in was a tour of more things familiar. An old man in a blue golf cap sat with two different pairs of eyeglasses—one on the edge of his nose, the other dangling from the beaded chain around his neck as he read the day's *Washington Post*. A coal-colored boy of sixteen or so changed out of his McDonald's uniform at the end of the car, revealing a pudgy midsection he should have kept to himself. A middle-aged woman with horsehair extensions bobbed her head to the gospel spilling out of her headphones.

Had time been on pause since I'd left? Even the ride itself was no different from what it had been on my evening journeys home from Sally Helen's, when I didn't have "overtime."

But I knew that all was not as it had been. Mom and Henry no longer hung their hats in the old neighborhood. They'd bought a house over in Southeast, a two-story with three bedrooms and a basement. And they had cable, something Dad had always been too cheap to spring for.

Hillcrest was a long hump from the airport. Even after you got off the train at Potomac Avenue, you had to take the 36 over the river to the end of the line up in the hills.

But I needed the time. I wasn't quite ready to face what was left of my family.

The stops came and went as the trolley crawled from elevated platforms into tunnels below the earth. Lit rectangular bulbs rushing by the windows at fifty miles per hour. Foggy Bottom, Federal Center, L'Enfant Plaza. A few hours earlier I might have seen a familiar face on its way home from the downtown grind.

Most D.C. folks worked for the federal government, funneling down to the center of our world to collect a paycheck. I'd always see them at the end of their days, as I was on the way to beginning my own. They'd gather underneath the ledge of the DOT building to avoid the rain or cluster near the fountains in the courtyard just to get a little mist in the summer heat.

I remembered the way they packed onto buses that might or might not have the proper climate control, only concerned with getting home, making it back to their own little pieces of the world.

It had been my own foregone conclusion that I was to be one of them, back before Sally Helen's and seven years on the inside. I dreamed of a GS ranking and a picture ID card to wear around my neck. They'd always talk about the benefits and the camaraderie, the sick days and leaves of absence: the idle chatter on those crowded trams at the end of each day.

Yet something inside told me that that wasn't going to be me, that the music or something else would deliver me from Chocolate City's usual path for the young, black, and practical. I knew too much about other places, about the music industry, about the Peace Corps and programs where you could get paid to teach English in other countries, even if you didn't speak the language. And I knew I could get into a college if I really wanted to go. I knew these things, but there had been no concrete plans outside of those made in Stevie's basement, when sound massaged my temples until the notes and words came out like music. But meeting Salamanca had been the clincher.

"There's no way I'm staying here for school," the girl had said on the night of our first Valentine's Day. Her breath hung in the icy air as I wrapped my arms around her, the bright lights of M Street everywhere we looked.

"So you gonna leave me behind?" I'd asked.

"I'll never leave you, baby. You'll just have to come a little farther to visit me."

"Maybe," I'd said with a smile. "Or maybe not."

"What do you mean?"

"A nigga might have to come with you."

"What? You're gonna go wherever I go?" she'd asked, trying to sound as if she didn't feel the way she felt, as if she weren't in love with me.

"As long as you'll have me," I'd said humbly.

She'd taken a moment to think it over, urging me to tighten my grip. Then she'd turned around and kissed me, her tongue sliding across my own.

"Good," she had said. "Good."

A power-doored 36 to Hillcrest was idling when I got to Potomac Avenue, its insides flowing with icy air, raising tiny bumps on my arms and legs as I entered. It was all pretty familiar once we crossed the Sousa Bridge. They still had the little gray concrete huts down in Anacostia Park, where Southeast people came to barbecue and set off fireworks on the Fourth of July. Then we crawled up Pennsylvania Avenue past what was left of the old Morton's department store and the Discount Designer Trading Post (DDTP), inching closer and closer to the city limits and the last stop, just four blocks away from my final destination.

12.

There were so many trees. Oak, elm, and maple, their vibrant leaves swaying in the August breeze. My gut was Tupperware for butterflies. My mother and brother might have been in a new neighborhood, but they were still the same souls, souls who'd had to suffer through the whispers of ridicule, through the dishonor of having the second "man of the house" become just another statistic.

I had been such a good boy before that last year of high school. I'd been a church musician since the age of twelve. I had spent hours at the Riverside soup kitchen, helping to feed the elderly and homeless on Christmas and Thanksgiving. And perhaps most importantly, I had been heir to Benjamin senior, son of the church deacon and layman, Eastern High All-City basketball star, the cop who made detective after only two years on the force. Yet I had still been pulled under.

You brought your family to Hillcrest when you made something of yourself, something that took you well beyond the fifty-grand-a-year mark. I had been up there a few times before to visit a girl, a flash of the feminine that had come and gone long before Sala ever existed.

Tamara Fowler's smile brought light to the darkest tunnel. And her chocolate behind wasn't a hard sell either. Time had stripped away many of the details. But I remembered that she had played drums in the school band and had asked me if I wanted to practice with her and *talk* about music.

Her father was the highest black something or other over at the main post office. But he wasn't much of a music fan. The family owned about twelve records. Eight of those were gospel. Two were disco, and her mother had practically warped the first two Whitney albums, as if the secret to eternal youth were hidden between their grooves. "I hear 'How Will I Know' in my dreams," Tamara had said once, laughing.

For a few weeks I'd made expeditions to see her, riding that 36 to the end of the line for endless sessions of advanced anatomy. They had a big basement covered in wood paneling, with two large oak bookcases and a fireplace that they burned wood in when company was over. And despite the limited music, the Kenwood system they had was superb, its speakers as clear as the glass in the windows.

"I like you a lot," she had said to me as Kool and the

Gang's first album played in the background, the first album I'd bought her. She needed to understand just how far they'd fallen off with all of the stuff from the "Joanna" era. She laid a slender hand against my chest, her brownie complexion a contrast to my own light almond.

"I like you, too," I'd said, knowing for certain that that was *all* I felt, though the uncontrollable organ in my jeans often argued otherwise. So I kissed her. And she kissed me. And our hands explored parts of each other far beyond first and second base. I remembered the sugary scent of the fluid that came from inside of her, though I was too afraid to taste it. I remembered the rush of coming into the latex around me, her walls milking me of all that I had.

Prison had kept that particular memory at the front of the file. Among straight men, even the vaguest pussy stories are more precious than platinum. While others had settled for sodomy, I was caught up in the rapture of sharing a cone with Salamanca at the lot carnival on Benning Road. I reflected on how she bit my nipples until I came, her breath on the back of my neck when she held me in our sleep. And I'd used those little snapshots to stroke myself in the depths of my dungeon, dreaming of the day when I would finally see the light.

The bulb on the porch gleamed with hundred-watt newness as the house came into view. I wanted Henry to answer the door. He'd be the easier one to talk to. He wouldn't ask about things I couldn't speak of. And he wouldn't tell me what I needed to do and when I should start doing it.

The house looked smaller than it had in the pictures. But it was still two times bigger than the old place. The outside of it was painted a blue green, and there were shutters on each of the four front windows. A low wrought-iron fence shielded it from potential invaders.

A concrete walkway led from the sidewalk all the way to the front door, which was made of dark cherrywood. And there was a driveway with room for two cars. I could see light behind the first-level windows. I raised my fist to knock, hoping to God that they both still loved me.

Part Three

1.

The print was so small that it strained Salamanca's eyes. But she made sure to read every single word, just to make sure. The signature space was a paved runway awaiting the landing of her new name: Sally Helen Baker. Her grandmother's first name. The love of her life's last. An unattainable past juxtaposed with the bliss she knew the future had to be.

"All you have to do is sign," her attorney, Allen Woods, remarked, his short, pudgy frame hidden behind the antique desk within the plain Sheetrock walls that made up his office.

Salamanca had met Woods

on the flight to Detroit a few weeks before, when she was on her way into the city from Atlanta. Woods had just quit his gig as a DA in New York to open his own firm back in Motown, where he and his significantly younger wife had been reared.

She needed someone to trust in this new place. And she wasn't sure about Pat after so many years. Woods had seemed so nice and concerned about her child that she felt obliged to tell him her story, and Ben's story, and the story of the child inside of her, tales that lasted nearly the full length of the hour-long connecting flight from Chicago to "the D." The only thing she'd revised were their real names.

He gave her a card and told her he'd love to help in any way he could, his shaved head gleaming from the reading light overhead. And she'd taken him up on it just a few weeks after Pat had taken her in.

She'd told her aunt as much as she could about all that had happened, about Ben and the baby, the man who'd followed her, Tahir helping her get out of town, and how she hadn't spoken to her father in more than six months.

"I don't know much about livin' underground," Pat had begun. "But that fake ID you used for the plane can't get you but so far. If you really wanna make a new life, you gotta get yourself a new name, as much as it hurts my heart to say it. Cuz then I won't be able to call you Sala anymore."

"You can call me whatever you want," Sala had replied. "I'll just have to get it right for the rest of the world."

Salamanca had smiled, excited by the brilliance of the idea, though she knew how hard it would be to come up with an entirely new identity overnight.

"It shouldn't be too hard, from what I hear," Pat had

continued. "You call up a lawyer and fill out some paper-work, and that's pretty much it. Then you get yourself a job, a little place, a credit card, all the things you need to look legitimate. Then you can set up wherever you want. It happens a lot more than you think. I don't think I could do it," she'd mused. "But you're the one with people looking for you."

The more Sala thought about it, the more insane it seemed. To her, fully false identities came with spy watches and cars that sprayed oil slicks. But that Mitchell name was the homing beacon that had brought trouble into her Atlanta home. And the uncommon first name didn't help matters, either.

But what about her child? How could she explain that change? And would she change it back once Ben got out? How would that work? And would all of this help or hurt them in the end? She wasn't sure. Then she saw a flash of the pear-shaped goblin who was almost upon her when Tahir saved the day, and she decided to put Woods's card to good use.

Three weeks later she was looking over the documents for a final time, subconsciously searching for some flaw or loophole that would make her lose her nerve. She was saying good-bye to the name her mother had given her, though she'd always given the credit to Alfonse Mitchell, because he had still been there and Viola had not.

Taking another name would free her from the binds of that person's life, of its rules, regulations, preferences, and pet peeves. But if she did this, certain things would have to cease: the nightly crying herself to sleep on the mattress in

Robert's room, the worry that Ben would not be there at the end of the years ahead, and the fear that her child, their child, wouldn't make it to the land of the living. She closed her eyes and asked the spirits of her elders to guide her hand. And they brought her pen to the solid line in exactly the right spot.

Sally Helen Baker handed the signed sheet to her attorney, who would put it on file with those who would make it official in one to two weeks' time, most likely near the very day that her child was slated to be born.

"Congratulations," Woods said as he reviewed the signature space.

"I didn't win a prize," she replied cynically.

"No, but it is a freedom," he said with a smile. "You are now free of everything you ever had to run from."

The short man's words brought a smile to her face, because she so wanted them to be true. But something told her that it might not be enough, that something beyond her power was out there stalking her, its ears attuned to the beating of her young and fragile heart. She shook Woods's hand and made her exit, remembering that there was a stop she'd promised to make.

She'd bought a car out of the classifieds in the *Free Press*, a 1988 four-door Accord the color of freshly fallen snow. After a few weeks she'd noticed that it ran a little hot in dense traffic, but it had otherwise proved to be a sound investment. She fired it up and shifted into drive, setting a course for the most painful block on the Mitchells' memory lane.

She hated that town. Three and a half weeks there and

she had already seen high school boys stomp the living shit out of a man twice their age, just because he'd attempted to cut in front of them at the popcorn line in a movie theater. A boy in nothing but boxer shorts had run out of a house with a shotgun to fire shells up in the air, raining buckshot on nearby neighbors, because there was nothing else to do. Women bubbled over with glee because they'd met a man with a job on the Ford assembly line, guaranteeing late-model cars at a discount and money to spend on them every other Friday. This was not D.C. This was the D.

Pat had written her directions on how to get there. But she would've made it regardless. The Motor City was pretty much a grid. A few blocks and a few turns and you eventually made it to where you needed to be.

The Palmer Woods were just as she'd remembered them. The endless stretch of cedars reached for the sky, beams of sunlight squeezing into gaps among leaves and branches. Lawns and gardens were manicured to perfection. And every car was buffed to a pristine shine.

The fifth house on the right looked exactly the way it had when she'd left it. The mailbox was painted a bright white, its placard telling everybody that the Miltons had a place in the world, a three-story house with a huge back-yard, a renovated basement with leather-cushioned stools, and a big-screen TV complete with satellite dish.

The Woodards, a childless husband and wife who both worked in Ford's marketing division, occupied the castle of an estate on the left. The Folsoms, a doctor, a housewife, and a pair of girl twins named Marley and Marla, held down the practically identical home to the right. And there were still signs for the Rudolphs and the Armsteads across the way. It was a neighborhood trapped in time.

The Miltons. It had been so long since she'd carried that name. She had liked being a Milton because there was a cute boy named Milton in her class who liked to tease her because his first name was her last. But she'd had to give it up when Daddy said so. Because the name Milton would not fit in their new place, the little town he said was the nation's capital.

She climbed out of the car and took a look at the place of her birth. Her father's memories had given her the image of an aging midwife and a lot of pillows in the master bedroom on the third floor, where her parents had lived in regal splendor for many years before she was born.

Alfonse Mitchell had been a minister at Greater Mount Calvary Baptist, the third largest church in the city, whenever he wasn't running that seafood restaurant out in Southfield, the one with the name she always had trouble pronouncing. Her mother was a lead saleswoman, and the only resident Negro, at the Benz dealership in Bloomfield Hills. And they had been a very happy family, for all that she knew, back then.

It was a nice neighborhood, though there was little nice beyond its borders. On longer walks she might see broken bottles and empty matchbooks, even the occasional used hypodermic needle, all of which her parents had implored her never to pick up. Sometimes she would even hear a pop or two late into the night or the screaming from the painted cars with the lights on top of them.

The memories intensified as Salamanca passed through the chain-link fence that surrounded the house. The grass was full, and there were even the same two plastic chairs on the front porch, which itself had been painted a fresh coat of the same gray paint she'd remembered. Coming home from school, she would always try to jump all three steps at once but ended up scraping her knee whenever she fell short.

She'd kept her key to the front door since the day they left. Back then she'd worn it on a beaded chain her mother had given her. She'd have to pull that chain over a thick head of plaits just to get it in the lock and open the door.

She pulled away from the past long enough to take a visual sweep of the area, making sure that no neighbors or cops or passersby might have ID'd her. She was only going to try the key and leave, just to remember what it had felt like the last time she'd called it home, before that strange Friday when she became a Mitchell instead of a Milton. The driveway was empty and the shutters were closed. It was just a dare to herself, to see how close she could bend her promise without breaking it. So she peeled back the screen door and pushed the key into the lower lock's slit.

And it went in perfectly. And then it turned without as much as a squeak. The inside was just as it had been more than a decade before, except for all the dust in the air. The splintered bookcase was still strewn on the carpet, its volumes in a descending pile leading toward the kitchen. The mirror-framed eleven-by-fourteen shot of her parents' wedding day was still broken into pieces at the foot of the staircase. And there was still that big stain in front of the TV, with the conspicuous wineglass laid next to it, to indicate a spill. But wine did not turn brown after ten years' time.

The next thing she knew, she was climbing the wooden stairs that led to the upper level and her room. The air was stale. The rooms reeked of their obvious neglect: two offices, her playroom, and the place where she'd slept since she was an infant.

The farther in she went, the more it felt like a dream, like the flashes she'd had for years of her daddy and that hole in the backyard, of the screaming and yelling that had followed her mother's declaration of independence and free will. The breaking of things. The screaming use of four-letter words a child her age was not to say for any reason. And then there had been a thud. Thirty minutes later she could hear her father out in the backyard, *working*.

Those flashes hadn't been dreams, because when they left her daddy had dirt all over him. He had thrown random things and some of her clothes into bags and dragged her to the car, foolishly believing that she had been asleep the whole time. The flesh rose on Salamanca's arms and legs. She so wished that she hadn't crossed that threshold.

"Where did Mommy go?" she had asked her father as he applied special pedal to the metal of his Oldsmobile.

"Your momma went away," he'd said coldly, his eyes obsessed with the road before him. "She went away and left us. But we'll talk about that later, okay? In the meantime you recline that seat and get some sleep. Daddy'll tell you the story in the morning."

And a story it was, a sugar pill of lies that went down easy in the girl's consciousness. But somewhere beneath the surface she felt something change during that ride. She saw the driver as something else other than "Daddy." And that something else wasn't good. Now, a decade later, in the house she was never to return to, all of the pieces had been reassembled. Ben or no Ben, she had to go home. She had to face her father one last time.

Yet she had promised Alfonse Mitchell that she would never speak of Detroit again, that it was a past life, and that the two of them were building a new one in a new place.

Sala heeded her father's command. As Daddy's little girl, it was her job to make him happy.

When awareness overcame her, she was standing in the mustiness of what had been her parents' bedroom. The sheets were still made. Her mother's oils and perfumes were still on the dresser. All of her clothes were still in the closets.

Pat had warned her that all had been left the same, except the yard, that she'd wanted to leave the place as it had been before, so that if Viola returned, she would feel right at home. She had obviously been in denial.

But what could you expect from the bereaved when there was no body to mourn? The Armsteads had told the police about the landscaping truck that came the day after Salamanca and her father left. The men went around the back of the house with tools and returned with something large wrapped in cloth, whisking it off to God knew where before the cops could even think about arriving.

Pat had fought tooth and nail to bring Alfonse to justice. Statements from the neighbors alone should have been enough to keep the case open. If he had left the state, the FBI should have been called in. If he had changed his name, there should have been people poring through records to determine the whens and wheres.

Viola's only sister was at police headquarters every day, depleting both her vacation and sick days. She worked with five different lawyers. She staked out the homes of investigating officers and badgered them on their way to and from their precinct. It was a miracle she didn't get arrested, that all of those who should have been able to help felt just as helpless.

Everyone gritted their teeth at the way the case was all but ignored. Pat couldn't understand why the cops could succeed in finding a booster in the worst part of the city but fail with a murderer in a place of privilege. She broke down, several times, and had been on medication up until a few months before Sala showed up on her doorstep.

It had taken years for Pat to understand the shadowy forces that had been against her from the start. In her first week in Detroit, Salamanca happened to mention that she remembered the tall, fat man with the gray Afro and the mustache like Magnum, P.I.'s, who had been Detroit's chief of police. Even as a little girl, she could recall his regular visits to the house for Sunday dinner. It was the same chief who five years later would be ousted from office for with-holding evidence in a major drug case — and then disappear as well. Sala would also tell her of the white man who came by from time to time, the lanky one with the bald spot in the back who once came to her school to speak as the owner of the largest newspaper in town.

Now that they were together, making the connections was the easy part. Accepting their magnitude was another thing altogether. In light of her talks with Pat, Sala could see that setting up Ben had been nothing, as had her father's murder of the woman he'd married. Salamanca was the child of an abomination no one could stop, except her.

She paced the room as she had as a little girl, searching for something new to explore and investigate. But there was nothing new, except the reflection staring back at her from the mirror. She still couldn't believe that her key still fit. Who'd kept the place up for all these years? Who'd painted the house without arousing suspicion from neighbors and cops alike? And why would they have kept the locks the same?

*

"I want to go home," she had said to her father when they'd first toured the new house in Southwest.

"This is our home now, baby," he'd said. "Our life, you and me, starts here and now. Nuthin' back there matters anymore."

It was a miracle that she hadn't cracked during all those years of school. How had she made it past all those teachers and counselors who had hunches that there was something wrong with Alfonse Mitchell's little star? But she knew how to elude such inquiries.

She played sports and joined clubs and introduced speakers at assemblies, and soon enough she was Miss Congeniality, the freckled light-skinned girl with titties at twelve, the lovely mask she'd used to conceal the real deal.

Starting back down the stairs, she thought that she heard the child inside her crying, its voice impossibly audible from deep within. She immediately wished she hadn't bet herself about the key and the lock. Making the switch to being Sally Helen Baker would have been a lot easier without it.

Then there was a savage ripple in her cervix. A moment later it came again. And then the pain started. Had it not been for the railing, she might have stumbled down the steps and killed herself. God must have been a sadist. She had just gone into labor.

2.

I prayed to God for it to be Henry. I must have asked
Him a million times between
the walkway and the bell. But
Henry did not answer.

My mother was a vision in
burnt orange as she took her
time in opening the door. She
wore a satin blouse with
matching slacks and slippers as
her gapped lips sealed into a
smile. There were light
whispers of Smokey Robinson
off in the background.

"Good God!" she exploded
as she took in the full view of
me. "What'd they feed you in
prison?"

"It wasn't the food," I
replied. "Just the weights."

"I just hope we can get you

through the door frame," she replied, backing away to let me in. I was barely into the foyer before she wrapped her arms around me, holding on as if I were about to go away all over again. I returned the embrace, noticing her frame was a little wider than I'd remembered it.

"You shoulda called, you know?" she murmured into me.

"I just wanted to get here," I said.

She looked up at me and smiled again. "Praise God you made it."

"God's the greatest."

"That He is. So you gonna stand there all day or come in here and sit down?" I trailed her into the first of many unfamiliar rooms.

The chairs and sofa matched her clothes: brown and orange against the gold on the walls. An enlarged photograph of her and Henry hung over the hearth, which had a real fireplace underneath it. Jade and spider plants crowded the window frames. And Smokey breathed through the entertainment center in the corner.

"It's as nice as you said it was, Ma. Way better than the old place."

"Mortgage is way bigger, too. But it's worth it. Besides, I told you how things were going to the dogs around the way."

The streets of Southwest had gotten even grimier while I'd been away, and Mom had weathered it for as long as she could. She even went as far as getting the windows barred and keeping Dad's old pistol in close reach after a pair of home invasions that came less than a year apart. But the last straw had been when someone stole her license plates in broad daylight.

The days of neighborhood games and block parties had

gone with the Old Man's disappearance. Now there were just dealers and users, thieves and black girls lost, many of whom my mother had taught in Sunday school.

She was tired of the broken glass on the streets, tired of seeing squad cars parked at the curbs. So when Stevie's brother, Malcolm, told her that place in Hillcrest was up for auction, she put her chips on the table and let it ride. In her mind that would keep Henry away from the black holes that were already pulling his friends into danger.

"I missed you, Ma," I said as we sat across from each other, though I wanted to say much more.

I wanted to apologize for the time I'd been absent, for not being there when Henry came home to find the window jimmied open, for being out of reach when they went to the cemetery on the five-year anniversary with the white roses Dad loved so much. I was sorry that she had a grandchild she'd never seen, whose voice she'd heard only for minutes at a time via staticky phone lines. I'd basically blown it all the way around.

"Sometimes I thought the world was gonna end," she said, her body sinking into the soft cushion underneath. She put her hand over mine and clasped my wrist with her fingers. "I thought God might take me home before you got out of there. But you had to do your time. And now it's done."

"Amen to that," I said. "You know, I'm glad you didn't let Henry come to see me."

Three years before, right after my transfer, my then-fourteen-year-old brother had devised a plan to come visit me. He had saved up $400 from his job at the Cinnabon in Wheaton Plaza and was going to take a plane and then a bus.

He didn't have a clue of where he was going to stay or whom he'd get directions from in a state so racist that it wouldn't celebrate King's birthday. But he'd just wanted to see his brother, the brother he'd always loved no matter what.

"Wasn't no way in hell I was letting that boy get out of my sight," she said.

"But he's out of your sight right now," I said.

"But he's seventeen right now, too. There's a big difference."

Time passed and we kept talking, about little things like that, about her promotion at the DOE and how I needed to go downtown and fill out paperwork so that I could get a job in her building. I didn't mention the money just then. I was still accepting the fact that it even existed.

We ran our mouths more than we ever had in our past life. Back then she went to work, and I went to school and work, and the three of us ate dinner in front of the TV on fold-up trays, barely speaking. When Dad had been there, meals had been reverent things taken at the big table in the dining room. There was no TV. No music. Nothing but four people talking about their lives. To Dad, we were all a part of one another and needed to know what was on the others' hearts and minds, because "no one in the world would care about us like us."

Dad kept the Bakers running like a well-oiled machine. He knew how to say and do precisely the right things, no matter who was away, or sick, or busy, or pissed off at somebody else. And he'd managed to do it without us even seeing him every day.

In that life, Mom and I had always been the ones with the most distance between us. From the cradle to the funeral we never really got past the usual mother-and-son jive, about cleaning rooms and ironing shirts, taking out the trash and keeping the grades up. We knew our birthdays and what we wanted for Christmas. But outside of that, we were perfect strangers.

Then Mom got that call from the precinct. There had been a fatal collision at the corner of Minnesota and Penn Avenue Southeast. And then the Baker machine broke down. Neither of us was that good at doing Dad's job.

"You been over to the cemetery lately?" I asked, clawing my nails against the sofa cushion.

She glanced down at the polished wood beneath her, caught completely off guard. "No, I haven't," she said solemnly, bringing her eyes back to mine. "But I don't need to. He isn't in that place anymore. He's with the Lord now. You know that."

"Yeah, I know," I said. "I just remember you used to go all the time. You know, to wipe the tombstone down with that rag and all?"

"I had to stop that," she replied. "Right after you went away. I didn't want your brother thinking that was what you did when people pass on."

On the inside I'd learned how to read people: their nervous tics, their avoidance of eye contact, their desperate pulls on an arbitrary square. It all had meaning, and I'd made a science of figuring it out. In Mom's case, I could tell that she was hiding something. But I didn't push.

"So how's work?" I asked, changing the subject. The dimple of tension eased between her jaw and teeth.

She loved being a supervisor, walking her floor in thick heels so they'd hear her coming and mind their p's and q's.

But she had gotten older and was in fact approaching sixty. And I could tell that she wasn't as spry as she used to be.

"I can't move in them heels the way I used to," she said. "Got me thinkin' about retiring. Sometimes I go in there and wish I had one of those pipes they use to blow darts, and hit every one of those knuckleheads in the neck and knock 'em out."

I couldn't imagine her not moving. After all, she had gone right back to work after four weeks' maternity leave, both times. I'd seen her go to work early, come home late, cook dinner, and still have the energy to make Dad scream and moan into the night a few times a week. Then she'd get up at five-thirty and do it all over again, leaving bacon and toast for all of us on covered plates at the kitchen table. That was my mama. That was who had brought me into the world.

"Now go and see the house," she said.

There were two bathrooms on the upper level. One was painted a deep blue and covered with laminated faces, their details mortally sharp. A top-heavy Latina with a wide nose and too much lipstick flashed a seductive grin at me. Two black boys threw up their neighborhood gang signs. A light-skinned man and his deep chocolate lady friend shared a kiss. And there were different poses of a slim brown girl with a poofy Afro and big doe eyes. Her smile was priceless. The bottoms of the frames were marked with the photographer's signature: H. Baker.

Mom's room had burnt orange walls with matching drapes flanking both windows. There was the oak armoire and the sleigh bed my great-grandmother had left her when she died. There was a tall bookshelf in the corner of the room, and above the bed was a framed picture of her and Dad, meant to let any other man know whom the woman who slept there belonged to.

The room that had to be Henry's was closed shut, as mine had always been when I was his age. But the room next to it was wide open and smelled of lavender and Murphy Oil Soap. I flipped the light switch at the doorway and entered. A moment later my heart stopped.

The guest room was larger than it'd looked in pictures. The plaques Pure Uncut had sent me were centered on the widest wall: two gold, two platinum, and two double platinum. "To Benjamin Baker Jr.," they all read.

I approached them cautiously, running a finger across the surface of the nearest one. It was proof that a dream could be made real. But that dream had been tossed away. The adjacent wall held laminated copies of every article where my name or picture had appeared. My little brother obviously had too much free time.

"Waiting for it to come off the wall?" a heavy voice asked from behind moments later. I spun around to see my little brother, who was far from little anymore.

He was an inch or two taller than me, his almond complexion a shade darker than my own. And he had Mom's pouty lips, with something that was supposed to be a mustache over the top one. His hair was cut close to his head all around, like mine, and he wore jeans, sneakers, and a gray T-shirt that had S.W. painted in graffiti script.

I looked him up and down to see if there was anything left of the little monster that used to scurry behind wherever I went. But that kid was gone. In his place was the young man I didn't have a clue of what to say to.

He didn't say anything, either. So we just looked at each

other. Then he smiled, and I smiled, and we rammed into
the hug that I needed more than air.

"I don't like it that much," my brother said from behind the
wheel of his '87 Maxima wagon. We were zipping down
Branch Avenue toward the freeway. "I mean, I love the house
and all, but I'm back around the way every chance I get."

"It's where you grew up," I replied, happy to be next to
him. "You don't never let the neighborhood go."

It was a little after ten, and people were all over the
summer streets, mostly teenage kids riding out the last days
of the season.

"I've just been out driving around all summer," my
brother confessed. "Most of the time it's over to my girl's
house. There's a picture of her in the bathroom. She's the
Spanish girl with the—"

"I saw her," I interrupted, feeling rather embarrassed
about having ogled my little brother's old lady.

"Yeah, her. And if I'm not with her, sometimes I take my
camera and my notebook and I end up where I end up. To
be honest, I'm not even sure where we're going now."

"It don't matter to me," I said. "I'm just trying to get
used to everything."

I kept my eyes on the sidewalks beyond the open window, studying passing frames and figures as they walked
and talked, drank and smoked, playing their music as loud
as they could to drown out all transgressions. Fewer perms
and more weaves on women. More braids and baldies on
men.

"Ain't that much changed," Henry replied. "We're all
just older."

"What you talkin' about, older? You're seventeen. You ain't nowhere near old."

"Not from where I'm standing," he argued. "High school is just a game, Ben, and I know you know it. I mean, you got all these cliques and crews, a buncha dudes tryin' to show out, a buncha girls that don't know what they want, except whatever dudes is at the center of attention. It's like one big circus."

I grinned. It was good to see that he'd gotten "it" long before I had.

"What's so funny?"

"Nothing," I said. "I guess I just remember feeling the same way when I was your age. The only thing that was real for me was the music. I didn't care about nothin' but what Stevie and I were doing down in his basement."

"See," he replied excitedly. "That's what I'm talkin' about! Mom always acts like I don't want enough outta life, 'cause all I wanna do is hoop and take pictures."

"That ain't it," I said. "She just don't want you to go the way I did."

"But she knows I know better than that. And besides, you got set up. That ain't even an issue with me. Speaking of which, Malcolm called and said he got somethin' for you."

"Yeah, Stevie told me," I said, having totally forgotten about his little find. "What's your day like tomorrow?"

"Wide open for you, man. What's up?"

"I need to get a bucket," I said calmly.

"I got you," he said casually. "You know me. I'll roll with you to hell if you want me to."

"We won't go that far," I replied. "Just need four wheels

and a engine. Somethin' to get me from A to B. And I need to get a cell phone, too."

"Sounds like you're stayin'?"

"Where else would I be goin'?"

He shrugged and lowered the volume on the stereo. "I don't know. I guess I figured you might move back out to L.A. with Stevie to do your music thing again."

"Nah," I replied. "I'm just here to find Sala and Sasha and start the fuck over."

"Ma said that she called the other day and left a number." In all of the emotion, I'd completely forgotten about those crucial digits. I would call her the minute we returned and tell her everything.

"Yeah, I heard. I can't wait to see her."

"Yeah, so you can get you some pussy before your dick blows up."

"Yeah," I said, teeth grinding into tongue. "Yeah."

The Kaffa House was a shoebox at the corner of 12th and U streets, only three blocks from where Sally Helen's used to be. We'd driven by my former place of employment. Wooden boards had been drilled over the entranceways. The neon tubes in the front sign were cracked and shattered.

Henry said the place hadn't lasted under the new management. Apparently it hadn't been the same without the Old Man. Nothing ever was.

Booths and tables fueled the chatter in air thick with incense and clove tobacco. A poet took the mike, some joker who had his face covered with a black shroud. Osama bin Laden meeting Darth Vader.

"The truth is a fuckin' joke!" he yelled pretentiously,

those words being the refrain that held his little ditty together. Where was Sandman Simms when you needed him?

My eyes wandered over to the Nubian princess in camouflage fatigues as she stuffed kale, carrots, garlic, and strawberries into the blender behind the bar. The contraption whirred and ground the ingredients into a thick brown liquid, which she then poured into a plastic cup that my brother paid $5 for and then began to suck down as if it were the greatest thing on earth.

"What the hell is that?" I asked.

"Smoothie. Cleans out your system."

"I'm clean enough," I said, and then we took in more than an hour of poetry.

I'd never been big on poetry, not even the stuff we read in school. I just didn't get it, even though it was practically the same as the lyrics I wrote. But lyrics needed sound to make sense. In my world everything had needed sound, from Sala's breath to the roar of a Metrobus climbing a hill.

For so long my ears had been the only thing that could make it all real. But I'd unlearned that on the inside, where there was no music and where the words in the books I read never rhymed.

Henry told me that he came there weekly for the event, often bringing his camera to take shots of the performers. He liked seeing people put their hearts into the work and the way they used movement to turn words into living things. But he mostly came because of his girl, Sagrario, who was a regular.

"So where's this girl of yours?" I said.

"In the back somewhere. Probably meditating before she reads."

"Is it that serious?" I asked.

"It is to her," he replied. "And I love her, so you know, I gotta be there for her."

He had met her at a house party the summer before. She had been the first Spanish girl he'd ever had a conversation with. He was from Southwest after all and had gone to Southwest schools, a world away from Columbia Heights, Hyattsville, or any of the other brown-folk enclaves.

"You love her, huh?" I asked, remembering what love had been for me at seventeen, an oh-so-conditional thing that could easily turn to dust.

"I don't have a doubt in my mind," he said.

"That's good," I said. "Love is a beautiful thing. But it takes a lot of work."

"Tell me about it," he said. "I mean, I can't even take a picture of another girl without hearin' about it."

"Women want loyalty," I said. "They wanna feel like you're blind to every ass in the world but theirs. At least that's the way Sala is. But she's never had to say it."

"I hope I get what the two of you got," he replied. His words held an innocence I'd once known well but would never know again.

"You will," I said. "Sounds like you might even have it already."

"So how do you feel, man? I mean, what's it like to be out after all that time?"

"It's like being a bird with broken wings. And then one day you get up and all of a sudden you can fly again. I feel free. But I'm real scared, too. Because when you walk out of that door you don't have any more excuses. All the rules that meant everything in there don't mean shit on the out-side. I don't ever want for you to end up in there, Hen."

"Don't worry. I won't," he said as if it were nothing. "I

mean, I learned too much hearin' what you went through, and what you wrote in your letters. You've always been tellin' me the right things to do. But you weren't ever preachin' to me. I felt like you was right here with me, lookin' over my shoulder at everything I did."

Something grabbed hold of me, and I took a moment to try to shake it loose. "What's up, man?" he asked, concerned.

"I'm sorry, Hen."

"Sorry for what?"

"I wasn't there for you. I mean, when Pop passed I was supposed to be the man of the house. I was supposed to look out for you and all, but I fucked up, and I left you and Ma all alone."

"You did what you had to do," he said firmly. "I mean, I know Ma put you through hell for gettin' locked up at first. But I know how it is, man, and I know that you ain't mean to get caught up. There ain't nobody who didn't know that. And there ain't nobody in the family that ain't wish they could do the time for you."

"That ain't the point, Hen," I started.

"You ain't never need my forgiveness," he continued. "Because like I said, I never felt like you weren't there. You ain't gotta beat yourself up over me and what happened after you went in. I knew where your heart was, and I knew you was gonna be back. That was all that mattered."

As usual I wanted to say something, even though there was nothing to say. So it was a good thing that God had the host call Sagrario to the stage.

The girl appeared from a dim corridor at the rear, throwing hips right and left as she approached the mike. Her waist was wrapped in a burgundy sarong, a white baby T with the word GODDESS covering the rest of her. Her breasts stretched the fabric to its limits. Her jet black hair was clipped into a bob as she stood before us all, armed only with a little book that could have been her diary.

All eyes were on her as she cleared her throat to begin. Her voice was warm and breezy as it told tales about loves lost, and a passion-filled night, and the cops choking her twelve-year-old brother with a nightstick until he almost died. Her words were the first I understood in that place, which helped me to further understand my little brother. We'd both inherited that same vision from my father, the one that saw what mattered in a woman, what was far beneath the surface, not the bouncing and jiggling on top of it.

When she finished the crowd came alive. Henry was a well of excitement ready to burst as his girl made her way toward us, shaking hands and mouthing thank-yous to her public as the host back at the mike called up the next person.

"I've heard so much about you," Sagrario said minutes later, within the lanky arms of the man she loved.

"What have you heard besides me being in jail?" I asked, stone-faced. My tone made her nervous. She was worried that she'd somehow offended me.

"I'm just playin' with you," I continued. They both relaxed, letting out little chuckles of relief.

"Henry does talk about you all the time," she said proudly. "About all the things you do. I love the Waterfront albums, too. When he told me you wrote the songs, I —"

"I'm glad you liked them," I interrupted. "I like the way you write, too." She blushed.

"Thanks," she said. "I mean, I haven't been writing for that long."

"It ain't the time," I replied as the relative elder at the table. "It's what you do with it. Where's your family from?" I asked.

"Costa Rica," she said. "But we've been here since I was a baby."

"I hear it's really beautiful down there," I said. "I read about it in a book once."

"Really?" she asked.

"Yeah. I tried to read about everywhere. Hopefully I'll get to go someday."

"Well, I haven't been back since," she said sadly. "Our house burned down there. So there's not much to go back to, even though I wish I could see it for myself."

"I'm gonna take her," my brother added as she passed him the final swallow of his smoothie. "I been saving up the money so we can go next summer."

Just then I realized that I could've sent them down that very next day, with first-class tickets, a hotel, and money to burn. After all, I was a rich man, and who better to spend my riches on but my only brother?

But I had to find Sala first. I promised myself that I wouldn't spend another dollar until I knew what she and the baby needed.

"I know you'll make it happen, then," I said encouragingly.

"You damn right," he replied. Sagrario giggled. "And I ain't fakin' about that."

"I know you're not, baby," she said. The kiss that followed was deeper than the bay.

"**So what do you think** of her?" Henry asked as he pulled into the empty driveway. Mom's car was nowhere to be found.

"I wonder where Mom is," I said. The clock on the dash said that it was well after midnight. My little brother hesitated in his answer, meaning that he knew something I didn't.

"I don't know," he said. "But I'm sure she'll be back soon. She's got work in the morning."

"I like your girl a lot," I said at the front door. Henry fumbled with his keys in the darkness. "Y'all look right for each other."

"This is like the greatest time of my life," he said. "I got her, and you came back, and it's my last year in school. Shit is damn near close to perfect."

He turned on the lamps in the living room and the darkness receded. Everything was as I'd remembered it.

"Guess I'm on the couch," I said.

"Nah, man, it's a fold-up bed in the guest room closet. Why don't you sleep up there." Remembering Stevie's, I didn't want to sleep around any more plaques from the past, especially not ones that actually had *my* name on them.

"I'm cool down here," I said. "Besides, I ain't tired and I don't wanna keep you up."

"Yeah, I do got work in the mornin'. So I better get my ass to bed. I'll holler at you in the mornin'." We hugged again and he disappeared up the stairs to his room.

I took a seat on the couch and turned on the TV. I was

in the mood for a cigarette, but I knew there weren't any around. So I just flipped through channels, mostly music videos and old sitcoms. If I hadn't glanced down, I wouldn't have seen it, the single sheet of paper on the glass table in Mom's squirrelly handwriting. I picked it up and saw the item I'd coveted more than anything in the world. Seven digits and Salamanca's name in blue ink.

I raced to the phone in the kitchen and dialed the number, my breath quickening with each ring. But after twelve rings no one answered. I hung up and tried again, only to get more of the same. I dropped the receiver three tries later, remembering the importance of patience and knowing that I would see Salamanca Mitchell soon enough, knowing that she was on her way to me.

3.

God had to be a sadist. That was the only way to explain the pain pulsing through Salamanca at rapidly narrowing intervals. The young woman was driving herself to the hospital, swerving from one lane to the next with each piercing contraction. It was a blessing that the hospital was closer to the Milton home than her own. But that didn't make a damn difference when she felt like someone was putting a sword through her privates.

This was not how it was supposed to be. She should have been on the backseat lying down while Ben took the wheel, nervous and panicky as he burrowed the car through traffic to ensure his first child's safe arrival. He should have been helping her through the various breathing techniques she'd learned in that damn Lamaze class, even if they didn't do shit for the pain. He'd had no problem putting his dick in her all those months ago and moaning, "This shit is so good, baby."

But now where was he? His useless hands were probably hanging outside a cell, holding a cigarette while he wrote songs about how "ride or die" she was when it came to him.

A pack of kids nearly became roadkill by assuming that she was just going to stop like all the other cars because their little basketball had tumbled into the street. Salamanca Mitchell had a baby to deliver. Even if it was on her own, even if that motherfucker she loved more than the child she was carrying couldn't hold her hand through the only true rite of passage for becoming a woman. And then she made her mistake. She looked down in her lap and saw the red stain on her cream-colored sweatpants.

Then she felt the blood running down her legs. And that was when she really lost it, cutting left down an alley so narrow that both sides of her car took a few scrapes, just to save the last ten seconds it would've taken for the red light ahead to change. A cluster of pigeons nearly lost their wings, fluttering toward the heavens just before she powered over them onto the next street, tears of anguish running down her angelic face.

Then she finally saw it, the entrance sign for Sinai Emergency Room. She popped the median and zoomed across the three-lane intersection, barely avoiding the onslaught of oncoming traffic, then raced up the ramp, screeching to a halt right in front of the electric-eyed entrance doors, totally and completely spent. That was when she finally passed out. Her last thought was of that mother-fucker Ben and how he better fucking love her for the rest of his fucking life.

When she came to, her stomach was a mass of concrete and her spine felt like it was in a vise. Her lungs barely in-flated as she gulped in the sterilized air. Her heart was beating out of her chest.

The three nurses surrounding her spoke in tongues, at first too fast and then too slowly to be understood. She felt like she was dying, that the smell in the air was the Grim Reaper's cologne bathing her for the ride into Hades. Twenty-four hours and she still hadn't dilated. The only word she made out before the clear mask covered her face was "C-section."

Even in her dreams all she could think of was that motherfucker Ben and how he should have been there, just so she could have the asshole in striking distance. Then she thought she saw her mother, sitting in the chair before her, the hair on her head still in a gigantic Afro, her arms and legs still as skinny and slender as they had been in the pho-tos of the life before her disappearance.

"Everything's all right," the mother whispered to her daughter, placing a hand upon the child's womb. That magic touch lowered the volume on all of the pain. "She's a beautiful girl."

She learned later about the team of doctors that had come and gone, frantic about her ruptured placenta and that the child might already be dead. Had she heard the words, she would have begged them to take her life instead of her little girl's. She would've cashed in her soul just to give that baby one roll of destiny's dice on the planet she'd grown to hate.

But when she woke up, all was well, and her mother was gone, and that motherfucker Ben had no idea of what she'd do the next time he laid eyes on her. They brought her the baby, and she instantly understood all that her elders had explained.

Bringing life into the world changes you. It puts you second. It shows you that all the petty things you had the nerve to think were pertinent can fall away so quickly when there's a mouth to feed, a question to answer, an empty mind to be filled with all that's needed for self-sufficiency.

On March 7, 1996, Sasha Salamanca Baker weighed in at nine pounds and six ounces. She had the arms and legs of a cherub, her mother's nose and mouth, and, as it turned out, her father's eyes, those narrow slits of brown that made her wet whenever she saw them, the ones that could ask anything of her and know that it would be granted.

"So how do you feel?" Pat had asked while Salamanca was nursing the child. Her little lips pinched the hell out of nipples more used to a man's touch. But that didn't stop the new mother from smiling wide.

"Beautiful," she'd replied, looking down at the butter-ball of a baby she'd delivered. Just then Sasha had looked up at her, stretching her eyes open as if to ask what was next.

"Put her on the phone," Ben had demanded through the receiver.

She put the phone close to the little girl's lips and Sasha

made a cooing sound, as if she knew who was on the other end. Male voices laughed and cheered in the background, more than likely lighting squares in celebration.

"And she's okay?" the new father asked. "The doctors didn't find nuthin' wrong with her?"

"She's perfectly fine, baby, our little gift from God."

She could see the smile on Ben's face way out there, and it gave her the strength to stay awake a little longer. The stitches didn't hurt as bad as her eyes. She needed to sleep.

"What about you, baby?" he asked with concern. "My little bunny all right?" He'd called her "bunny" because of her obsession with Bugs. She'd seen every cartoon with the character and kept a stuffed version on the bed where she slept.

"Tired," she murmured, her eyes closing on their own. Knowing the drill, Pat pulled Sasha out of her mother's arms and away from the breast poking out of Sala's gown.

"Then sleep, sweetie," he'd said. "I love you."

"I love you, too," she whispered before fading away. The little girl cried her lungs out when Pat put her back in the hospital crib by the window, annoyed by her maker's lack of stamina.

Pat smiled at her new niece's feistiness, knowing that she was definitely a Davis at heart. She hung up the phone and put Sala's breast back into her gown. Then she sat down and drifted off herself, resting patiently until the next time she was needed.

4.

Alfonse Mitchell exploded into consciousness, his tank top soaked with sweat. But the slender twenty-year-old stripper next to him did not stir, her blond extension braids spread over her face in sleep. There was a pain deep inside him, and it was not from the Ethiopian meal he'd finished just before he'd met the girl outside of the Zulu Cave.

The sweet young thing had an ass as smooth as butter and the suction of a DustBuster. He barely remembered the specifics of their interlude. A doggy-style thrusting that ended with him pulling out and exploding on her backside, just because he could.

He hated the shitty apartment he'd rented in Dean-wood. But shitty meant stealth for a man of his stature. In two days he would meet Provenzano out in butt-fuck Pennsylvania to get started on the next venture in a long and industrious career of hustles and subterfuge. But that had nothing to do with what had brought him awake before dawn.

There was this pulling inside of him that he couldn't describe, as if the hand of God were trying to snatch his soul from the body that contained it. It was as if something had been shaved from his spirit and carried off to some other realm. And then he thought of his daughter, as he did a hundred times a day.

He constantly checked in with the legion of thugs and PIs he'd hired to find her. But there'd been only one blip on the screen, that 'Bama ass hick down in Georgia who'd gotten his ass kicked for talking instead of getting that chloroform over her face.

He knew he was wrong for what he had done to the girl, striking her in the womb when he'd promised never to strike any woman again. He'd said it in that old Toronado as they drove out of D-town, stopping in a motel for the night so that he could empty his safety-deposit box the following morning. That box held the near two hundred grand he'd skimmed from the restaurant in little chunks during his decade plus of service. The money had been there for a rainy day. Killing his own wife had summoned up a hurricane.

It had been an accident. She'd found out about the skim and about that whore in the choir who made a habit of sucking him off in the church parking lot before early morning services (doing the job exceptionally well on the days he had to preach). Viola, one of the two things he loved more than anything in the world, said she was leaving. And he couldn't take it, particularly when she used the word *divorce*.

Because he was from Rocky Mount, North Carolina, the South. And in the South, husbands and wives prayed and stayed together. No alimony. No white lawyers and judges trying to tell whom and how much he had to pay to keep his family fed and clothed. She wasn't questioning just his authority, but his whole belief system. As a matter of fact, she was questioning his manhood, and that just could not be.

The power of the word brought a husband's fist to his wife's nose, breaking it instantly. A shard of broken bone pierced her brain, and she was dead before she smacked against the bookcase, before all of those positive black titles she loved came tumbling down upon her, making it ridiculously hard to lift her corpse without causing enough ruckus to wake his little girl.

But he did it somehow, dragging her out inch by inch. A pool of blood stained the carpet where her head had lain. Yet he wasn't frantic. He wasn't even afraid.

Because he was from Rocky Mount, North Carolina, the son and nephew and cousin of men who'd had to deal with a body or two in their day. The fence in the backyard was wide and the ground was soft from the week's rain. Digging would be easy, and getting out of town would be easier. There were a set of Ohio plates he kept just for something like this, because you never knew.

He'd collected his things and his daughter, all that he had left in the world, and departed, fully intending never to return to the scene of the crime again. He'd changed his last name and used cash to buy off his boy, D-town's chief of police, and falsify a few records. He'd always liked D.C. And he'd always wanted to live among the black and powerful.

The only hard part had been lying to his little girl, staring into his wife's face incarnate at eight, wrapped in the footed Barbie pajamas he'd bought her for her seventh birthday. She was too young to know the truth, too fragile to know that Mom was four feet deep in the yard, likely to be exhumed in no less than a day and a half. He promised the girl's fluttering eyelids that this was his last sin, that they were headed to a Promised Land where all would be different, and he kept talking until she was fast asleep.

Only then did he finally begin to breathe normally again, as he sat on the curb in that motel parking lot, crying his eyes out for the crime he'd committed. Then he went into room 246, lay down next to his daughter, and slept like a baby.

Men without conscience covered his tracks, removing the body from its temporary resting place so that it could be hacked into several pieces and buried in as many locations.

He didn't sell the house. But he did transfer the deed to one of his dummy companies. Every few years he paid men to maintain the paint and fences, to trim the hedges and mow the lawn. Every now and again a moving truck might appear and, for the sake of neighbors, either load in or remove empty boxes from the residence, to create the appearance of normalcy—on the outside, at least.

Alfonse Mitchell had it in his mind that the house would one day be his daughter's. So he wanted it kept just the way it had been before, down to leaving the same locks on the doors. He wanted her to go home someday, even though she had promised him she wouldn't. He wanted her to put her key in that lock and see all the things he'd shielded her from on the night they'd left Detroit forever.

It was passive-aggressive psychology, a punk move in comparison with a lifetime of engaging the enemy head-on. But Salamanca was not his enemy. She was all that he had left. Yet still he owed her an explanation but knew he'd never have the heart or the humility to explain.

His hope was that fate would bring her to the scene of that long-ago crime. Then she would ascertain the truth for herself. It would be found in the broken bookcase and bloodstained carpet. The act of murder would still be hanging in the last piece of Detroit he had ever set foot in.

Once she got there she would know what he was, if Viola's sister didn't tell her first. She would have more questions than even he could answer, more rounds to load into karma's clip. She would hate him, even though that was the last thing in the world he would ever want.

On the night Sasha was born, the Old Man stood in his kitchenette guzzling iced H_2O. But the cool liquid only made his gut feel worse. The pain grew into a burning, a kicking at his insides like the child in his daughter's womb. So he poured himself a shot of Teacher's and enjoyed the sting as it went down.

Then he went to the living room and got out the album of Salamanca's pictures. From drooling and babbling infant to high school sweetheart—he had it all in there, even the shot of her in her prom dress next to Benjamin Baker, the spark that had burned his old life to a crisp.

He flipped through the book until fatigue took him over, bringing him into a doze out on the couch, the album still clutched in his arms. Behind his eyes he saw his wife's face, that final scowl before he sent her to the heaven where she belonged. She appeared to him sometimes with spit and curses, but just then she was smiling. "It's not about you anymore," she said. "It's not about you."

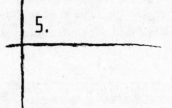

5.

I heard the rumbling of feet on the staircase and the distant melody of a Prince song. But Henry had long since departed by the time I found the waking world.

I had that nasty feeling you get when you sleep in your clothes. Rancid breath, stiff spine, sleeves and cuffs wrinkled and twisted from shifts in dreamland. But the more I moved, the better I felt, particularly once I saw that Henry had left me breakfast and a note.

Ben:

I know I said I'd take you to see Malcolm. But I guess I forgot that I'm doing time and a half

today, so I won't be back until eight. And I don't think
you want to wait that long. So I'll see you when I see you.

Hen

He'd left a plate of cinnamon toast and turkey bacon
underneath a sheet of plastic. And I tore into the meal without even heating it up.

A shower and a shave later, I was wandering the new
house again in search of clues, markers of what I'd missed
while I was away. Something was different about my family.
And I had to know what it was.

But aside from the new rugs and carpet, the disc player
in the bathroom for shower listening, and a few unfamiliar
faces in Mom's most recent photo album, everything
seemed to be the same. Mom still kept her jewelry neat and
polished, arranged by style and type in the African box I'd
given her for a birthday. Henry still had his favorite stuffed
bear from when he was a little boy, the one dressed in car-
penter's overalls with tools on his belt.

There was a small box of my things in the basement beneath the staircase. Inside, among old clothes and crumpled
Right On magazine pinups, was my old binder of sheet music, a huge bin of CDs and tapes, and a few snapshots from
my prom. I went through the pictures one by one, grinning
at the way I looked in a white tuxedo jacket with black
pants, posing with Stevie in front of the limousine his parents had rented for us and our dates.

But at the bottom of it all, in the depths of my former
life's remains, was the most precious treasure of all. The $1
instant photo booth had given Salamanca and me four shots
for three bucks. But only one of them had come out right.

In one, my mouth was wide open. In another, Sala's eyes were closed. And in the third, there were streaks of motion on the image as we both laughed hysterically at how stupid we were going to look.

But that last frame had been perfect. She was resting her head against my shoulder and smiling the way only she could. She had taken the others, but I had kept that one in my locker for my last few months of high school. I blew her a kiss every time classes changed.

Those were the first pictures we'd ever taken together. And while there had been plenty of others since, they had always remained my favorites. I slid the image into the empty plastic window in my brand-new wallet, so happy to have her with me again.

"What did you say your name was?" the receptionist asked me, her face shiny with moisturizer. The green in her eyes was artificial. And her hair was in one of those synthetic "I didn't have time to braid it all" ponytails.

"Benjamin Baker," I said, envisioning the beauty beneath the tacky. "I told him I was gonna come through." The look on her face said that she didn't buy it.

"Have a seat," she said with an uppity air. "I'll see what I can do."

The office was what I'd expected for a private eye/bounty hunter: four gray walls with a few frames of generic art hung for good measure. The receptionist had a desk with nothing on it except for the phone, a stack of papers, and the trash novel she had bookmarked halfway through. Two sliding doors separated guests from the host, and just then those doors rolled open.

Malcolm Turner hadn't changed one iota. He was still skinny and still not much for dressing up. A CEO in khakis, a gray T-shirt, and a pair of low boots. But then again his line of work, finding what didn't want to be found, was dress-down to say the least.

"Well, goddamn," he said, happily surprised. "I heard you got big, but what the fuck?!"

"Survival of the fittest," I said as I stood up to meet him. We hugged and then he ushered me into his office.

Malcolm Turner Investigations focused more time on bail bonds than anything else. That money came in faster than any of the private dick work. So he spent his days tracking down bail jumpers, with a few surveillance gigs peppered in every now and then.

His steel desk was cluttered with various forms, message slips, and newspaper clippings. His computer was layered with dust, its casing yellowed from years of use. There was barely any wall visible, most of it being covered with framed and enlarged news articles with highlighted mentions of Malcolm's outfit and its involvement in high-profile arrests and convictions.

There were also signed glossies of local celebrities he'd done work for. One was of D.C.'s new mayor, Anthony Williams. Another was of go-go godfather Chuck Brown. And of course there was one of him and his little brother with the rest of the Waterfront. It was the one in the most expensive frame and had been signed by each and every one of the group's *original* members, including me.

"Finally face-to-face, huh?" he said as he eased into the chair behind his desk. I sat in the cushioned seat across from him. There were a few gray hairs in his manicured beard and a couple more in his caesared crown.

He took in a breath of air, as if about to speak, then stopped himself.

"What is it?" I asked.

"Nothin'," he said, grinning. "It's just that you grown-up now." He stopped again, reaching out for a cherished memory. "You know, I never forgot about that tape."

I hadn't forgotten it, either. Stevie had done the track, but I had written the words and sung the vocals. Malcolm had been two years into his bid at the time, and he had written us a letter. For me, at sixteen, it had been the most serious piece of writing I'd ever read.

Malcolm had said that he wanted to die. He'd said that he was coming up with a plan for how he was going to do it. He might hang himself with his drawers or try to do it with the fabric from his pillow. And it was going to go down in the middle of the night when the COs would be watching him least. Or maybe he'd try going out in a blaze of glory by starting something with any random man he couldn't beat.

He'd said that death was the only way for him to truly be free. He'd been fooled by the foolproof plan that had convinced him he was untouchable. He didn't want us to end up like him. He wanted for us to do the right thing, stay in school, and chase after our dreams until we caught them.

But we didn't care about saving ourselves. We cared only about saving him. So we put our hearts into a song, a song called "Lock Down," one of the first few I'd ever written. Then we recorded it and sent him the tape. He wrote us back a few weeks later saying that he played it every day and sometimes twice a day. He continued to do so for the eight years that followed, sneaking it into whichever tape deck he could get to and hitting "rewind" enough times to tear the cassette to shreds.

Two weeks before I went inside, the day before my own verdict was handed down, Malcolm sent me a postcard to declare that "Lock Down" had saved his life, that *I* had saved his life.

"I know you didn't," I answered, remembering how much it had meant to him back then. He looked at me for a long time, still thankful, still indebted to me.

"You hungry?" he asked. I nodded.

"Good," he said. "Because I'm buying you lunch."

"Outta all the jobs I coulda picked, I don't know why I picked this one," Malcolm said with a mouth full of chicken teriyaki. We were in the food court at the Shops, ogling the many employees stretching one-hour lunch breaks into two.

"Sometimes I feel like a traitor," he continued. "I used to be on the inside. And if I had had the bail, I mighta jumped it. Now I track 'em down and bring 'em in, like I don't know what I'm bringin' 'em in to."

It had been two whole years and he was still adjusting. He'd put the last of his drug money into ten-year Treasury bonds, which gave him close to a hundred grand when he got out. He'd chosen the bounty business because it was easy for an ex-con to do. No credit checks, no background investigations. No one cared about the past as long as you took care of present business.

"Nobody puts us anywhere but ourselves," I said. "And it ain't got nuthin' to do with the people who bring us in."

He ran that thought through his head for a moment, trying to figure out how much truth there was in it. Then he cleaned the plate before him as if it were his last.

"Looks like you had some time to think, Main Man," he said, sucking his Sprite dry. "You seem like you got your head in a good place."

"Ain't no other place for it to be," I said. I was happy to see him again and even happier to know that he was doing all right. But I had come for information. And I needed to stick to the script.

"So what you got for me?" I asked.

He smiled. "Straight to the point, huh?" he asked. The look I gave him didn't require an explanation. "It's just a shot in the dark, man."

"Give it to me anyway, even though I probably won't need it. Sala called the other night, but I missed her. Says she's on her way back to the city."

"Well, that's good to hear," he said. "Means I probably won't have to get the Crew together."

The Crew was a trio of homeboys Malcolm "consulted" from time to time. They were men he never named but whose actions made them known in all the places that mattered.

"Like I said in the letters, it's like your boy Mitchell just up and vanished. Everything got sold: the restaurant, the house, all of his real estate holdings. There's no driver's license renewal, no credit report update. But no death certificate, either. So either he's alive, living as somebody else, or he's in a hole waiting to be dug up." The furrow in my brow told him to continue.

"But an Alfonse Mitchell still owns a beach property house off of the bay near Annapolis."

"What's the address?" I asked.

"You're gonna need a ride if you wanna go out there," he said.

"I'm gettin' a bucket today," I said.

"No, I'll take you if we gotta go," he said adamantly. "You just got out, and I ain't lettin' yo' ass go right back in. Besides, like you said, Sala's all right. What the fuck you wanna go pokin' around out there for? Especially if the wife and kid are good?"

I pictured the Old Man posted outside that beach home, lying in some lawn chair basking in the August heat, a young tramp lying next to him, her phat ass browning in the sun. I wondered if he ever thought about me or if he even knew he had a grandchild. But most of all I wondered why he was leaving his tail out. Why was he making it so easy for something he owned to be found and uncovered?

Maybe he was expecting me. Maybe his old ass was sitting right out on that stoop with a small arsenal, hoping that Benjamin Baker would come out there to put him out of his misery.

"Like I said," I reiterated, "only if I have to. Now give me the address."

Stevie shook his head.

"Why not?"

"Because that way you won't be stupid enough to try and go out there alone."

The Department of Motor Vehicles was even more of a mess than I'd expected. A woman with inch-thick glasses yelled at three Hispanic men who just wanted to get their learner's permits.

"You don't have the proper ID, understand?!" she blurted. The men were as embarrassed as they were clueless, having obviously hoped that a conversation wouldn't have to be part of the exchange.

The license renewal line stretched the length of two walls and corridors. Luckily I'd gotten there just before the big rush, and the tiny men under fire were half of what stood between me and renewing my piece of plastic. Soon after, a pretty dark-skinned girl barely out of high school came around the counter and cleared up the lines of communication. Within ninety seconds the men were on their way, and I was one step closer to being a functional driver again.

Minutes later, I read letters through an optical viewer as the same woman with the thick eyewear quizzed me for potential blindness. Luckily I still had twenty-twenty, and I was out of there a half hour later with my first piece of ID for my second life on the outside.

"**Hey, man,** where I know you from?" the man asked from the Metro seat across from me. I barely looked at him. My mind was an imaginary slide show of that house on the bay.

"Nowhere, I don't think," I muttered. I looked over to see his beady browns squeeze together as he searched for some vague shred of recall. Then it hit him like a nightstick.

"You went to Eastern, right?" he asked. Eastern High School, to be exact. High school. The life before my last one.

"Yeah," I said plainly. "What? You went there, too?"

"Yeah," he said. A scraggly beard and cornrows garnished his almond-shaped skull. And he wore a Wizards' jersey with Jordan's number on the front and back, showing off flabby arms and a Michelin tire of midsection. "I don't think we had no classes or nuthin'. I just remember your face."

I started to ask for his name, but he cut me off before I got the chance.

"Wait a minute!" he exclaimed, loud enough to turn heads through the whole car. "You was in the talent show that year, with those other dudes, the ones that got the record deal."

Commuting eyes turned my way as I did my best to pay them no mind. The Old Man had been right. D.C. was small, too small. What kind of life had this man been living if he remembered me and some song I'd sung at a $2 talent show nearly a decade before?

"Yeah, that was me," I said. "But what made you remember that?"

"Because I was hatin' on you," he said with embarrassment. "I was there with my girl on the front row, and when y'all came on I might as wella been there by myself. Cuz she was all on your dick. Y'all was almost like Jodeci or somethin'."

"Yeah," I said, revisiting the moment. I had been bold enough to jump off the four-foot-high stage and sing to a few girls in the front row, including his. We only did the one song, "Promises in Pieces." But when it was over we were all dripping with sweat.

Looking out at the crowd, at the way the packed auditorium moved and swayed to our sound, I felt wings on my heels, feathered protrusions pushing me toward the stratosphere.

"We was all right that night."

"So what happened, man?" he asked. "I mean, you was singin' lead. How come you ain't get a record deal?"

"It just didn't go that way," I said, knowing the answer wouldn't satisfy him. But I also knew that the train was slowing to my stop.

"Stay up, man," I concluded just as I zipped through the parting exit doors.

the day had been, her little girl would always have a story to lighten the load of her ten- and twelve-hour shifts. And the child was always growing wider and taller, her feet bursting out of brand-new shoes every other month.

Freckles had formed on the child's nose, much like her mother's. Once-fat limbs had slimmed, making Sala wonder if her child might be made for ballet or gymnastics, as she had been. And if not, there would always be track years down the line. She walked back over and pecked the child on the cheek, her narrow eyes shut tight as she dreamed her dreams on a Wednesday night, one week shy of her mother's twenty-third birthday.

Pat had owned a bungalow up on the North End for years, the only thing Kenny had left her before his departure. Sure, it wasn't exactly prime real estate, sandwiched between a crack lab and a crack house. But it had a big cast-iron tub in the bathroom, central heat and air, and a yard for Sasha to play in. Plus it was about as inconspicuous a crib as the Motor City had to offer.

But the place was silent only when her child was asleep. Sasha's only-child energy always converted itself into some sort of sound. It was the television, or the computer, or her voice asking a million questions about why life was the way it was. Or her cackle of a laugh, as the little girl attempted to sing along to any CD her mama might play, particularly the songs her daddy had written.

Sasha's mother was always talking about the man with the muscles in all those pictures. She always called him "Daddy," though all the daddies she knew from school and the playground were men who lived in houses with a mother and a kid, or at least came to visit, or at the very least sent money in the mail for bicycles and Big Wheels and even trips to camp. But for some strange reason, these things did not make little Sasha feel angry or insecure or even curious. She trusted all that her mother said was true, particularly the fact that she would see her daddy someday and that the minute she saw him all his time away would seem like nothing.

Salamanca, however, was having more doubts than ever before. In the evenings, after she'd put her daughter down for bed, she would retreat to the tiny bathroom and find herself staring in the mirror, posing questions that she was always unable to answer.

Could she make it for another year until he came home? Would they get along after all this time? Would prison make him try to beat her when things didn't go his way? And perhaps most importantly, would he still even want a woman? Had he succumbed to the next best thing in the shadows of that correctional abyss?

There was a gigantic zit on her left cheek, a sign of stress. Alternating between bartending and substitute teaching left very little room for balance. But she somehow managed to squeeze in thirty minutes of yoga before Sasha came awake with her questions and views and hopes for the day ahead. The days became identical aside from changes in wardrobe, meals, and the kind of homework the mother had to help her daughter with.

There was no more passion, no more dates. No more shirts and sweaters that still held Ben's scent. There were no strong fingers (aside from her own) to relieve the com-pounded tensions of double duty on arms and limbs. She was truly alone, except in name, and trying to raise a child to love a father she'd spoken to only in minute-long snatches on monitored lines. And she couldn't take it anymore.

She removed the black T-shirt with the word *Survivor*

across the front, the gray sweatpants, and the white under-wire and matching panties she'd bought in a pack of three for $5.99. She looked at herself in the wide mirror that took up most of the bathroom wall.

She'd lost most of the weight from the baby. But there was still a little pouch around her navel. And her breasts had swelled even larger. Her hair still hung well past her shoulders, dark and silky curls still the subject of scrutiny every time she went to get it pressed. She could still have had any man she wanted. But she only wanted Benjamin Baker.

She plugged the drain and started the hot water, placing yellow glass candles at every corner of the tub and lighting them. She added jasmine and peppermint oil and removed the half-smoked blunt she'd taped to the inside of the sliding door to the medicine cabinet. Then she lit up and pulled, climbing into the water cautiously, as if it were filled with creatures other than herself.

This was as close to heaven as this life could bring her. A Scorpio soaking in healing liquid, five days of the grind easing out of her flesh. She closed her eyes and leaned back, her hair pinned above the waterline. She kept her mind focused on nothing but her own breath as she took herself into a yogic sleep.

But there was more than the breath behind her eyes, more than the toxins leaving her through the hard and fast breaths. She felt those pianist fingers around her breasts, his thumbs encircling her nipples. She could hear him taking in the air as he ran that dick of his across her abdomen, tracing the incision scar from which his child had been delivered.

And then he was inside her, so wide and thick and

throbbing that it opened her like a flower, bringing forgotten nectar into the warm water all around her. He moved it in and out as he whispered how much he loved her, how bad he needed her to hold on, to wait for him, to hold their torch until it had burned itself black, all the while slamming into her with perfect timing and bringing her to the hardest orgasm she'd ever felt and a wash of dizziness that almost made her faint.

"I love you, baby," Salamanca told him. But the only answer came in the form of a tiny knock on the bathroom door.

Salamanca opened her eyes and removed the hand from her special place. There was sweat on her forehead and the imagined smell of him all over her pores. The knock came again, followed by a frantic jiggling of the locked knob.

"What!?" Salamanca demanded.

"I gotta go pee, Mommy. Can I please come in and pee?"

The child's mother remained silent for a moment, half-embarrassed and half-disgusted. Couldn't she at least masturbate in peace? Knowing the answer, she reached for a towel and pulled the plug in the drain.

7.

I opened my eyes to the dusk outside. The pits of my shirt were soaked through. I'd had a dream about Sala. Someone had cut off all her hair. But it actually looked pretty good.

I put my feet to the floor, my head still swirling. But there was little time for recovery as I heard the sound of a key in the front door: Mom.

I hopped up and headed toward the foyer, noticing the upright piano parked against the living room wall. I must have missed it upon my arrival the day before. Or maybe I'd wanted to pretend it wasn't there.

There was this sense of urgency in the moments it took to get there. A nest of questions multiplied with every step. Where had she been the night before? Why was she out so late? Why was she getting home at summer's dusk when she got off at four in the afternoon?

I got to the door just as it came open. But it was not my mother standing at the threshold. And thus many of my questions were instantly answered.

He was about six feet, a little shorter than me, and definitely not as built. Patches of gray appeared in his short 'fro. He was a deep tan color, wearing a short-sleeved dress shirt and gray linen slacks that matched it. The shoes were mud-colored wing tips.

"Hello," he said politely.

"Why you standin' at the door like that?" I heard my mother's voice say from somewhere behind him. But I kept my eyes on him the whole time, determined not to let him into a house to which he appeared to have keys.

"I think I just met Ben," he said, cracking the slightest smile as he turned to my mother.

"Yeah," I replied with a skeptical frown. "You did."

This isn't the way I wanted for you to meet Carl," my mom remarked from the kitchen as she and her new *friend* put away the groceries they'd just bought.

"I'm sure it isn't," I said sarcastically, staring across the room at the portrait of *my* family: of *my* father, Mom, Henry, and me.

"But a meeting's a meeting," Carl said with a chuckle. I peered into the kitchen and scrutinized him even further than I had in the minutes that had already passed.

"Whatever," I said with a shrug. Nothing he could say to me was going to matter. From where I stood he was utterly useless, a wannabe Richard Gere in blackface trying to worm his way onto the deed for my mom's new house. And I wasn't having it.

A minute later, Mom had put everything away and come out to sit with me at the dining room table. Carl was two steps behind her, presenting me with a glass of homemade iced tea to go with theirs. It was the best I'd had in seven years. But I didn't say it, just in case he'd been the one to mix the brew.

"I was going to tell you about Carl," she began, now nervous. "But I guess I was so excited to see you that I forgot to bring it up."

Mom never forgot anything. Therefore, the only reason she hadn't told me was that she didn't want to, or maybe she was afraid to.

"So how long you been goin' together?" I asked, assuming my father's voice.

"We're not dating, Ben," she assured me unconvincingly. Carl looked as if he'd been kicked in the chest. "We're just friends."

"Just friends, huh?" I asked, my eyes locked with hers.

"Yes, son," she replied. Her actions made her a liar. I glanced down to see their arms forming a V shape, indicating a clasping of hands underneath the table. I wanted to vomit.

"You ain't gotta lie to me," I said, raising my voice. I stood up, unable to bear what I was seeing, unable to comprehend the fact that she and Henry had conspired to sneak another man into our family without even telling me. She didn't answer as I stood up, towering over them both. Carl looked as though he wanted to cry. I just wanted to leave.

The front door slammed behind me. And then I realized there was no car to get me to wherever I was trying to go. I had no clue of when the next bus might arrive or whom I could call to Calgon me away from all this madness. But by the time I reached the sidewalk, it didn't matter. I was drowning in a sea of my own thoughts about what was, far away from the warmth and comfort of what should have been.

I made my way toward Iverson Mall, the climb up the slopes of Branch Avenue to its strip mall plateau. Woodward & Lothrop, Montgomery Ward, and Up Against the Wall were only a few of the plaza's retail treats. But now the Woodies had closed, replaced by a Value City discount store. There was a Wendy's where the Hertz Rent-a-Car used to be. And the Sizzler had been turned into an $8 all-you-can-eat Chinese buffet.

I passed the Carriage Hill apartments and the roller rink that once upon a time had been known as Crystal Skate, another home sweet home to city shootings, stabbings, and go-go jams that went well into the next morning. I'd never been old enough to go, but Malcolm had told us the stories of all the carnage, of the big-bootied girls dancing onstage in hiked-up skirts and thong bikinis, taking it off to the chants of the crowd and the musicians behind them.

The Howard Johnson on the right had become the Branch Avenue Motor Lodge after the chain had massive cutbacks. And the motor lodge was the kind of place you went for either a quick roll in the hay or an even quicker money-for-weight exchange.

Why hadn't Henry told me? Why hadn't he given me some kind of a warning? With all of the letters and calls, how could he have glossed over the fact that my mom had a new man, that she had left Dad behind for someone in the land of the living? And this man, this Carl, had taken my place, the place my father had left for me to fill. The Old Man had already taken my time. Now this motherfucker was trying to take my family from me.

I went from Branch Avenue to St. Barnabas Road, strolling past the Blockbuster and IHOP and the Little Italy Pizzeria. My eyes never grew bored with the familiar sites and the countless strangers I crossed in passing. This was Prince George's County, the paradise beyond the city's southern borders.

For so many of us kids, PG had once been the Promised Land. When your parents got that big promotion, or when your mom was about to have one child more than could fit in that apartment, you packed it up and headed out to the green lawns, school buses, and shopping malls. Stevie and I never admitted, even to each other, how nice it was out there. Because it was Maryland, which meant it wasn't D.C. And if it wasn't D.C., then it wasn't worth our time.

I had been so proud of where I was from. We'd all used the same slang, worn the same clothes, driven the same cars, and lusted after the same girls. Then I went inside. And there, in that cramped and controlled space, I was finally able to see just how big the whole world was.

On our cell block alone there had been Trinidadians and Costa Ricans, a one-armed boy born on the island of Cape Verde. Scores of different languages were spoken in hushed corners: Portuguese, Spanish, French, Italian, Yoruba, and

Hausa. All so no outsider could understand an insider's words.

Walking on the outside, toward nothing in particular, I found myself smiling at how delicious it was to be free of those politics. Even if Mom had laid Dad to rest, and even if my brother had kept me in the dark about it, I was still moving, gaining ground toward the dream that had kept me alive, a realized fantasy heading my way at the speed of light.

"You sure you want this one?" asked Ponytail Dan as he stood beneath the hand-painted sign that welcomed the world to his dime-store version of a dealership. The oscillating fans in the office said he was too cheap to spring for air-conditioning. The gray-streaked hair slicked and rubber-banded to the back said that he needed a stylist, badly.

His lot was a cemetery for lemons and losers: junkers with sun-bleached paint, rust infections, and exhaust pipes that kicked out smoke the minute you turned the key. Stereos and speedometers were missing. And more than a few of his prizes didn't even have all their wheels.

Yet I still managed to find "the One": the 1978 hunter green Datsun 280ZX. It had been on my list of dream cars back in the third grade, when I got a Transformer that turned into one for my ninth birthday. Sure, there were key scrapes and a small dent here and there. Sure, the exterior doors were a different green from the rest of the car. The stereo had a push-button AM radio, and the tires were as bald as the spot in the middle of Dan's head. But it had a good heart under the hood, and that was all I was looking for.

A swipe of the debit card made her mine. And as I backed her onto the road, $2,500 poorer, I was still pretty sure I'd gotten the better end of the deal. Backing out was a little awkward, though. I hadn't driven in seven years.

Her engine hummed as if she'd just come off the line. And that hum didn't break when the car hit thirty, or forty, or fifty-five. Even at seventy she was still holding her ground, despite the rattling dashboard and the radio that got only two stations.

We pushed into no-man's-land, burrowing deep into the boondocks and the sticks beyond them. I saw the silhouettes of horse stables, and cows, and rolled mounds of dried grass, and two white kids with funny haircuts rolling down a hill in a little red wagon, the setting sun behind them. I ran races with invisible jets on their way to Andrews Air Force Base. I drove for nearly four hours, almost emptying the tank and then refilling again.

"He's a good dude," Henry assured me between slurps of a strawberry shake from the drive-thru we'd just left. Disgusted by my choice in automobiles, he'd insisted on driving when Mom left a list of things she and Carl had forgotten at the grocery store. The couple in question had since vanished, more than likely taking refuge at Carl's secret hideaway home.

"I mean, he ain't Dad. He'll never be Dad. But he's good for her, you know?"

"Then why the fuck didn't you tell me?" I asked. "I mean, all those damn letters and you just forgot to mention Mom's sleepin' with another nigga?"

"Hey," he replied curtly. "Mom already has a daddy. And he's in Virginia. It ain't for you to judge her."

I put the requested box of laundry detergent into our basket. Next up was a trot to frozen foods to replenish Henry's sacred stash of frozen waffles.

"It wasn't my place to tell you. That was her business. All I could tell you about was my business."

"But it's your business, too," I argued.

"Why? 'Cause he comes through the house every couple of days? 'Cause we have dinner sometimes? To be honest, I ain't never even seen 'em kiss each other. I *know* he ain't my father. And I know he ain't tryin' to be my father. So if he makes Mom happy, then that's that."

"Why you takin' up for him?" I charged, still angered by the scene so many hours before.

"I'm not takin' up for anybody. I'm just tellin' you where I'm comin' from."

Through the years, letters aside, Henry and I had rarely talked about Dad, unless we'd been going back to some family memory that he happened to be a part of. But it had been my little brother, at ten, who handed me a cloth for my tears at the funeral, as the two of us wore matching suits to mourn alongside Mom, my two grandmothers, a grandfather, and what seemed like a million cops in full dress uniform.

"You don't even miss Dad, do you?" I asked without any sort of a segue.

The question took him by surprise as he closed the freezer case door behind him with an institutional-size box of waffles under his arm. He looked up at me with his usual nonchalance.

"No," he said, tossing the box into our basket. "I don't have to."

"What do you mean?"

"I don't miss him because he's with me," he began as we moved our cart toward the registers. "He's been with me ever since he left. So I don't have to miss him."

Now I'd read Native American philosophy, and the Qu'ran, and the Bible two times through. I knew about the spirit continuing on long after the body turned to dust. I knew that fathers and mothers and their children and their children were grapes on the infinite vine of spiritual and metaphysical ancestry. I knew that our elders were always there to help us. All we had to do was call out to them. I knew all of that. But I wan't sure if I really, truly, believed it.

"Don't get me wrong," my brother started up again, taking my silence as a request to elaborate further. "I miss him in the physical sense. I miss him being in front of me at dinner and hearing his voice and the way he used to walk around the house in his drawers and a T-shirt 'cause it was his house and he could do that."

The waffles and half gallon of butter pecan Breyer's brought us to ten items, two more than the eight Mom had on the list. "He's with you, too," he said in finishing.

He placed a hand on my shoulder, and my head cleared. Then I saw my father's face as it had been that last morning, shaven and smiling in his undershirt as he gloated about beating me in push-ups again, forty-five to twenty-eight. I felt his hands on my back as he embraced the two of us at the door that last time, promising that he'd rent the *Star Wars* trilogy for us all to watch on his next day off. A soothing warmth oozed through me, and I closed my eyes, feeling it massage the tops of my eyelids. He was with me. And he wanted me to stop fighting and just be happy.

"Give it some time," he said, sensing the goings-on within my soul. "You just got home. You can't do it all at once."

"Do what?" I asked as we joined the end of the "15 Items or Less" lane.

"Live," he said. Then he reached for the latest issue of *Jet*. As always, the bikini'd beauty, a sugar brown twenty-four-year-old from Mitchellville, Maryland, was on a page in the thirties. "It takes a lot to start livin' again."

The sounds of closing cabinets and the wrinkling of recycled plastic were all that didn't make the place feel like a black hole. I wished that my mother would come home. And I wished that I hadn't left. Henry went up to his room after the food was put away. And I was alone again.

I flipped through the four hundred channels of the same thing, idling on the old episodes of *The Cosby Show* and *The Real World*, Jeff Smith's *The Frugal Gourmet* and *Batman: The Animated Series*. That was when I thought I heard a woman's voice call my name.

I turned off the TV, but there was silence. I spun around, but there was no one. I peeled back the drapes to find that my mother's car was not in the driveway. The ground level was deserted, except for me and that piano in the corner.

It was right there, maybe fifteen or sixteen feet away. The stool was still adjusted to the same height. The same nicks and scratches inhabited its polished surface. Time had not changed its physicality. But now it was nothing more than an instrument.

The voice called me again. But this time it was muffled, almost as if it were coming from within the wooden box itself. I moved to investigate. Each step brought about even more caution, and the memory of a time when that stool had been a second home, a haven for a boy who often felt misunderstood, even if that had been his own delusion.

The piano had been my woman when there were only stupid girls with their fickle wants and desires, neighborhood niggas destined to either knock them up or beat them down—or, in the worst cases, both.

Before I knew it, we were facing each other, myself and that dead mouth of ivories. I felt the urge to reach out, to touch what had once been all I'd cared for in the world. But then I pulled away. Because there was no sound.

There was no music in my mind. And without the music that thing didn't matter. It couldn't matter. I began to reach again, this time just about to make contact. But the phone rang.

I thought of Salamanca, of Stevie, of Malcolm, of anyone and everyone who might deliver me from the urge. Then I heard Henry answering upstairs and figured it was for him, until he called down to me.

"Ben!" he yelled excitedly. "Get the phone. It's your girl!" The Lord had delivered me out of Egypt.

I snatched the phone off the kitchen wall, out of breath from a ten-step trudge.

"Hello?! Sala?" I asked frantically.

"It's me, baby," she said, her voice lower and raspier than I'd remembered it. "How's my baby daddy?"

"I'm just fine now. Where you at?"

"Route Twenty-three south, on my way to you," she said. "I'll be back in the city by six a.m. Your daughter wants to know if you want to have breakfast with her."

"Is she there?"

"Yeah, but she's on the backseat getting a little nap. But trust me, you'll get more than enough of her mouth when she sees you."

"I'd believe it. Especially if she's your child."

"And what does that mean?"

"That means that Mama can do some talkin' when she wants to."

"And so can Daddy. You miss me, Mr. Baker?"

"More than words could ever say," I replied. "I can't wait to see you."

"We can't wait to see you, either. But you know how I am about phones."

"Yeah, I know."

"And you know how Daddy is."

"Yeah, I know."

"Then meet us at Memorial Hill Park. Seven a.m. just to be safe?"

"God, I love you."

"I'm not God, but I love you, too."

"Smart-ass."

"Convict."

"Don't be late."

"I never am."

I wanted to dance, sing, sneak Henry into the closest bar to have a drink with him, to celebrate the long-awaited reunion of lovers and daughter, of the family that no one, absolutely no one, could keep apart.

But when I climbed the stairs I found the door to

Henry's room closed to a crack. The lights were off. But his voice was lowered to a murmur as he whispered sweet somethings to the love of his life, trying to sound suave. I let him be.

Then I went to my trusty bag and dug out seven years of photographs, a stack of prints documenting the evolution of my family, from girl and infant to woman and child. I flipped through them a hundred times before I drifted off. All they needed was a man to make them perfect. And that man would be there in less than seven hours.

8.

There was only one week left. Seven days. One
hundred sixty-eight hours until
her man came home. She
should have been packing. She
should have been coaching her
daughter about what to say
when she met her father for the
first time. She should have been
worrying if the Old Man could
sense her the way she sensed
him.

But instead she was dressed
to the nines in a dive called D's
on the West Side. The lavender
bra she'd chosen made her
titties look twice as big,
especially in contrast with her
tiny waistline.

"You need a light?" he
asked. His name wasn't

important. Neither was his occupation or the pin-striped suit and the two-grand-plus alligator shoes and derby that matched it. She just needed somebody, just once. For seven years she'd handled the solitude like an original gangster, more than willing to put in work in the name of love. But that morning she'd awoken to see the narrowing days on the calendar, the closing of that once endless gap between her and Ben. And it scared her.

"What's your name, baby?" the gentleman asked. His head was shaved bald, a goatee circling his lips and chin. Six two, maybe 215. Tall and slender. Marlene, her obstetrician and homegirl, was always saying that they were the ones with the biggest dicks. And here he was in front of her, Mr. Ebony Man himself: an ivory toothpick swirling in his mouth as if the maneuver were some kind of proof that he knew how to use his tongue.

"Yeah, I work over at the plant," he said proudly, lighting the cigarillo Salamanca had removed from her purse. She took in a deep pull, watching him flame a Newport. A three-grand outfit and he was puffing the cheapest smokes in existence. Go figure.

All the clichés she'd heard and read were true. She knew that this chump was going to be the one, the one to break her in again, the one to give her a final fuck before she spent the rest of her life making the kind of love Whitney Houston didn't know the half about. All he had to do was avoid the words *bitch, ho,* and *I just want you to suck my dick* and he'd have something to tell the boys about at the plant the following morning. But first, she just wanted for him to shut up and finish the drink she'd bought for him.

"What are you thinking?" Salamanca interjected, blowing smoke over his shoulder at the scowling hag in heels who'd been hoping for the action she was about to get.

"Huh?" he asked in response. She pictured him in a loincloth, carrying a club and dragging some unlucky girl around by the hair into his cave.

"What are you *really* thinking about?" she probed. "I mean, forget about all of the bullshit. And tell me what's really on your mind."

His brain came alive as he filed through all of the *Penthouse Letters* moments in his head for the perfect scenario to suit him. Then he found it.

"I'm thinkin' about kissin' you up against your front door," he said, tilting his head to the side, his lower lip folding over his teeth. "And then you put the key in the lock, and maybe I pull up your skirt from behind and—"

"Let's go," she said with a sigh, anxious to get the ball rolling. She couldn't wait for him to shut up. Sasha was with Pat. And this had been Pat's idea.

"Get it out of your system," Pat had said as Salamanca was on her way out. "Find some man that means nothing and give him everything you don't want Ben to have. All that anger. All that fear. Dump it all on some poor fool that just wants some tail, and leave it with him when you send him off."

Pat must have been born to give advice. Or she had at least been through enough to want Salamanca to learn from her mistakes. In the years since Sala had come to Detroit, Pat had told so many stories about the family. About her and her mother drinking and dancing all night long. About how hard it was to teach kids when their parents needed lessons themselves. About how proud she was of her children for chasing their dreams. And about how thankful she was to the Lord that He'd let her live this long, allowing her to survive wrong turns and bad choices that would've gotten anyone else six feet deep.

But she never talked much about Kenny, the only man she'd ever had, or at least mentioned. Salamanca knew that he had been there to love her and to give her children and to be the only man who'd ever had her heart. And then he'd disappeared, more gradually than suddenly, leaving her with two scrapbooks full of memories, two houses, and two children, who only saw him now and again over the years.

The man with no name looked surprised at Sala's suggestion, a hunter with no previous kills to his credit.

"For real?" he asked, looking left and right for the candid camera. She saw the weakness behind his eyes, the fear shrouded in silk and alligator skin. He was not an equal or a partner. He was prey.

"I ain't gonna say it twice," she uttered, throwing back the final swallow of cognac in her snifter. He tripped over his own feet following her out, almost forgetting the 1994 Escort keys he'd left on the bar. A gatored player with very frugal taste in automobiles.

Salamanca drove him in her car, taking him all the way up to the North End, at the top of the city. He'd have to find his own way home in the morning.

Marlene's theory had been proven true when she saw the thing erect, when she sucked it and pushed it inside of her, feeling it part her waters like the staff of Moses.

Seven whole years without dick, she thought as he pounded into her, giving her sensations she'd all but forgotten through those long years past.

She liked his shoulders, particularly the cuts between the deltoid and triceps, and the way the veins pulsed in his neck as he went in and out of her. She liked the Altoid-heavy breath that filled the room. She liked the fact that she wasn't alone anymore, for the night.

She bit his nipples and sucked his neck, burying her nails into muscled buttock, riding it like an urban cowgirl, smiling at the blissful friction between her thighs. But when she came it felt empty. The rush and the tingling were so distant, as if the sensations belonged to someone else.

His orgasm was loud and sloppy: a lot of sweating and trembling and self-commendation on his performance. He called her "baby" and "mama" and the currently popular "mami" as he collapsed onto the mattress, curling into a ball as the rubber dangled from a tool that didn't seem as big upon a second viewing. He closed his eyes and drifted off while she sat cross-legged at the foot of the bed, unsure of the hows and whys that went with her feelings.

The only thing certain was Ben's face, a hovering visage in front of No-Name's grill. She closed her eyes, trying to dismiss it as a figment of the afterglow, though she wasn't glowing. But when she opened up it was still there, looking just as sad, hounding her just by being and telling her what she had to do without a word.

She obeyed instantly, knowing that it was best, rushing from the bedroom into the kitchen. She filled a glass to the brim with cold water and then rushed back to the scene of the crime, this time noticing the stench of intercourse in the air. Then she dumped the liquid all over the man with no name, jerking him into frigid consciousness.

"What?! What?!" he demanded as he scrambled to wipe away the water in the dark, using her sheets.

"Get the fuck out!" she yelled, as if she hadn't invited him there, as if she hadn't wanted all that he'd given. But upon those words, Ben's face faded and it was just the two of them again.

"What's wrong, baby?" he asked innocently. She thought of him causing problems and of the pepper spray on her key chain on the dresser, just a lunge away. She really hoped that this asshole wasn't dumb enough to try her, not when she felt like this, not when there were spirits in her bedroom.

"Please leave," she said, more calmly this time, hoping to appeal to the sense of chivalry that had brought his lighter to her little cigar all those hours before.

"All right," he whimpered, gathering his things. He wrote his number on a scrap of paper, only to have her ball it up right in front of him without so much as a word.

"Well," he said at the front door. "Good night."

"It's morning," she said coldly, seeing the image of Ben smiling the night he took her to his prom, looking sharp as a razor as he'd led her to the limo. That man's love was deeper than the bay. What the fuck was wrong with her?

"The bus don't start runnin' till six," she said, seeing that the living room clock read 5:15.

"I'll be cool," he said as he went through the door, closing it behind him and leaving her alone with the mess she'd made.

She had to work quickly. The smell of him could be easily erased by hot water and shower gel. The sheets would be thrown into a bag and taken out to the cans at the curb. The condoms would be flushed, the incense lit. The yoga would remove any remaining traces or toxins. But even after all those things were done, she could not sleep.

She paced the house naked until well after sunrise,

knowing that there was work in the morning and that this would nag her all through the day, and the next, and the one to follow, until she saw her man and could confess to the crime. But the worst part was that the fear was still there, still grating against her like nails on a chalkboard.

What if, after all of this, Ben wasn't where he was supposed to be? What if her father had men waiting for him? What if he'd changed his mind and wanted to start all over again? Find another woman, have another baby, make another life, like so many of the no-good niggas she'd seen and heard about in beauty salon chats and barside confessions? What if he was no longer the man she needed him to be?

Her eyelids could not dam the tears as they streamed down her face in the new daylight, reminding her that the love was still real and that she had just betrayed her lover based upon the advice of someone who'd lost a man and never gained another. She was so stupid. So naive. So impulsive. So human.

She ended up in the bathroom looking at her naked self. She ran fingers through her mane, mimicking all those white-girl shampoo commercials on TV.

"God bless your great-grandma for bein' half Indian," her father would say many a Sunday morning as he looked the girl over, admiring the elaborate ways she'd done her own hair at eight. "I knew my little girl was gonna get the 'good' hair."

"You could cut all that hair off and I'd love you just the same," Ben had said in the shower with her once, his shampooed fingers scrubbing her locks, bringing the tender flesh beneath to a boiling point.

She'd wanted to cry when he'd said that. And now, eight years later, she was finally letting the tears go. Thinking of what she'd just done with Mr. X brought on streams and sniffles. And then she stopped.

She removed the clippers from under the sink, where they were stored in the same box they'd come in. After a few slices of the scissors in the kitchen drawers, she used her Wahl brand shears to remove all that remained, leaving nothing but an eighth of an inch all the way around. And then it was done.

She'd come out of the womb with more hair. Her grandmas were turning in their graves. Those lame-ass Detroit niggas wouldn't look her way for another ten years, unless she got a weave. But fuck all of them—even Pat, if she had something to say about it. They were all the past. Ben was her only future.

"Mommy?" Sasha asked confusedly at the door to Pat's house. The aunt's jaw dropped, while the little girl began to smile.

"You cut your hair," her daughter said.

"Yes, I did, baby."

"But why?"

"Because I wanted to start over. Have a new beginning."

Sasha studied her mother's new look and began to cheese as wide as she could.

"Well, I like it," Sasha said, touching the barretted plaits on her head. "Can I cut mine, too?"

Salamanca smiled back, knowing that her child would follow her into hell if she asked. "Maybe when you get a little older," she said to the child, then turned to her aunt. "And what about you?"

Pat's eyes studied the shape of the girl's skull, touching

her own in comparison. "Well, it ain't like you can glue it back on."

"Nope," Sala replied. "I can't."

"Then come on in here and explain yourself."

"So you just gonna go without knowin' nuthin'?" Pat asked after the girl revealed her plan. Pat wore a pink-and-green sweatsuit, her braids wrapped on rollers to achieve a curly look she'd seen in one of those hair magazines.

"I gotta go see Daddy," she said. "And I gotta be there when Ben comes home. I don't wanna hide anymore."

Sasha pretended to build a fortress with the pail of Legos before her. But her ears were wide open. They were leaving Detroit, leaving their friends and their house and everything she'd always known, maybe even forever. And that put a million questions in her six-year-old mind. But she pushed them all to the side. Because she trusted her mother and knew that Mama knew what was best. And besides, the kids at school were just okay. But they cheated at all the games and couldn't read half as well as she could. Even second graders had to have standards.

"Hidin' ain't always a bad thing," Pat replied. "Especially when you don't know what's out there. And when you got a crazy-ass daddy that ain't seen you in seven years."

Salamanca knew that she was right, to a certain degree. But she wasn't worried. Something inside of her said that it was going to be all right.

"I'm all Daddy has left," she replied. "He just wants to see me again, know that I'm all right."

"But he doesn't want to see Ben, now, does he?"

"That'll change when he knows he's a granddad," Sala said, lowering her voice so the child did not hear. "He'll owe Ben then. I'm sure of it."

"You want me to go with you?" she asked.

The younger woman shook her head. "No, I want you to stay right where you are. Cuz you know I might need you."

That was the point when they held each other as if it were the last time.

"I know you're gonna need me," Pat replied. "Maybe even sooner than you think."

In the next five days mother and daughter packed up all they needed to take with them. Mother sent letters to the phone and power companies, and to Sasha's summer camp, and had a yard sale for all that she would not need. And then she removed the remaining $3,000 in her safety-deposit box and left Ben's mother's address with her supervisors to forward her final paychecks.

Sasha said good-bye to those three or four who mattered, who'd had her at their birthday parties or shared their dessert during lunch at school. She gave hugs and kisses on the cheeks, somehow knowing that their names would eventually fade away, leaving only faces to stamp in her memory.

Then, on the twenty-fourth of the month, two days after Ben's release, Salamanca called his mother's home to learn that he was on his way back to the place of his birth. She left her home number but knew that she would leave to meet him right away. She had waited long enough.

Part Four

out there playing game after game of spades, casually awaiting his orders.

The Old Man looked up at the protégé he viewed as a son—the baby blue velour that covered his lanky frame, the $1,000 sunglasses, and another ten grand on his wrist. All of that, and the boy still wanted to live with him out at the beach. Maurice claimed that he wanted to be right there if anything jumped off. But Mitchell knew that was bullshit. The truth was that the boy was afraid to be alone.

The pain had become a constant, dulled only by Teacher's laced with a sizable amount of his own product four times a day. His stools were a stew of bright reds and undigested food. But he'd be damned if he let *them* see any sign of his weakness. He'd take one in the head before he ever gave off the impression that he needed anyone but himself, though he knew this to be the biggest lie of all.

He needed his daughter, for she was the only part of him that would live on. The men he'd hired to find her had returned with nothing again and again until he'd stopped writing checks. He took every picture from the albums and transferred them to his bedroom, where they were pasted into a two-part collage on the east and west walls. He needed her to be with him while he slept. He needed her to hold him through the sleepless nights and never-ending days.

What had become of his grandchild? Had it been vacuumed into a biohazard bag? Was it trapped within the transparent walls they had at all the social service setups, wishing it hadn't been left behind?

Or maybe the kid had made it. Maybe it was still strapped to his daughter's back like a little papoose, eating and growing and being taught to hate him. Maybe she was preparing that kid for the day when it would be brought to his grave and told to lay down a bouquet of dying petals, a gesture that would mean nothing to him down in the lake of fire.

After all, he knew that he was going to hell, for more reasons than even God Almighty could count. He'd killed men, and a wife, assaulted an only daughter, and fed the boy she loved to the wolves to save his own precious ass. And to make it even worse, for seven years he'd failed to bring his only child home so that he could say he was sorry.

The cancer had come from his own evil. He had more than enough money for the surgery, radiation, chemo, and any other goddamn treatment that would make him well. But what would he be doing it for? Why should he hold on to a life filled only with things that no longer moved him? Cash in those boxes all over town, the Cadillac, the real estate, and the round and brown behinds of girls younger than his own child.

There were no letters, no more kisses on the cheek, no more I love yous and breakfast to greet him when he awoke in the morning. No more frilly Easter dresses and ribboned hair braided with grown-up precision. No more of the dandelion and lavender she sprayed on her sheets.

What was a life without those things? What was a life without the only living woman he loved?

"I'm all right, son," he said to the pretty boy before him.

"You think he's comin' home?" Maurice had asked for the tenth time in the past two days.

The Old Man found himself smiling. Maurice's ignorance had to be bliss. "I *know* he's comin' home," he replied.

Mitchell could feel the same chill that ran through the boy's brittle frame. And it made him smile again. He thought of all the times he'd watched the kid act like he was the Man, untouchable, an enforcer not to be reckoned with. He'd listened to him tell the others stories of murder and mayhem, of cop interrogations and high-speed chases through the streets of the nation's capital, lying through his teeth because the truth was too pathetic. He loved the boy, even though he was weak, even though he was nothing without the man who treated him like a son.

"You want me to take care of him?" Maurice asked, an insanely forced grimace on his face. Mitchell dammed the flood of laughter welling inside of him.

Ben could have probably killed him before. Now, after a long stretch inside, the outcome would be that much more predictable.

"Not yet," Mitchell replied. "We'll see what he's gonna do first."

The outer door opened and both men turned toward the two-way glass. Al was back from the carryout. It was time to go and eat.

But something went wrong when the Old Man got to his feet. His legs folded under him, and the worst pain yet shot out in all directions, sending all six feet of him hard to the tiled floor. His head collided with the broken money counter they'd replaced a month before, and he had the quickest flash of Benjamin Baker smiling big and wide, so happy to see the tables finally turned. Then it all went to black.

2.

I didn't have to wake up because I hadn't slept. All night my eyes had opened and closed to peek at the numbers on the wall clock in the living room. I cackled in the dark as I pictured myself standing in a sun-washed Memorial Hill Park, joyfully awaiting the reunion that would bring a dark era to an end.

I chose a short-sleeved button-up and a pair of cargo shorts. I showered and shaved, using Henry's clippers to shape the stubble on my scalp. I had orange juice, strawberry Pop-Tarts, and a mint from the tin Mom had left on the kitchen counter. Then I fell to my knees in the living room and prayed to the Lord for my dream to come true.

"Lovely Day" came through on one of my radio's two audible stations. I backed out of the driveway, grinning at the bona fide fact that I would not be returning to Hillcrest alone.

It was six-fifteen when I started down Branch Avenue. The sun had already begun its blinding rise toward the heavens. Yet my mother's car had still not returned to its proper driveway.

Crossing Sousa Bridge, I saw a little girl of six in the white Honda Accord across the lane, her hair pressed and curled as she waved at me. Her eyes begged me to save her from the lip-synching post-teen mommies in the front seat. A smile was all that I could offer. Then the baby offered one in return. She made me think of my own little girl, the one I was about to meet for the very first time.

I cased Florida Avenue, searching for a toy store, or a five-and-dime, any spot where I might be able to buy my daughter some kind of gift, some little token to say that I'd thought of her, that she was the most important thing in Daddy's life equation. But nothing was open, and the vendors had yet to set up their tables on the sidewalks.

The only merchant on the street was an elderly Hispanic woman selling red and white roses wrapped in ribbons and plastic shields. I bought two dozen whites, my dad having convinced me years before that reds were for clichéd suckers and women who fronted salsa bands.

I grabbed a pack of gum at an Ethiopian corner mart and then headed toward the park, moving against the flow of traffic, noticing all the new cars and their shapes and sizes, packed and stacked on their way to the twenty blocks of madness that was downtown. I was more than happy to be going the other way.

Memorial Hill Park was a garden encased in stone: walls of mortar and exposed brick wrapped around benches and trees far older than I would ever be. An elevated platform that provided the perfect view of 16th Street as it stretched toward the peaks of the Gold Coast, that overpriced oasis for the truly dark and lovely.

Sala and I had been to the park only once—strangely enough, in the middle of winter—when the S2 bus had broken down and there wasn't another transport in sight. We'd traveled the labyrinth just to kill time and keep warm, leaving footprints in the fallen snow as the bare branches above us glistened with frozen water.

We had kissed there, overlooking Adams Morgan, speaking of life as if the two of us were all that mattered in the world. I wondered if that was why she'd chosen the place. Did she want to see if I remembered little moments like that, if a little twenty minutes on an otherwise boring day would stand out in a mind that had made it through seven years of prison? Or maybe it had just been a coincidence. Maybe there was some other reason that I couldn't think of because of the time of morning, or my lack of sleep, or the ball of nerves I became as the minutes passed. It was six forty-five.

I lapped the entire park. Two old white men tossed bread at a gathering of pigeons. A robin squawked at a sparrow lighting too close to her nest. A young woman in a short skirt crossed her legs while she read from a tiny Bible before a giant of a man pulled her onto tiptoes to give him a kiss. I followed them with my eyes until they exited the park, hand in hand. And then I headed back to the elevated platform.

7:09. 7:23. 7:59. Why were women always late? She knew that I'd be there early. She knew that I needed to see her face more than I needed air. So where was she?

8:12. 8:29. 8:43. 9:02. Maybe there was traffic. Maybe she'd caught a flat. Maybe she took a wrong turn and had to stop for directions. Had she said Memorial Hill? Maybe she'd meant Rock Creek, or Candy Cane, or maybe even Anacostia Park. Had I written it down? Had I double-checked before we ended the call? I needed to find a pay phone. Maybe she'd called the house. Maybe she'd left a message with Henry.

I went down to a pay phone at 16th and Meridian streets. I dialed Henry just as he was leaving for work. No, she hadn't called. But he would change the voice message to tell her where I was just in case.

9:43. 10:15. 10:58. This wasn't like her. She'd chosen the time. She'd chosen the place. There was no way in hell that she would've missed our meeting. She would've killed if she had to. Stolen another car, jumped over the moon. Something was wrong. Something was very wrong.

11:29. 12:33. 12:58. A runaway heartbeat. A cacophony of voices and questions. Fear. Insecurity. Paranoia. Delusion. Evil was at work. And that evil could have had only one name: Alfonse Mitchell.

He'd gotten her before I had a chance to. He'd traced that last call or gotten a tip from one of his people. He'd had her run off the road and thrown into some burlap sack to be transported in a car trunk along with my child.

He was torturing them, brainwashing them with magic

spells and lies. He was doing everything he could to shatter that which I held most dear, aiming to turn all that I had left into his.

But I was not going to let him. I was not going to let him get out on me again. I raced out of the park and back to that pay phone. But this time I dialed a different number, my only spade in a hand full of possibles.

"Is Daddy coming back to Detroit with us?" Sasha asked her mother from underneath the blanket over the backseat.

They'd left the motel two hours before. But the little girl was still sleepy. She'd only jump into consciousness when the car hit a bump or picked up speed. Salamanca had needed the five-hour pit stop, having almost run the both of them off the road. She'd tried to swerve away from the lights of an imaginary tractor-trailer in her rearview, and almost hit the railing in the process.

Now she was alert again, her eyes carefully reading the signs as she counted the miles between her and her man, who was now less than three hours away. She had to stop somewhere to do her face, to brush the short hairs on her head, and to get out of the scuffed white Reebok Classics she normally only wore around the house.

Sasha had finally posed the question her mother had been anticipating for weeks, since she'd first told the little girl that they were leaving. Now it had arrived in the dark of the early morning, as they drove between two seemingly endless stretches of greenery.

"I don't know what Daddy wants to do," Sala replied. "But we'll all talk about it when we get there."

The child processed this new data, not knowing exactly

how to feel about it. Her life ahead seemed so uncertain, so confusing. But at least she would be spending the rest of it with her father.

"I hope Daddy still loves me," Sasha said, pushing herself into a seated position.

Salamanca lost breath upon hearing the words. But she knew what to do. She stretched her right arm back to its limits to rub her little girl's thigh.

"Your daddy loves you more than life itself, baby," she said. "That's why he wants for us to be with him."

"Then why hasn't he been with us since I was a baby?" she asked, unconvinced. "Daddies don't do that. At least not Paula's or Tarik's or Jasmine's."

"The only reason your daddy was away was because he made a mistake and had to make up for it—"

"In jail, right?"

"Yes, baby. He had to go to jail. But he didn't do everything they said he did."

"Then why didn't they say he was innocent? Ms. Thomas always says that in America you're innocent until proven guilty."

"But Ms. Thomas is a white woman from Livonia. Things work different for her."

Sasha didn't have to ask what that meant. Her mother had given her too many lectures on the life that she would live as a black woman, on the histories of people of color and how America almost always tried to bring them down, just as they'd done to her daddy. And she knew that her daddy hadn't done everything they said he did. And she knew that he loved her with all his heart, because she'd been hearing it from the both of them for the whole six-plus years she'd spent on the planet.

"Well," the little girl said in response, "I just hope he's not late."

Salamanca smiled so widely that Sasha could've seen it from behind her.

"I know your daddy," the mother assured her. "He'll be as on time as on time can be."

"Okay," Sasha said, nodding in the darkness as she faintly recognized the song on the radio. Living just enough for the city. The car's peaceful journey made her eyelids heavy. She soon closed them.

The more Sala drove, the more awake she became, fueled by the glorious light at the end of her journey's tunnel. It was about to be over. All of his years away. All of her running and ducking. The void deep within her—the one since the bailiffs took Ben away and since she'd walked out of a house for the second time in her life, uncertain as to whether or not she'd ever return—was finally going to be filled.

However, Ben was only half of the equation. There was a part of her still wandering through that murder museum of a house back in Palmer Woods. Another part still lying on the floor after that blow to her midsection. And still another lying on the backseat of that Toronado almost twenty years before, hopelessly waiting for an answer to the question of when she would see her mother again.

The horizon turned from black to blue to tangerine. She found her way to 363 and then to the Beltway, picking up speed with every mile, maneuvering the ride as if it were a part of her own body. And she was doing fine, just fine.

But the driver in front of her was not. A tractor-trailer

fifty yards ahead somehow lost a tire. The tractor then detached from its load, which skidded at a forty-five-degree angle and hit the bright red Ford Explorer head-on. The two cars behind it swerved out of the way. One cleared the runaway caboose. The other crashed into the median, clipping the bright yellow Beetle and sending it into a spin. Salamanca slammed on her brakes, but she knew it was too late as she saw the Beetle barreling toward her.

"Stay down!!" Salamanca yelled to Sasha. Lying across the seat, the girl instantly came awake and covered her head with both hands as the Beetle made impact. Glass spilled everywhere as the Honda tipped onto its side. Salamanca glanced at the dash clock before the air bags opened. It was six-fifty.

Damn, she thought. I would have made it.

3.

The plan had been foolproof. Yet his fool of a

surrogate son had foiled it
for him, by trying to save
his life. Alfonse Mitchell had
never liked doctors or
hospitals and had enjoyed
the good fortune of having to
spend little time in their care.
Minor surgery for a hernia
at twenty-seven. A broken
arm after one of those fights
in one of those Carolina joints
that had a name he could no
longer remember. And there
was that slight concussion
after that bat to the head
outside of D's on the East
Side, for flirting with a
piece of ass with a ring on

her finger. He should never have left his pistol in the glove box.

Such violence had been typical in his young man's life, years so far behind him they often felt like a dream. This time they'd brought him into the emergency room in one of the wheelchairs they saved for the old and crippled, all because he'd hit his head on that goddamn money counter that Maurice swore to God he could sell on eBay in a week. And the thing had still been collecting dust four months later.

The uniformed orderlies and nurses rushed to him before the corn-fed white boy he saw with the broken nose and the screaming pair of twins cursed with either colic or fever, or both. Maurice had slipped a Benjamin to a "friend" of the family on duty, and the next thing Mitchell knew he was behind a curtain, a doctor with graying blond hair stitching the gash on his skull.

Mitchell focused on the long white legs beneath her doctor's coat, remembering that that was one line he'd never crossed. Sistas had always been good enough for him.

Dr. Weiss fixed him up and was on her way to her next victim when she happened to glance down at the same time the Old Man was standing up. She saw the wide stain across the seat of his pants. And then there was that smell of blood and feces that turned Maurice's face into a wrinkle. And that was when the Old Man knew he'd really been caught.

He'd had dreams of dying in his own office, right in that leather chair where he'd spent most of his life, doing work, putting in work, and giving orders for all kinds of shit to get done. Sometimes he'd hated that chair as much as he'd loved it, because it was as much prison as it was paradise, doom, and salvation in the same sitting.

He'd always wanted to blame his father for the way he turned out, for offering him that toke of a joint when he was twelve, for teaching him how to clean pistols at fourteen, for schooling him in all the ways of Hades before he had a chance to choose whether or not they were his ways. He blamed his daddy for taking that slug in the gut before the conspirators kicked the two of them off that moving pickup, leaving them for dead while the others took the loot for themselves.

But it hadn't been his daddy or Maurice that had gotten him there. It had been that damn Hippocratic oath. He could've cried broke and they still wouldn't have let him walk back on the street with the cancer inside of him. But the sadder thing was that he probably couldn't have walked anyway. Every limb was half-dead, as if all the life had oozed right out of him.

So there was nothing to do but lie there, and watch TV, and suffer the utter discomfort of having a catheter up his dick and ten million other lines flowing in and out of him. If this was the rest of his life, then he wanted to die all the more. But it was hope that made him hold on. Not the hope of healing. Not the hope for survival. Just the hope that Salamanca might have the mercy to appear out of the nothingness and give him her blessing. If she would come and kiss him on the cheek one last time, he could stroll into hell with his head on high.

He thought of all the sci-fi flicks and the James Bond films, wondering if there might have been some way to put a tracer on the child from birth, some chip he could have put in her hand so that she might have never been lost. But she *was* lost, and his time was dripping away like the fluid in the bag above him, destined to be depleted at a point in the very near future.

4.

"There's some things we have to talk about before I
turn the key in this car." The
look on Malcolm's face was a
cancer kind of serious.

It was two-thirty when he
finally pulled up, dressed in the
same T-shirt and jeans I'd seen
him in less than two days
earlier. His afternoon shadow
was in need of a razor's edge.
There was also a zipped leather
bag on the backseat. I
immediately wondered what
might be inside.

I brought him up to speed
as best I could. The question
now was what would come
next.

"Talk to me," I said, already
anxious. In my mind I was

already parked in front of Malcolm's mystery address, waiting to get my girls by any means necessary.

"Are you sure you want to do this?" he asked.

"Yeah," I said. I don't think he expected that answer. He sighed and lit a Black & Mild.

"All right," he said, exhaling sweet smoke. "We're just goin' out to look. We see somebody, we follow 'em. Nothing else."

"Even if we see her?" I asked.

He hesitated, not having thought that far ahead. "We'll deal with that when we come to it."

A minute later we were off down Bangor toward Suitland Road. From there we'd take Silver Hill to the Beltway and then hit 50 all the way out to the Annapolis side of the beach.

It took the better part of an hour to get there. Mile after mile of dotted yellow lines and the same ten songs on the radio. We passed the time with smoke and idle chatter about the old neighborhood and Malcolm's past life as a local kingpin.

"I don't know why nobody ain't pop me," he grumbled.

"Cuz you knew how to handle your business," I replied.

"Bullshit," he said. "I was just lucky."

"You must've had some skill about you. I mean, luck only gets you so far."

"Well, then I guess I pushed it to the limit. I mean, buyin' that condo right in the neighborhood, in my own name. A drop-top Carrera when I was supposed to be workin' for Public Works. Like I said, somebody shoulda shot me."

"You still think about it like that?" I asked, figuring that he'd clean-slated it all the minute he'd stepped into the fresh air of his first free day.

"Every morning," he replied, spitting another cloud out the open window. "I get up and I look at my little boy, and I can't believe how fuckin' stupid I was. To put everything that mattered on the line for some shit like that."

I smiled. "I can't wait for that feeling."

"Which one?" he asked.

"The one I'll get when I finally see what I have, when I can hold my ladies and walk off away from everything else. Start over, you know?"

"Yeah, but what you learn is that you never really start over. Life is one long stretch. You move until you stop."

The house at 3807 Woodley Court was a duplex sandwiched between two larger homes, both of which had lighted walkways and side entrances that led to small swimming pools and/or hot Jacuzzis. We parked in surveilling distance and killed the engine and the stereo, rolling down the window to take in the sounds of the second ocean I'd come to know on my journey. No dogs barked. No car alarms, just the echoes of moving fluid and the animals that made it their home.

The Old Man's place didn't look like much. No pool or porch lanterns. The front windows carried a heavy black tint. It was far less impressive than what I'd expected.

"So what do we do now?" I asked, already restless.

Malcolm shook his head and reached for that mystery bag on the backseat. He pulled it over the seat and into his lap, studying it for a quick moment before pulling the zipper back to reveal an assortment of food items: fat-free potato chips in a can, a few bottles of water, and four different kinds of sandwiches, all on wheat bread and sealed in plastic bags. And I'd been thinking pistols and a pump-action twelve-gauge.

"We wait," he said. A reach of a hand under his seat produced a pair of binoculars, which he gave to me. "There's only one way in and one way out, unless they're coming in from the bay. So you're on first shift."

"So what are you about to do?" I asked, prematurely. I knew as soon as he reclined the seat.

"Wake me up in two hours," he said. Five minutes later he was out like a light.

We did shifts well into the night, earning suspicious stares from neighbors light and dark. We both got the feeling that trouble might be on the way. And sure enough, just before midnight, we got a visit from the expected green-and-white, one of Paragon Security's finest, in a 1993 Mustang 5.0.

"Are you guests of the Whitmores?" the rent-a-cop asked. His pitted face was a dermatologist's nightmare, with a blond buzz cut on top. He also had a steel .38 on his hip.

Malcolm didn't sweat it in the least. He crunched on barbecue chips as he fished a small billfold out of that bottomless bag of his. Then he flashed what looked like an FBI badge with his name and picture on it. Pit boy took a step away from the car.

"Yes," said Malcolm in a gentle and relaxed voice. "We

are, at least as far as you're concerned." I forced my face into an *X-Files* frown for the bluff. He went for it.

"You guys need anything?" he asked. "I mean, this is my last patrol. Maybe I could—"

"Get home to the wife and kid," Malcolm charged, bringing the power window back up as the words hit the air.

"But I don't have a wife," he said, his face still just beyond the glass. Malcolm took his finger off the button long enough to hit him with a finishing uppercut.

"Then you better get one," he said, and then closed the remaining gap. Two seconds later Officer Pit was backing into the night, more than likely on his way to the nearest porno house.

"FBI?" I asked.

"Yeah, Fake Badges Incorporated," he remarked slyly. "You gotta be ready for anything."

Six hours of nothing nearly had us ready to throw in the towel. By the time night fell we'd scarfed down everything in the bag, run through the entire CD wallet three times over, and calculated an accurate average of the property value in the surrounding subdivision. Then the beginning of the end showed up.

It was a dark blue Honda Civic, with chromed exhaust pipes and a tacky spoiler on the back, a later model than I'd been free to see. The sole man inside it was blasting Rare Essence at a "call the cops" level as he pulled into the driveway and parked. Yet for him there was no Pit Boy to speak of.

The driver killed the engine and climbed out, his face shaded by the tree limbs above. But I knew it wasn't the

Old Man. Even from the rear I could see that he was about my age, his hair in manicured cornrows going straight back, a Timberwolves short set surrounding his legs and torso.

He started toward the house but stopped halfway there and headed down the driveway to the mailbox, which he found to be empty. But just as he leaned in to check the postman's pouch, the low beam from a passing Benz blew the shadow away from his face. And I saw the last man I'd ever expected to see: Maurice.

He slammed the box shut, seemingly disappointed, and jogged up the walk to enter the house without incident. I started breathing again as soon as he was fully out of sight.

"You know him, right?" Malcolm asked me.

I nodded. "He's the nigga that signed the affidavit against me."

"Ain't that some shit," Malcolm said, sucking his teeth. "I guess he's still down with Team Mitchell?"

"But not for long," I said, moving toward the door. But Malcolm had me by the arm before I could get there.

"What did we say?" he reminded me. "This is recon. We look or we follow. But we don't do shit."

My synapses fired up dreams long forgotten, those curdling revenge fantasies of me snapping the boy's neck and ripping his head away from the torso before I poured myself a wineglass of his blood. All I had to do was kick in that lame-ass front door and make it a very satisfying reality, just after he told us where to find Sala.

"You know better than that," Malcolm chided. "We don't know what the fuck's behind that door. Guns, pit bulls, fifteen niggas gettin' paid to whip your fresh-out-of-jail ass. If Mitchell's everything you say he is, you know he's gonna have somethin' up in there. And your boy knows what and where it is. While we don't know shit. So what does that mean?"

I eased back against the seat cushion, knowing that he was right, no matter how much it pained me.

"That we wait again?" I asked with a sigh. There was a soreness around my tailbone from sitting too long.

"Yeah," he replied. "We wait again."

But before I could recline the seat, and before Malcolm could play Frankie Beverly one more time, our target removed himself from the house by the sea, armed with nothing but a nylon tote, a bag of chips, and a bottle of water. He got back in his car and drove off. We were right behind him.

The little Civic took us farther than we'd ever expected, up past Baltimore and across the state line. Even in darkness I could see the change taking place all around us. The complexions and features of our fellow drivers got increasingly whiter. SUVs turned to pickup trucks and outdated minivans. And all of the radio stations I'd ever known faded into unbearable static by the time we crossed from Delaware into Pennsylvania.

Malcolm didn't so much as flinch during the tail. There were no words to me. Not even a quick buzz on the cell to check in with the wife. He was ready to follow Maurice into hell if he had to. And so was I. But as it turned out, our journey fell short of the lake of fire as the Civic pulled into a strip mall in Lancaster, Pa.: Dutch country.

Maurice pulled around the back of a two-level building at the far end known as "Pop's Hardware." There was also a hair salon, a religious bookstore, and a restaurant.

A plastic banner announced "Pops' Grand Opening," though the raggedy look of it implied that someone had forgotten to take it down a long time ago. Maurice's silhouette climbed a thin metal staircase that led to the rear entrance and disappeared inside.

"A little late for hardware shoppin', ain't it?" I said. Malcolm smiled. But I could tell it had nothing to do with my words.

"What?"

"I can't believe it."

"You can't believe what?"

"That this is where your boy's been hidin' for all this time."

"Shit, Maurice ain't my boy."

"I wasn't talkin' about Maurice," he said, grinning. "I'm talkin' about the Old Man."

At eighteen, I'd've found the idea more than preposterous. There was no way in hell that the Old Man would ever go to hide out in the middle of fucking nowhere, especially not in Amish country. This was a guy that drove a Cadillac, a man who wore Stacy Adams and alligator shoes, who craved action and prestige as his life's blood. There was no way I could ever see him holing up in horse-and-buggy land.

"I shoulda done some shit like this," Malcolm continued. "Set up a front where nobody's gonna look for it. Pay off the cops or whoever and just run shit."

"Run what?" I asked.

"The drug game."

"Out here?"

"Especially out here. Think about it. No competition.

And even if there is, he's probably got 'em outgunned two to one."

"Who are you? His biggest fan?"

"Nah, but you gotta respect it. Even if we do burn this place to the ground before we're done."

"So you were thinkin' that, too?" I asked. We shared a quick laugh and then plotted out the watch shifts for the remaining hours until daybreak. We were both pretty sure that Maurice would stay put into the morning.

"Hey!" Malcolm shouted. I jumped into daylight, unfolding my arms from the hug in my dreams. Malcolm was wide awake and slightly annoyed.

"You shoulda told me you was tired," he said, sucking his teeth. "Your boy's gone. I did a quick pass around the building and he ain't parked no more."

If Maurice was gone, then I'd blown it. We might have to go back to the house and start all over again.

"My bad, man," I said. "I ain't even feel myself dozin' off."

The bounty hunter swallowed a ball of emotion before he finally spoke.

"It's all right," he said. "But it's after ten now. What's the last time you remember being up?"

"I think it was like seven-thirty."

"He could be in Canada by now. That means we're gonna have to go in."

"Go in where?" I asked.

"Where do you think?" he said, gesturing toward Pop's Hardware. "Maurice or not. At least some of what we need to know is in there. So we need to go in and see how much."

"What if he just stopped in to get some hardware?"

Malcolm shook his head. "I'm not even gonna dignify that with an answer."

An Amish couple left the automatic doors as we entered, their eyes seemingly glued to the concrete below in lieu of greeting our "Good morning" nods.

The place was all but deserted, yet cashiers were working all four of the registers. Merchandise was stacked neatly in the rows, and the air-conditioning was up so high that you could see your breath. We pretended to browse, poking our way through each aisle, looking for doors or passageways. But it all seemed pretty normal, or at least as normal as any front could be.

The second level was even more deserted than the first. Of the six or seven aisles, only two or three even had product on them. A giant stand-alone bathtub was on display without a price. Latex paint was on sale, as were several marked-down screen doors in a sample area on the east wall. But there was one door in the rear, a metal one tattooed with a sign in bright red-and-white letters that read: MANAGEMENT ONLY.

"You thinkin' what I'm thinkin'?" I asked.

"You know I am," he said, smirking.

"So what do you want to do about it?"

It only took a light tap on the metal to get the attention we wanted. A kid of seventeen flung the door open, decked out in black basketball shorts and a matching white T. The look on his face said that we were obviously not welcome. Over his shoulder I could see at least two other kids his age, both of them crowded around something I couldn't make out.

"If you need some fuckin' help, go ask a nigga with a name tag," he said. "This is shipping and receiving in here." The Old Man's customer service training had fallen off in recent years.

"We just wanted to know how much the Sheetrock was going for," Malcolm added with rather believable naïveté.

"And how the fuck am I supposed to know?" he charged.

"Our mistake," I said.

"Yeah, sorry. We'll just ask somebody downstairs."

"Yeah, whatever," the boy grunted, immediately pushing the door shut. And we were off, to the escalators and then out front to the car.

"So what do you think?" I asked back inside our vehicle.

"I think recon time is over."

"What? You wanna go back up in there?"

"Nah, not yet. We need some more dudes."

"Yeah, I saw two over his shoulder, plus Maurice makes at least four."

"Then we should count on six, and a nice little arsenal to go with it," Malcolm said. "Sala's not in there, though. She must be somewhere else. Maybe back in the beach house, or even somewhere we ain't heard about yet."

"But if there is another somewhere, we'll have to get into that office to figure out where. So either way —"

"Shit could get hectic," Malcolm finished.

"Yeah," I said. "It most definitely could."

———

Salamanca came awake in a dark room with no windows, her arm pierced with an IV. She felt her bare ass against the stiff fabric of hospital sheets. She tried to get up, but the pain stopped her. It was a liquid ache that flowed from one side to the other like water in a shifting glass. She eased back against the pillow to get her bearings, finding a light switch that set the room ablaze.

Sasha was curled up on the cot at the foot of the bed, without a scratch on her. The child shifted to avoid the light overhead. A half-finished Happy Meal lay on the tray next to her. There was no clock in sight.

It took a few minutes for Sala to gather her thoughts. She remembered that yellow Beetle spinning toward her. Her head had smacked against the steering wheel before the air bags fired, giving her a nice fat concussion. But by lying down, the little girl had been shielded from much of the impact.

There were flashes of cops and paramedics, of ambulances and wheeled gurneys, unfamiliar faces in a rainbow of colors. Purple spots and joints that all ached. Now she was here, in this unknown room of an unknown place. A finger to the lit orange button might have brought answers all at once. But there was the risk that they might come with questions, unwanted questions. And there was no time for such an inquisition. Not with Ben so close. And not with her father possibly closer. She had to move.

So she swung her legs over the side of the bed, lowered her feet to the frigid floor below. That was when the swimming pain intensified. And this time it came with a tickling sensation along her arms and legs. She tried to stand erect, but her bones turned to rubber, and she slid and then stumbled back, using her hands to catch herself before she stumbled to the floor. She wasn't ready yet.

She climbed back into bed and pulled the sheets over her, breathing deeply until the pain murmured away. She told herself that it would only take another minute or two. But she knew it might be a lot longer.

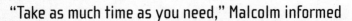

5.

"Take as much time as you need," Malcolm informed
me as I stepped out of his truck
and onto the lush green beyond
it. I was so tired that my head
ached. But this was something
that I needed to do.

I wasn't sure if it was only a
coincidence that Mom's new
house was less than five
minutes from the cemetery. But
what I did know was that I
needed to see him. I hadn't seen
him in a long time.

I knew the plot by sight,
having been before it more
times than I could count. But I
wasn't there to pay my
respects. I was there to ask for
help.

Graveyards teach you the

most important thing about life: that it ends. And there were so many endings on that sloped field off Suitland Road. Paul Wormington, Raymond Preston, Myra Fontaine, and Carla Huddleson. Lives that had come and gone generations apart from one another.

Benjamin Baker Sr. was in the last plot on his particular row, bordered by Dionne LaRoux on one side and a wrought-iron fence on the other.

"Whassup, Dad?" I said, stooping before the polished marble with his name on it. Someone had left three white roses for him.

I knew that there weren't words for what I needed to ask. How does a first son tell his hero of a father that he failed, that his family has been broken, all of his freedoms purged, because he failed to understand the lessons his father had tried to teach him?

"Shit has gotten really out of hand."

How could you tell a career cop that his recently released ex-con kid was about to posse up for a vigilante mission with another parolee in the heart of Pennsylvania Dutch country? All to save the daughter-in-law and grandchild he'd had to leave behind when he went away for a crime caused by nothing but his own stupidity?

"But I know I gotta do somethin'."

And how do you ask him to be with you? How do you ask him to add the strength of his spirit to yours as you go to do everything that he would not have done?

"And I need for you to be with me. Even though this ain't your way, I need you, Dad. Cuz all the heart I got in me came from you."

I didn't say anything after that. I just stood there and waited, as if the dead man might answer me from six feet below. And then I remembered those words of his from long ago, words that then and there made more sense than they ever had before:

The sooner we start, the sooner we finish.

There were so many other things I could have said. I could've told him about Carl and what Henry had said about Ma being happy. I could've said how much Sasha was going to miss him, even though they'd never met.

But those were all things I was sure he knew, as he did the outcome of the night ahead. But whatever it was, I just hoped that he'd stay close. I hoped that he'd be with me until the end.

My eyes came into focus in the guest room, smack-dab in the middle of the Ben Baker wall of fame.

The dwindling sunlight informed me of the lateness of the day. Car horns echoed from the rush-hour traffic on Branch Avenue. Night was coming, and the inevitable with it.

Baked chicken was in the air. The garlic and sage were as pungent as ever. Everything in me ached.

"Whassup, Big Ben?" Henry asked as I passed the entrance to his room. I crossed the threshold to find him lying on his bed. His matchstick legs almost stretched from one side of the room to the other. Sagrario was right between them, spooning into the curvature he'd created, her braided head against his bird chest.

I crept in, doing my best not to disturb his little missus. It was the first time I'd seen his space unlocked since my arrival. An abundance of dirty laundry had been piled into a single corner, its funk covered over by the burning Nag Champa in the air.

Jerry Stackhouse and Allen Iverson took it to the hole on the two large posters behind his head, each identical in height and width. A wide desk and matching armoire held a massive Macintosh equipped with all the works, covered in more Post-it notes than I could possibly count.

The rest was photographs, three walls covered with color and black-and-white prints, each depicting one drop in an ocean of times and places: solitary shots of squirrels and pigeons at McPherson Square, his girl balancing on the brick wall outside the Fort Davis Library, and a wash of exploding purples from the Fourth of July fireworks show, just to name a few.

"How long did it take you to fill up the walls?" I asked, ogling the endless picture show.

"Aw, man," he said in a pseudoshy sigh. "I think I did most of 'em last year. Last year was a big year for pictures." He wiggled out from under the sleeping girl, gently bracing her head for his departure from beneath it.

We wandered back into the guest room, where he asked me about our little excursion. I told him that Salamanca hadn't shown up at the park, and where we'd been since. If she showed up at the house and something happened to me, he would have to make Sala understand why we had done what we did.

"We goin' back up there," I said confidently. "And this time we bringin' some backup." Henry nodded like a soldier, though I could see the fear on his face, the fear of his losing me—again.

"You sure this is what you wanna do?" he asked.

I nodded.

"Then I'm goin' with you," he declared.

He wanted me to see that he wasn't ten anymore, that

he was a man. Because after all, brothers had to stand behind their brother. They had to be there for each other
when the beef came. And that might have been true in the
rest of black America. But not on my watch.

"Nah, Hen. This shit is too big for me," I said. "That
means it's way too big for you."

"But you don't even know these dudes you goin' in
with," he argued.

"And that's a good thing," I said. "Shit gets hot and the
only person I gotta get out of there is Malcolm. The rest of
'em got their own back to look out for. But that doesn't
mean I don't need you, man. If Sala calls, you gotta tell her
everything I told you. And you gotta tell her where I am."

"Hey, man, I got you," he replied. A hug sealed our pact.

Mom was in her usual place: seated at the dining room
table at six p.m. sharp, her nose buried in the day's *Post*
while the dinner—baked chicken, wild rice, and kale—
cooled on the stove. Her usual glass of Chardonnay was
half-empty.

"What you got your eyes on me for?" she asked, looking up.

"Just watchin' what you're doin'," I replied, as always.

"You sleep okay?" she asked as I came up behind her.
She stacked her papers and put them to the side as I sat
across from her.

"Yeah, real good."

"So what's up?"

"I wanted to say I'm sorry for what happened yesterday."

She cut her eyes away from me before she spoke, a move that negated everything she was about to say.

"You don't have to apologize," she began. "I knew how you were going to react."

"I know you still love Dad," I said.

Her eyes fled again, this time toward the black-framed photo on the wall, the one of all of us.

"It ain't no romance," she said. "It's just havin' somebody that's there for me. Carl's a really good friend. I met him at a conference last year. Lost my quarter in the soda machine and he gave me another one, and it worked. So when my soda came out, I went over to the table and got a cup and shared it with him. He didn't want to take it, but I made him.

"We talk on the telephone and we go out and see things. And like you saw, he even helps me with the groceries, but I don't want him *with* me, Ben. I don't want him in your father's bed."

"It's all right if you do," I said.

"I know," she answered. "But I just want you to know where I am. I didn't have to have this talk with Henry because he just understands things."

"Tell me about it," I said. "It don't seem like nuthin' gets under his skin."

"You too?" She chuckled. "Sometimes I think the boy is the Golden Child or somethin'."

"He might be," I said. My response gave her the moment she needed to think something through.

"And I didn't stop goin' to the grave because of Henry. I did it because God told me to," she replied, simple and plain. "The Lord came to me in a dream one night and asked why I was buyin' flowers every week to stand over a box. I couldn't see him—God, I mean. He was standing behind me and we were at your daddy's headstone, and the next thing I knew I was digging up the ground, with nothing but my hands. And I was tearin' it away like it was papers, pullin' away layer after layer until I got to the coffin, with God eggin' me on the whole time. Then I got to the casket, and I opened it. And wasn't nothing in there of Benjamin Baker Sr. Not even the suit he was buried in. And then the Lord said, 'Myrna, you gotta look inside yourself. Cuz he's with you and he's with me, and he's with your children, and their children. But he's not in that box. So stop comin' there thinkin' he is.' "

I had to change the subject. This was a discussion for another time.

"It was hard in there without you," I said.

"It was hell out here without you, too. But we both made it. And now we both gotta make the best of it."

I came around the table and she pulled me to her, her arms stronger than any others.

"Now sit down and eat your dinner."

Little brother and his little lady descended moments later. Plates and silverware were arranged in their proper positions. But that chair at the far end of the table, my father's chair, remained empty.

It was the best meal I'd had since I'd been on the outside. I cleaned two plates and welcomed the *-itis* that soon followed. Mom went to her room to catch her favorite show, *Star Trek: Enterprise*. Henry and Sagrario went out to a movie. I hit the showers, shaved, and went to meet destiny.

My Datsun zoomed south on the freeway, veering off

toward the 7th Street exit. I was excited about getting back to the old neighborhood. I couldn't wait to take in the sights and sounds that had been the be-all and end-all in my last life.

Sometimes it takes an extra month for D.C.'s summer heat to dissipate. And the ninety-six-degree habitat at the end of August more than proved that point. I had stripped down to a tank top and a pair of khaki shorts and a pair of low-top boots with no socks. A khaki baseball cap covered my dome, its bill pulled down to cover my eyes.

I could smell the change in the air as I cruised past the Waterfront. Many of the restaurants had changed their names. But most things were just as I remembered them: Jefferson, Amadon, Bowen, Riverside Baptist, and the post office at Half and K.

Five little boys, not one of them over nine, did their best to climb the crabapple tree in front of Waterfront station. The pudgiest of them dangled from one of the lower branches, swinging back and forth, overjoyed by the feeling of weightlessness. The others had already scaled up a ways and sat perched on branches like oversize sparrows.

They probably thought that they were the first to attempt such a feat, as we had long before them. Climbing that particular piece of living history had been a rite of passage for every Waterfront boy in history, and even a few girls, too.

But the memories darkened with the setting sun as I drew close to South Capitol. Dilapidated strips of abandoned town homes and burned-out buildings brought back things I hadn't minded forgetting: Muhammad Whitfield getting shot in the head for his Filas on the first day of ninth grade. Stevie and Malcolm's cousin Randy OD'ing in a rundown suite at the Skyline Inn. And there would always be Bebe's old storefront, with its ancient sign still loosely bolted to the redbrick wall, still marked with a decade-old graffiti tag from one "Cool Disco Dan."

But though I knew the streets, it was easy to see that they were no longer mine. The faces I cruised past were all foreign, their eyes firing back stares demanding to know what I was doing around *their* way. Those I knew had ended up out in Lorton, or other parts of the city, or early coffins.

But after a turn here and there and a stop for cigarettes came 1st Street, my street. I parked in an empty space at the corner toward the middle of the block: six units down from the first place I'd ever called home. Anticipation crackled through my limbs as I hit the asphalt. I hoped that seeing the old place again would put everything into the perspective I needed.

The whole block had been the victim of some gigantic shrinking ray. Giant trees had become shrubs. Houses that always seemed five stories high were now less than three. But as it turned out, the block was the same. It was I who had grown up.

Our front lawn had become little more than a dirt pile. The exterior blue paint was chipping from the brick almost all the way around. The flower basket on the tiny terrace held nothing but dry earth, and the bars on the front windows had rusted from black into a reddish brown.

I climbed the walk for a closer look, remembering when Dad had driven us all to Hechinger's for that flower basket and how Henry and I both loved grinding our fingers in the bag of potting soil every spring. I could still feel that cool earth between my fingers. And I could still see Dad up on that tall ladder as he painted our whole house all by himself. I thought of all the hours of all the days I'd spent running around that yard, with Henry, and with Stevie, but mostly with just myself.

Then I remembered something that Jimmy Stein had told me on the inside, more specifically what he'd said on my first Arizona Christmas.

"What I wouldn't do to be home right now," I'd muttered as I moved my knight two to take his rook. Anticipating my move, he dragged his bishop three diagonal places to the right, leaving my king with nowhere to go. Checkmate again.

"Home is never in the neighborhood," he said. "It ain't no block, and it ain't no address."

"What do you mean?"

"I mean that home as the place always changes. But the home in your head is the one that never leaves you."

Years later, Stein's words finally made sense. I tipped my hat to him as I turned away from the real estate my mother had sold years before. She had made her home somewhere else. And so had I.

I turned left, then right, and then went straight. I passed the senior citizens home across the street from what used to be the Capper Projects. There was the KFC/Pizza Hut that had once served only chicken. There was the Navy Yard and the long brick barricade that hid most of it from public view. There was the narrow tower called the Environmental Protection Agency, and the Waterside Towers that still marked the line between two very different worlds. Sala and the Old Man's house looked the same. But I couldn't look at it for too long.

And finally there was the park, a block-long stretch of stone and grass where the Waterfront had officially begun on another Christmas morning, when we sang to the crowd of parents and friends who had gathered in the freezing cold just to hear us.

It had been my idea, cooked up after I saw a team of Boy Scouts butchering Christmas carols in front of the HUD building a day or two earlier.

"If we can rock it here, we can rock it anywhere," I'd proposed. Stevie had seconded my motion, and the four of us had gone to the phones.

A week later a concrete bench was our stage as the thirty-degree hawk wind sliced our padded layers to shreds. But I'd been right. The people, our people in blood and spirit, came and heard. Faces and hands turned red and then blue. But they'd all stayed until we were done.

I shook off the memory. Those years, that group, that life, were as far behind me as the old house and that crabapple tree. I had to stop reaching back. I also had an appointment to make.

"I still don't remember you," a ten-year-old Dante complained, scrutinizing my face while he picked at his food. He had his father's eyes and lips, Bebe's nose, and a head that couldn't have been anything but a Turner's.

"That's because you were a baby the last time I saw you," I replied while chewing the best steak I'd had in more than a decade. And that was all of an answer a ten-year-old needed.

"Oh, okay," he said, pushing the oval frames up on his nose before returning to his meal.

I'd been at Malcolm's for a little over an hour. They had welcomed me into their lovely home on the other side of the park. It was a three-bedroom off 38th Street that had been damaged by an electrical fire. Malcolm bought it for forty grand in an auction and took out a loan to redo it from scratch. From the Sheetrock, to the windows, to the red-brick fireplace, it had all been remade to suit the new lord and lady.

"So how've you been feeling?" Bebe asked from the kitchen as she sprayed cleaner onto the stovetop.

"I'm finished, Ma," Dante said as he brought his plate in to his mother. She kissed the boy on the cheek and he headed for his own upstairs heaven, stopping only to hug his father on the way.

"Nice to meet you, Uncle Benjamin," he yelled when he was halfway up the stairs. Uncle Benjamin. I liked the sound of that.

"So I hear you're makin' a run tonight?" Bebe posed from the kitchen. I looked at Malcolm, but he was more focused on cleaning the plate before him.

"Yeah, girl," I replied. "We rollin' out. But I promise I'll bring your man back in one piece."

She twisted around to grin at me. Her behind was as round as I'd remembered it.

"Oh, I ain't worried about that," she said as she walked back into the dining area and eased onto her husband's lap. The arm that wasn't stabbing at steamed kale wrapped around her in a concrete grip.

"My boy's come out of plenty worse than what y'all got ahead of you. Ain't that right, baby?"

If you took away ten pounds, it would've been 1992 again, back when I'd see them walking around the neighborhood arm in arm. I'd watched the way they held each other, kissing as if it were their only way to breathe.

"Then we need to get rollin'," I said, feeling a burst of emotion I would rather have avoided. "But let me piss first."

I scaled the stairwell and closed the john door behind me. I dropped the cover on the seat and removed the photos of my two little ladies. I took in every feature, as I had countless times before. Tears fell from my eyelids, salty drops that stained the hands that held them.

I didn't know where they were or what shape they were in. They could've been sitting in a morgue off some interstate, burned to a crisp in some freak accident. They could've been starving and bleeding to death in some basement, with the Old Man dangling food and water just beyond their reach. All I knew was a house on the bay and a goddamned hardware store in the middle of Quaker land.

It wasn't anywhere close to being enough. But it was all I had to work with.

"So what's the deal?" I'd asked Malcolm, just out the front door.

"We gotta pick up the Crew."

The Crew was waiting at a bar called Below over by the bridge. I remembered when the place had a pink exterior and advertised an all-male revue. Things had obviously changed.

"Nah, they ran them up out of there," Malcolm informed me. "Cop raid or somethin'. Now it's a little lounge or whatever."

"So who are these dudes, anyway?" I asked as we pulled into a parking space behind the place.

The closest streetlight flickered as we got onto the street. I tensed at the sight of the moving shadows before us and the entrance littered with people, more men than women. A few seemed familiar, but not enough for anything more than a nod.

"Everybody's got friends like these," Malcolm said. "The kinda dudes you don't always wanna be around, but you know'll be around you when you need 'em, especially when you're offering a cut of the money."

"Of what money?" I asked as we went through the open entrance door.

"Dope on the table is money in the bank for these niggas," he said as we traveled the narrow corridor that separated outside from in. "And even if it ain't dope, they'll find somethin' up there to make it worth their while."

We entered Below unfrisked and unchallenged. A guy that could have been Morris Day's little brother was manning the bar, sporting a conked-out perm combed to the right and a red satin shirt unbuttoned down to his rib cage. The decor was all mirrors and red velvet. Morris's ringed fingers poured drinks double time.

"Whassup, Randy?" Malcolm said in greeting.

"Whassup with you?" he hollered back.

Malcolm grinned, shrugged his shoulders, and kept it moving. There was a little stress when I bumped shoulders with a light-skinned dread with a hooked nose. But it didn't last. I did notice the sawn-off pool cue poking out of his jeans. Someone stood a good chance of catching a bad one. I was glad it wasn't me.

There weren't too many women in sight, outside of a

pair of two-hundred-pound dykes in doo-rags and baseball jerseys. Perhaps the guys in the Crew went the other way, though it didn't make a difference to me.

Malcolm's men were crowded into one of the leather booths at the back of the place, right next to the doorless bathroom. After the first whiff I decided to breathe through my mouth.

On sight I could tell that they'd all done time. One had a cell block number tattooed on his neck and a V-shaped chunk missing from his left ear. This was Raymond. The short and bald block of muscle in the middle was Terry. And the third and lankiest of the three was Marvin, a dark-skinned kid with thick eyebrows, a huge nappy Afro, and his right forearm in a cast.

Greetings were exchanged. Fingers locked with friendly hands before being pulled away in a snapping motion. Marvin remembered me from the neighborhood. Raymond wanted to know who was driving, and Terry only cared about how much money they had in that Dutch country hardware store. I didn't say much. They were Malcolm's boys, so I let him do the talking all the way there.

We left our cars at Below and walked a few blocks to a black Villager parked at the corner of 3rd and H. Terry took the wheel. Malcolm was at shotgun, and the rest of us slouched along the two rows of seats in the rear. Raymond had removed a nylon duffel from the trunk of his 1989 Thunderbird before we left. I could only assume what was inside. But then again, assumption had made the ass of me not long before.

The ride seemed twice as long the second time around. Terry took Route 1 to reduce the chance of cop problems. Everyone else knew one another, except for me.

I just looked out the window at the road, at the yellow and white paint running beneath our wheels, as I'd done on that bus to prison, the last time I'd sung, the last moments the old me had drawn breath. But that had been bright and early in the day. This was the deepest night. And in the night anything could happen. Anything.

"Hell, yeah, the city done changed," Marvin said a quarter of the way toward our destination. "White people all over the place, buyin' up everything. All the rich black niggas is going to the club snortin' H just 'cause they can. Mayor sittin' around lettin' it happen."

"But that shit ain't all his fault," Raymond started in. His lion's growl overpowered all others present. "I mean, you gotta look at what Williams had to work with, just like Kelly. All that time Barry was in office he was fuckin' shit up, all that corruption, makin' jobs for people just so they could stay quiet. He wasn't thinking about keepin' all the people here that was movin' out to PG County. He wasn't thinkin' about startin' up initiatives for black people to get their own houses. All he was thinkin' about was smokin' rock and fuckin' models."

Even I had to laugh at that, because there was nothing else to do. We all remembered that infamous tape, that embarrassing exhibit A of our balding, skirt-chasing commander in chief "beaming up Scotty" in a downtown hotel room. It was the most humiliating thing imaginable for a black man in public office. And it had gone down in our city, in Chocolate City.

And at the time no one had wanted to believe it, even when it was right in front of their eyes. Even my father, a man of logic and levelheadedness, sported a T-shirt on his off days that read: THE BITCH SET HIM UP.

———

"If you're horny, let's do it, r-i-i-de it, my pony," Maurice sang along with his favorite single of all time. His hips and legs simulated the grind Ginuwine had performed in the song's music video. He snorted the last line of blow from Halle Berry's breasts, or at least the glossy image of them on the magazine cover in his lap. Then he shifted into drive and pulled off the shoulder.

As usual, there was nothing on either side of the paved travelway, just the tall silhouettes of trees older than the state they grew in. But it was his domain. He was the fucking man now, or at least until the Old Man returned. So he had to take care of business, meaning he had to pick up a package from the supplier, which meant a long trek to Lewisburg and back in the dead of night.

Maurice missed D.C.: those amber white lights on the sides of the Sousa Bridge, the apple martinis at DC LIVE and Jasper's, and his ex-girl Tamay, the one he swore had the prettiest pair of chocolate titties in the world. But he had been a nobody there. Even with what happened at Sally Helen's. Even when he was managing some of the Old Man's properties, he was just another nigga with a nine-to-five. But up there in Lancaster he was a thug, a dangerous man, the underboss of the only crew making real paper in powder. And now the whole operation was his, to do with as he pleased.

He turned onto a narrow dirt road and flipped on his high beams for the rough terrain. The Civic buckled and bounced over the uneven earth, its twenty-inch rims making the ride even rougher. And then he saw it up ahead.

It was a utility shed about two hundred yards out from Provenzano's farm, a little weekend hideaway he'd bought for the family with the spoils from his war with the DEA. It was he who had come to the Old Man with the idea of moving weight for him. Provenzano knew that Alfonse Mitchell didn't really need the money, just the thrill, that warm endorphin rush that pumped through him whenever he got away with doing something dirty.

The Old Man played it all like chess, accepting casualties when and where they came. Sometimes they were painful and often crippling. But they meant nothing in the face of true power. Maurice had learned these things in his seven years in Mitchell's shadow. And now it was time for him to show and prove, as this was the first time he'd be making the exchange himself.

The shed was rented by a dummy third party, just in case the sheriff got antsy and ever decided to ask any questions. But that would only happen if their monthly envelope stopped being enough. And it was always enough. After all, what the fuck were they going to spend their money on out in the middle of this muck, anyway?

He left the engine running outside the shed as he got out to turn the combination lock right, left, and then right again to get the doors open. Inside sat a champagne-colored 626, with its rear facing him. He walked over to the car and checked the trunk. The package was there. He was happy.

He removed the Mazda key from his pocket, got inside his new vehicle, and backed it out. Then he drove the Civic in to take its place, halting only to remove his Ginuwine CD from the changer. The trunk of the Honda held Provenzano's payday. Maurice locked the doors behind him and shifted into drive. The switch was always easy. The make-up back at the store, however, was going to take all night. But at least there would be *plenty* of people to help him.

A whole day passed before Salamanca woke again. Her child wore a different shirt and pants, a stack of coloring books and what appeared to be a tiny portable TV cradled inches away from her diaphragm. She slept peacefully, her body recharging after a long day of life without a mother to guide her, something Sala swore she'd never let happen again.

"Sasha," she called in a whisper. But the child did not stir. Someone else, however, did.

A tall blonde of thirty entered mother and daughter's space. Seeing that she was awake, she walked over and cued the light switch beyond Sala's head.

"How are you doing, Ms. Baker?" she inquired. Sala just stared at her, almost forgetting her legal name change.

"Where am I?" she asked as she began to feel a dull pain at the front of her skull.

"You were in an accident," she replied, her ocean blue eyes radiating condescension wherever they looked.

"I asked *where*, not *why*," Sala replied.

"Oh, you're in Prince George's Hospital Center. You have a concussion and a few minor—"

"Honey, I didn't ask for a diagnosis," Sala replied as she put her feet to the floor. They felt steadier this time. "I just need to know where my car is."

Chrissy Snow froze in her tracks, as if the patient were asking too much of her all at once.

"Well . . . I don't know. I just work the night shift. But if you were in an accident, I don't know if your car would even be drivable."

"You know, that's the smartest thing you've said since you came in here," Sala said, chuckling as she moved to her feet. "Just give me three Excedrin and check me out of here."

"I'm sorry, Ms. Baker, but you're in no shape to be released just yet."

"I'll take my chances."

"Any release requires approval from the chief resident, and he won't be back until—"

"Fine," Salamanca said with a huff. "Then I'll wait until he gets here. Just make sure that he knows I'm ready to leave."

"I'll tell him you want to be processed first thing in the morning," she said.

"You do that," Sala replied. Chrissy backed through the doorway and closed the swinging wood quietly behind her.

Salamanca had no intention of waiting until morning. She reached over the bed for the phone on the other side, picked it up, and dialed the only number that mattered.

She'd committed it to memory long before. And as it rang she waited for her dream of all dreams to come true. And she was close. But there was no cigar.

"Baby?" a groggy voice inquired. It had Ben's bass, but not enough of it. Henry.

"No, Henry. It's Sala. Is Ben there?"

"Sala?!" the boy said, awakening instantly. "Ben hoped you were gonna call."

"Yeah, it's me. But I really need to talk to him."

"Damn, he left a couple of hours ago. He and Malcolm went to find you. When you didn't show up, he thought your dad might have—"

"Oh, Jesus," she said. "No, I was in a car accident."

"Are you all right?" he asked with genuine concern.

"Did he tell you exactly where they were going?"

"Nah, but I know it's out of state. They found Maurice out at some beach house on the bay your father owned and followed up somewhere else. He didn't tell me exactly where, though. And he didn't give me Malcolm's cell number. He said he wanted you to come here and wait for him."

"I'd be glad to if my car wasn't wrecked," she said, thinking of her man and what he was walking into.

She thought of the beach house he'd mentioned. Could it have been the one she'd spent her summers in before high school? Could there be that much coincidence in the world at one in the morning? Did she still know the way? If so, perhaps there was still time to head off impending doom.

She looked over at Sala, her sleeping ray of light, and knew that it was too dangerous a run to make with just the two of them. Someone would have to keep her little girl safe. And there was only one candidate.

"Do you need a ride?" he asked. "I can get my mom's car."

"Yeah," she said. "I'm at PG Hospital Center. But I also need a favor."

"Anything for my sister-in-law," he said earnestly.

"Well, we're gonna need to make a stop or two on the way to your house."

"No problem. Where you gotta go?"

"I'll tell you when you get here. I'll be at the corner in twenty minutes."

"I'm on my way," he said, hanging up the phone and leaving Sala to the hum of her hospital room.

She found her clothes and bags in the closet against the far wall. All her cash was still there. After she was dressed, she finally woke the girl. They crept down the hallway, made two turns, and were soon in the elevator toward the street, two women on their way to the only man who mattered.

6.

Terry parked us behind a trash Dumpster against the
outer edge of the strip mall. It
was three a.m., and the
Pennsylvania air was cooler
than we'd expected. In
summer clothes we all
struggled to keep warm.

"It shouldn't be taking him
this fuckin' long," Malcolm
grumbled, referring to Terry,
who'd been itching to use the
reconnaissance skills he'd
learned in the army. So we'd
sent him down toward the store
via the woods on the opposite
side of the road. It had been
twenty minutes and there was
still no sign of the man, until he
materialized right behind us
without a sound.

"Hey," he said. I jumped a little, startled, while the others just turned in his direction. But then again, none of them had anything to lose.

"So what's it lookin' like?" Malcolm asked.

"Ain't shit out of the ordinary," Terry said. "Two cars in the back. A green Escalade and a Corolla. There's only one way in from the back. Metal stairs two stories high and one metal door without a handle."

"No handle?" I asked.

"Saves the trouble of leaving a lock for somebody to pick," Raymond said.

"You gotta respect it," Marvin added.

"Then that means we gotta go in through the front," I said. "And you know they got an alarm."

"Yeah, it's risky. Set off the alarm and the cops get in the mix," Malcolm noted. "But then again if they think it's the cops, they might run out the back and right into us."

"Yeah, but remember. This ain't a hit," I reminded them. "We're tryin' to find out information."

"Then why don't you try and knock on that fuckin' door and ask 'em?" Terry challenged. "From what I hear, they'll be pretty happy to see your ass, now, won't they?"

"You got a problem, nigga?" I challenged.

Terry grinned. "If I did, it'd already be on the ground."

I took a step forward, but Malcolm stopped me.

"Why don't we save it for the niggas in there who might try and shoot at us?"

Terry nodded. I just stepped back and kept my eyes on him.

"So what's it gonna be?" Raymond asked. "The front or the back?"

"Why don't we do both?" Marvin proposed.

"Yeah," Raymond said. "That's what I was thinking, too. Three through the front. Another two on that door."

"I can live with that," Malcolm said, turning to me. "What about you?"

I still wasn't clear on what exactly our plan was. We could storm the place all we wanted. But if the forward three ran into trouble, the other two wouldn't be able to do a thing about it. And if the two at the rear got the heat, it'd be the same thing. But then I thought of something that no one else had.

"Wait a minute," I said. "I've got a better idea. But first we need to get suited up."

"We already got our vests," Terry said for the others.

"Then it's time for me and my man to get ours," Malcolm said with a smile.

He opened the back of the van to reveal a few tools of the trade. Raymond popped a clip into a black Sig 2226. Marvin had a black Desert Eagle fitted with a custom-made stock for his uninjured forearm. Terry reached into the side of the van storage area and pulled out a nylon case that held a pump-action twelve-gauge, some shells, and an ammo belt, which he clipped around him before tossing the wrapping back into the trunk.

"Here," Malcolm said, offering me the butt of a .45 identical to the one in his other hand. I froze.

The last time I'd carried one had been the day of my death, that fated Saturday when the Old Man had sent the cops to bring my life as I had known it to an end. The little bullshit .25 Bebe had strapped me with was enough to add two years to my sentence. And here I was, barely a week out of jail, and Malcolm wanted me to pick one up again. Fuck that. I'd take my chances.

"Nah," I said, waving the gun off. Malcolm only nodded and tucked the piece back in the van before he handed me a Kevlar vest, which I gladly accepted.

"Nigga, is you crazy?" Terry demanded. "You ain't gon' strap?"

"I just got out," I said.

"Ain't a motherfucka here that ain't on parole or probation. What you gonna do if they start bustin' in there?"

The others muttered similar complaints. But as great men had said long before me, the only weapon one needed was one's mind. And my mind had just assembled the best plan it could possibly come up with.

"I'm goin' in last," I said. "Somebody has to set off the diversion." They all glared at me at once.

"What diversion?" Marvin asked.

"The one I'm about to tell y'all about," I replied.

Twenty minutes later they were all positioned as instructed. Terry was right next to the rear door with the pump-action. Raymond was posted low behind him at the first landing of the staircase. Marvin was on the ground, with a clean shot at the door from the parking lot. And Malcolm was with me, crouched low on the right side of the 2002 Cadillac Escalade.

One of the funniest stories I'd ever read on the inside was about some silly dude up in New York that had blown up a jeep to get some attention from some rapper that beat his ass over some article he wrote. It was the silliest thing I'd ever heard of, some kid with a college degree that didn't have the good sense to cover up and take his beating.

This particular guy had felt as if he'd had something to

prove. But by the end of the book, the only thing he proved to me was how fuckin' stupid he was. Or maybe he hadn't been that stupid, because I had remembered the story. And it had given me the idea to pop the lock on the Caddie's gas tank, stuff a rag in, and, when the time came, blow it sky-high and bring all the people inside to the outside.

"I wish we had some radios or somethin'," Malcolm said.

"Yeah, but we don't," I replied. "Somebody's gonna be salty about their jeep, though."

"As long as it ain't yours or mine, I don't give a fuck," he said. "And neither should you. This is a good-ass plan."

I gave Raymond and the others the signal for them to cover their eyes and ears as best they could. Malcolm gave the rag a light, and the two of us retreated to the corner of the building as the blast shredded the truck into a billion flaming pieces. The door came open three seconds later. Five minutes later we were all inside, rather surprised at what there was to see.

"Who the fuck are y'all, anyway?" the little punk from our last visit demanded as Raymond put the gun barrel to his skull. Armed with a MAC-10, he had been the only pro-tection for the Old Man's team of baggers, four scrawny white girls in Kmart bras and panties, all of whom we'd corraled into the room's rear office.

"Does it really matter when your life is on the line, player?" I asked. He quieted down as he looked up at me from the floor. His legs began to tremble. "Now where's the Old Man at?"

"He ain't here—" the kid started before Terry smacked

him across the mouth with the butt of his pistol. Blood and a fragment of tooth spilled onto the tiled floor.

"Where's the shit?" Terry demanded, having seen the cutting agents on the table at the rear of the room. "You got the make-up girls and all this mix, but no shit to make up."

"It ain't got here yet," the kid spat as Marvin bound his hands and feet. It was obvious that he was more afraid of us than them. Maybe the Old Man was getting soft. "Maurice got it."

"And where's Maurice?" Malcolm asked calmly.

"On his way back here. He just called like twenty minutes ago. Said he was on his way."

"What's your name, anyway?" I asked.

He hesitated, obviously trying to make something up. "Uh . . . Luke," he said.

"Luke what? Skywalker?" I joked. "Where's the Old Man?"

"I told you, he ain't here."

"Then where is he?" Raymond demanded, pushing the boy's skull with his gun barrel. His hesitation said we were getting closer to what we came for.

"He in the hospital," he finally confessed.

"The hospital?" I asked.

"Yeah, man, the hospital. I don't know which one. But he fell out in here like just the other day."

"How long's he been there?"

Luke had to think about it. And Raymond didn't like that. So he jabbed him in the gut hard enough to make him double over.

"Since Monday," he whimpered from the floor. "Look, man, the stash is back in the office. I don't wanna die. Please don't kill me."

The Crew headed for the office while I leaned in closer, thinking of what to ask next. But I drew a blank. So I decided to head into the rear office, where we had the girls tied up.

When Malcolm and I got there, the three men were tossing the place like pros: papers flying everywhere, cracks and crevices checked for contraband. All with the girls on the floor in the midst of them, their eyes welling with tears.

I stood on the edge of the room, taking it all in. This whole storming into the drug lab thing wasn't my cup of tea. Sure, I'd been apprentice to a thief. But now we were blowing things up, smacking people around, and putting guns in their faces. This shit was worse than the music business.

I scanned the walls and floor for clues the others might not have noticed. But it was mostly flotsam and jetsam: shipping receipts and invoice orders. Just like the old office at Sally Helen's. Just like the old burglary scam. A foolproof front with the big score in the back. From fencing to powder in less than a decade. The Old Man was something else.

There was a glint of silver beneath an accordion file. Raymond yelled something, but I was more focused on the item on the floor. I moved the wrinkled box away, reaching just beyond the creamy leg of one of our captives. And I found what I was looking for.

Salamanca looked like she was ten or eleven. Her hair was braided into a thousand sections as she smiled for the camera in a lavender Easter dress, a wooden basket filled with candy in one hand and a church purse in the other. This was the Old Man's little girl, immortalized in the way he always wanted her to be.

I looked around for other mementos, but that was it. One picture in one frame covered in the debris of a heist interrupted. All the effort and stealth and pyrotechnics, and all I had was an old picture to show for it.

We'd had it all wrong. Or at least it seemed as if we did. If the Old Man had been in the hospital, then where were Sala and Sasha? Maurice had apparently gone to pick up product. So they probably weren't with him, either. But he had to know something. He was the only person who could've grabbed her. But asking him meant waiting for him to get there. And since we'd just blown up a car for the entire state to hear, time was something we didn't have.

We locked the white girls in the back room. Raymond had found over a hundred grand stacked in perfect rows in the Old Man's bottom desk drawer. I let Malcolm and the others split it among them. They'd earned it. And I had money of my own. Plenty of money, but no answers.

I cracked the back door and looked out at the flaming wreck of an automobile. Burning shrapnel had started a small fire in the woods across the street. Someone had probably heard that explosion. And though no alarm had been triggered, I had a feeling folks would be coming soon to see about the commotion.

"It ain't safe to be just waitin' around," Terry said.

"Tell me something I don't know," I replied. "But this nigga Maurice is my only lead."

"You can catch that man another time," Marvin added. "Better that than some hick cops violatin' us back to the clink."

Just then I pictured the most horrible thing imaginable: my two babies without the light of life in their eyes, their corpses being covered by the fresh soil of some hit man's shovel. Or maybe the Old Man had checked himself out and done it on his own. I had taken my shot and missed. I hadn't saved them. I hadn't even found them. And now they wanted me to walk away from the only person who might be able to give me some answers.

"We won't get another chance. They'll see this shit we did here and make a run for it."

"Then what's it gonna be?" Malcolm asked, resting what could have been his choice on my shoulders. "You know I'm wit' you whether you stay or go." The others waited for me just as patiently, each over twenty-five grand richer.

I thought about it for another moment. I thought about beating Maurice's face in with my fists, about twisting every bone in him until it splintered and shattered. Then I saw my old cell, and the old prison yard, and the days that passed like months. Even a life alone was better than one on the inside.

"Let's roll out," I said. The boys gathered their weapons and their cuts of the cash and we all went out the back door toward the van at the other end of the lot. The flaming wreck was still burning bright. Terry was about to say something when we saw the headlights approaching.

"You got a lotta nuts, Ben," Terry said. That was when the shots rang out.

The best thing about living in the sticks was that you could see everything coming. Maurice had seen the light from the mall nearly two hundred yards out, when he'd pulled over to do a few more lines on the shoulder of the straightaway. He snorted first and then saw the trouble up ahead.

Something was off, and this wasn't the night for anything to go wrong, particularly when there were twenty pounds of weight in the trunk and enough cut stashed in the office to supply their clientele for the next few months. The girls were in position, stripped down to their drawers so there'd be no stealing and a galvanized focus on getting the job done so the niggers in there could stop staring at their flabby white asses.

And now there was this weird orange light up by the mall. Maurice wasn't having it. He unholstered the Glock 9 in the small of his back and popped off the safety. There weren't going to be any problems on his watch.

It took less than a minute for him to see his flaming wreck of an Escalade, the one he'd just had fitted with a DVD player and a stash box in the front dash. Then he saw the five men casually exiting his domain. And none of their profiles looked the least bit familiar.

Of course, he wasn't thinking clearly. The coke had made sure of that. So he proceeded to do what he never would've done if the Old Man were there. He opened fire through the open window, right there out in the clear, his wrist aching with every slug the pistol discharged. Then he hanged a U to get a look at his quarry, only to see that three of them were still standing. And they were all pointing things that looked a lot like guns right at him.

The slugs were red darts screaming through the darkness. The first made a crackling sound as it exploded into my chest. The second hit Malcolm in the arm as I went to black for a few seconds. Deafening gunfire was everywhere. Someone had transformed a quiet country road into the hottest block around the way. There was the screeching of tires, and then Marvin's voice yelled, "Shit!"

When I came to fully, Terry was checking my vest. "Like I said, you got nuts," he said, showing me how the bullet had landed dead center with my breastbone. Malcolm had torn off the bottom of his shirt to use as tourniquet for the wound through his bicep. And Marvin had apparently taken one in the leg.

"Nigga was movin' too fast," Raymond said. "I barely had a shot off before he was outta there."

"Then I guess that was Maurice," I said as the others helped me up. "He had the drop and he took it."

"You can say that shit again," Marvin said. "I ain't been hit since I was like eighteen."

"I ain't been hit since now," I said. I looked over at Malcolm, and he didn't look good. His whole body was trembling, and blood was spilling from the wound.

"I gotta get to a doctor," he said to me more than the others. "But I know if you let him get too far away—"

"I know," I said, thinking of Bebe and my promise, and then of Sala and Sasha and that other promise. I looked back into the lot at the parked Corolla. The side of it was slightly scorched from the explosion, but it looked drivable. I also saw that we'd left the rear door to the office wide open.

"Y'all get him to a hospital. I'ma take that car over there and try to catch up with Maurice."

Malcolm staggered, and Terry caught him. "Let me know what happened," Malcolm said as Terry started him toward the van.

"Take this," Raymond said, offering me his pistol. "You on your own now."

Remembering the incident at hand, and the pain in my chest and the wounded men hobbling back to the van without me, I knew he had a point.

"Thanks," I said as I took the gun and tracked away from them, back into the lot and up the stairs to the office, where I removed the car keys from Luke Skywalker's right pocket.

"I'll bring it back," I said. He muttered curses through the duct tape over his lips. I would've flipped him off, but I didn't have the time. There was only one chance left, and Maurice had a twenty-minute jump on me.

7.

Henry Baker wasn't sure of what to expect when he took 295 toward Cheverly. It was pushing one in the morning, and he was supposed to be at work in a matter of hours, the blessed $13-an-hour telemarketing job that was going to help him buy a car of his own. No more begging Mom for the keys. No more taking Sagrario all over the city on the Metro.

But in order to make it work, he couldn't miss a day in the nine-week cycle. And he'd have to jump at every chance for overtime there was. But it would be worth it, even if he only had enough to cop some twelve-year-old bucket with a bullshit sound system. Because it would be his.

But a car meant nothing when it came to a brother in need, the big brother he'd always worshipped and wanted to be like, even after he went to jail. Because Ben had always had this determination about him, this superhuman drive that was like something out of a comic book. Even as the smallest boy he could remember him seated in front of the family piano, playing his heart out for hours at a time, stroking the instrument as if it were his woman.

And the music Ben made always soothed the ears that heard it. It would lull his father to sleep on the leather couch in the family room. It calmed his mother's unebbing nervousness as she prepared reports and projections for the next day. Henry missed that music. And he prayed every night that his brother might change his mind about giving it all up. He might even settle for just one more song for his wedding day.

Salamanca had been the other half of Ben's beauty, the warm wind that enhances the sun on a perfect day. She always gave Henry a hug and a kiss on the cheek, pulling his head close to the most beautiful bosom he had known at ten years old.

Salamanca was everything he'd wanted for a girlfriend when the time came, everything he'd seen in Sagrario that first night they'd met beneath the blue light of that basement party up on the Gold Coast, dancing to Dru Hill's "Beauty." He had found his love that night and was willing to do whatever Ben needed to help him reunite with his own.

The hospital came into view a few moments later, and

he saw her standing at the curb. Her hair was gone, but he knew it was Sala. It was the curve in the calves that stretched out of her capri pants, the small hands with long fingers clasping the child next to her, her child, his niece. He'd almost forgotten that he was an uncle.

He pulled up to the curb and they got in. Sasha gave him an apathetic glance and then curled up on the back-seat, falling under the Sandman's spell before Henry could even say hello.

"Damn, you grew up," Salamanca said with a grin as she climbed in. "All tall and handsome."

Henry blushed as he turned his head toward the road and pulled off. "Thanks," he replied. "Where you need me to take you?"

"You need to get on Fifty to Annapolis," she said.

"Annapolis? At one in the morning?" he asked.

"Not Annapolis," she said. "We're going to the beach."

"What's at the beach?" he asked.

Salamanca hesitated for a moment. Her head still ached as she leaned it back against the cushion behind it.

"My father's house," she said.

All the points met in Henry's mind. But there were still a few holes. He had the impression that Ben and Malcolm were heading farther away than the beach. If Salamanca was going to this house to find them, then she was waaay off track. And he'd be driving her way out of the way, particularly since he had work in the morning.

"I don't think that's where they went," he began. "They went there and they saw Maurice and they followed him somewhere else. I think they went wherever they followed him to."

She didn't want to tell Henry it was a shot in the dark or

that it flat out didn't make sense. If Ben was somewhere else, she was helpless. If he was at that house, if anybody was at that house, she'd at least have something to do. She couldn't stand any more waiting, no matter what the reason.

It even took her a moment to realize that they hadn't begun to move. Henry was holding the pause button on her destiny. She couldn't tell him what she might have to do out there at that house. Maybe that was because she hadn't fully thought it out yet. She knew that her father was a murderer, and that he'd tried to kill his own grandchild, and that he would more than likely be gunning for Ben the minute he knew where he was.

And now Maurice had been mentioned, which further solidified her fears that things hadn't done too much changing since she'd left the neighborhood. Daddy's forces were still in position. And she felt that she was the only thing in the entire world that could stop them. She and Sasha were the only semblance of a future he had. So she had to see him, talk to him, give him the hugs he'd probably missed during all those years she'd been MIA.

And maybe, after all of that, after he learned that Ben had fathered his only grandchild, and that Ben didn't want revenge, and that they were going to get married and he was going to take care of Alfonse Mitchell's daughter, maybe he'd pull the plug on the beef, and Ben and Malcolm would have nothing to look for and no one to battle against. And then they would come back home. And Ben would come to her and Sasha, and it would all be right again. This was what she told herself, right before she told Henry what she needed for him to do.

"That's where I need to go," she reiterated. "And I need you to take me there."

Henry looked over at her and wondered how in the hell she could look so much the same after too much time. Then he wondered what might be waiting for them out on the shores of the Chesapeake. Then he stopped wondering and shifted the car into drive.

"What's it been like?" Henry asked as they drove. The Maryland sky was clear as a bell, its surface covered in a billion specks of light.

Salamanca twisted back to check on her little one, who was still in the ball-like position she'd assumed a half hour earlier.

"Hell," she replied to her brother-in-law-to-be. "Pure hell. Never felt safe. Never felt anything except when it came to her. That girl's the only light I've had for seven years, that and your brother's letters and calls and pictures. I don't think I could've lived through it without the both of them."

"Well, he can't wait to see you," Henry replied. "You're all he talks about."

She knew the way as if she were twelve again. She'd committed every twist and turn to memory, giving names to the biggest trees and the most elaborate houses. But she could mostly tell by the sound of the sea through the open windows and how it changed with the accents from various winds and echoes. But there were many turns in that labyrinth, too many dead ends to remember. Just because you'd been there once didn't mean you'd get there again just as easily.

But after a while they finally found it, the little cabin between two mansions bordered by that fence fitted for a fortress. The driveway, however, was empty, which meant she was going to have to wait.

"You might wanna close your eyes, Hen," she said.

"Why?" he asked.

"Because we might be here for a while."

There was no more blow in the packet by the time Maurice made it to Interstate 50, and his high was fading. Sure, he still had the product, but their whole setup had been compromised. The week's take was gone. His jeep was up in flames, and God only knew what they'd done to the girls.

He couldn't go back there now. Not with the Old Man or even with God Himself. The cops would clean it out. He was finished. So there was only one thing to do: exactly what he had done all those years before. He was going to run.

There was fifty grand in the emergency safe in the basement at the house. And there were clean guns all over that place. He'd drive the Mazda into Annapolis and hop the first Greyhound leaving the station. It would all blow over. Maybe the Old Man wouldn't be so mad at him. Maybe he saw the end coming anyway. But the first thing was get to the house, and then to the safe, and then out into the great wide world.

8.

"You're not that far off," Arnold, the hundred-year-old white man, proclaimed at the Exxon station. The place had been the first sign of life I'd seen in miles. I'd apparently missed my turn for Route 1. And with time ticking, I needed to find a faster path as quickly as possible. He wrote down three different interstate numbers with notes on turns and landmarks. I gave him a twenty for his gas and trouble and was on my way.

I was driving to break the sound barrier, believing that my midsize vehicle could splinter the time-space continuum and put me right in front of that cabin in

.4 seconds. Yet the trees stretched on forever, and there were hints in the gray sky that morning was closer than it had been. I followed Arnold's commands and found my way to 95 south in less than forty minutes, and Maryland soon after.

It was a long cruise to the Bay Bridge exit. But the radio helped to pass the time. Nelly was apparently feeling the same heat that I was.

And that was when I saw it. It was just a flash, but I saw it plain as day: a small, fair-skinned hand with long, elegant fingers lying flat on a chocolate carpet, a gun just beyond its reach as the fingers twitched helplessly. I saw it as if I were standing right before the scene. And I knew whose hand it was.

I skinned the rear tires turning onto the Bay Bridge exit. And then I prayed.

The Old Man had gotten rid of the jungle gym he'd built for her at the rear. And he'd had the windows changed to the eerie black tints even her eyes couldn't penetrate. She'd loved that place. When she and her daddy had come there, she'd truly believed that he'd bought them their own ocean.

Sometimes she'd played with the dead jellyfish that washed up against the shore. Other times she'd built elaborate sand castles. And others she'd just lie out on the shoreline, reading a book like the old white ladies she'd see resting yards away, never really speaking to her, as they hoped that she and her father would always remain on their side of the property line.

But then she remembered something she hadn't thought about since it happened. As an only child, she often felt obligated to play games to keep herself entertained. And her favorite had been hiding things to see if her father would ever find them. Sometimes it was his sunglasses or the last bottle of the liquor he liked.

She'd only move them slightly, a few feet, or maybe to the adjacent room. And they were usually bigger things that weren't hard to see. But once she'd been a little more daring. Once, at ten, she'd taken the spare house keys from the rack in the kitchen and hidden them in the sand beneath the rear porch of the house.

But he'd never looked for them. He'd never even seen that they were missing. Maybe it was because he'd kept his original set close. Or maybe he'd just gotten tired of playing his daughter's nerve-racking games. But he'd never gone to get them. And neither had she. So what if they were still there?

Henry and Sala were fast asleep when Salamanca closed the door behind her and trekked up the driveway toward the rear of the house. A neighboring Doberman watched her without a sound, respecting her need for stealth on the most important night of her life.

The rear porch seemed the same in the moonlight, though the wood had gone brittle from exposure to the ocean air. She ducked under the wood structure, to the right rear column, and dug for treasure in the earth just beyond the sand. The two keys were still less than half an inch beneath the surface. They were rusty and gritty, but they might still work if the same locks were in place.

She scaled the steps to the porch and tried them out on the bottom lock. And once again, they actually worked. She was in, though she wasn't exactly sure of what she was going to do inside.

She flipped a switch to reveal a stove and counters un-used, a fridge filled with every kind of takeout imaginable, a half-killed bottle of Rémy Martin, and a six-pack of berry Alizé. These were not her father's, for she knew that he never took his liquor cold. Nor did he ever eat a thing that wasn't served on porcelain plates.

The living room was a little more familiar, mostly be-cause it was made up of things she already knew. The same credenza and shelves, the same pictures of her in frames all over, each gleaming in the light from the lamps she'd turned on. There were the same couch and chairs, along with a new flat-screen TV against an otherwise blank wall, a home theater system beneath it. Nothing out of the ordinary. Nothing she hadn't expected.

But when she took a look at the glass table in front of the sofa, there was something: the disassembled baby Glock 9 mm and the full clip that went with it. It was just sitting there, in plain view for any neighbor, any cop, or any bullshit home security guard with a flashlight to see.

Salamanca had never seen her father go near a gun. But that didn't mean he didn't know how to handle one. And she still had her fetish for weapons, though she had not been this close to one since target practice with Tahir all those years ago.

She picked up the two pieces and made them into one, folding her fingers into a fist around its handle. She liked the way the grip eased into the space between each finger. The trigger was hard, restrained by the all-important safety. She popped in a clip and cocked it, placing bullets in the chamber. She'd keep it in her hand, sit that hand on her lap, and wait.

What a sight it would be for a father after so many

years. His little girl with his gun, waiting for him after another long day of doing dirt. She saw the stairway leading to the upper level but decided not to explore it. She liked where she was. She liked the feel of the cushion beneath her ass. And she liked the view she had of the door. There was no way that he could get away from her.

She had come here to talk, but she somehow knew that talking would not be enough. Her mother had probably tried talking. And look what had happened to her. Ben had stayed his hand and look what had happened to him. Now it was down to her and him. And that was just the way she wanted it.

And just then, as if on cue, she heard a car pulling into the driveway.

Maurice saw the light on inside as he parked. And he knew he hadn't left it on. He never left the lights on. And it wasn't the Old Man, because his car wasn't in the driveway. No one else knew about the place. And with all that had happened up in Lancaster, he had no plans to take chances. He lifted his gun from beneath the seat and approached the house carefully.

Salamanca wanted to smack herself for not killing the lights again. But as she gripped the gun, she was more concerned with the look she'd find on the Old Man's face when that door swung open. It would be so sweet.

Maurice tried the door and found that it was still locked. So he inserted his key and opened it, a little less tense. Maybe he had left the light on. But as he was pushing at the door, there was the honk of a horn behind him. And since no one honked horns out there at that time of night, it startled him, and he almost dropped his piece as the door came open, catching it in midair before it fell.

Henry, who had just come awake in the car, had meant that horn blast as a warning to Sala, who he knew had gone inside. But as he saw, he might've been too late.

"What was that?" Sasha asked sleepily from the backseat.

"Nothing," Henry said to shut her up. Even from where he was, he could see there was something in the man's hand. But he wasn't sure of what it was until two moments later.

Maurice didn't see Salamanca on the couch. He saw what looked like a short-haired man with a gun. Salamanca saw Maurice instead of her father, armed with a gun he'd just gotten full control of. This was all wrong. But it was too late to do anything about it. So she removed the safety and raised her gun, as Maurice did with his own piece.

Maurice knew it was his gun the guy was holding, the one he'd been keeping in the Civic while he drove it around before the exchange. Why the fuck had he left it on the table like that instead of putting it in the safe upstairs with the money and the rest of his little arsenal? Hindsight was the twenty-twenty you hated having.

Henry heard four shots and assumed the worst.

I made about twenty wrong turns once I got into the subdivision. After all, it was dark and I had been there only once, and even that had been when Malcolm was driving. But I'd used a garden of tulips as one landmark and a rusting 1964 Mustang as another. And the next thing I knew, I was looking at the champagne-colored 626 that had been the scourge of my night. I screeched the Corolla to a halt. There were lights on in the house. And the door was wide open.

Neighboring homes were burning bright: silhouettes peering through curtains at the Old Man's residence. I kept my weapon at my back as I started toward the house, hoping not to arouse any more suspicion.

"Ben!" Henry's voice yelled. I turned to see that he was in the driver's seat of my mother's car. And there was someone in the backseat. I didn't know what he was doing there. And I was too rattled to make all the connections.

My only focus was that twitching hand on the chocolate carpet and on Maurice and Malcolm and the seven years I'd done on the inside. So I made a dash for that open door and moved toward the light, each step bringing me closer and closer to some kind of resolution.

I crossed the threshold to find Maurice on the floor before me, a bloody hand to his gut as he lay facedown on the carpet, his breathing desperate and shallow. And then I saw the woman I'd come for, her hair cut as close as it had been in my dreams. She was still beautiful, even when she was on the chocolate carpet slumped against the tacky-ass couch I'd told the Old Man to toss nearly seven years before. There was a bullet wound between her clavicle and shoulder. And it was leaking blood all over the rest of her. The gun was just as I'd seen it, right beyond her twitching left hand. It took all her strength to look up at me. And out of all the things to do in the world, she grinned.

"Damn, baby," she said in semidelirium. "You got big."

I rushed over to her and took her in my arms, putting as much pressure on the wound as I could, though I should have been watching my back.

"This shit really hurts," she growled. Two fingers to her neck and I could feel her fading away.

"I know," I whispered. "But you gotta stay with me. We're gonna get you outta—"

The bullet broke a rib as it entered my side and came out the other way. My body screamed without making a sound. I stumbled to the floor, falling directly into Sala's lap. I couldn't reach the gun at my back in time. But hers was another story.

Maurice tried to stand as he kept pulling the trigger on his pistol, not realizing that he'd just hit me with his last shot. The wound was fire spreading outward. My nerves twitched. My vision blurred. But I had enough left to finish what Sala had started.

His head popped back as if it were on a spring as the bullet pierced the side of his skull. He was dead before he hit the ground. Then Henry came through the doorway with my little girl in tow. The six-year-old had to take it all in so fast: the guns and their loud bangs, all the blood, and seeing her mommy and daddy together for the first time in her life, just before they were about to die. Her perfect face rained tears in every direction, its color flushing from chestnut to cherry in a matter of seconds.

Sala's eyes were closed, and mine were on the way. Henry was frozen with fear. And Maurice was no longer anything at all.

Here we were, all the key pieces on the Old Man's board. And he wasn't even around to see us checkmate one another. Seven years of dreams, and it had ended like the climax of some bad hood movie. God must not have loved me. Because He kept killing me.

But as I died for a second time, I felt something different. In the void behind my eyes I heard a sound, a single tone playing sharp and clear. Then it was followed by another, and then another still. A melody. There was music inside me again, the most beautiful piano I'd ever heard, even after the sirens drowned it out, and even after I lost track of Sala's heartbeat and my own. The Old Man had made his play and come out the winner of all winners.

9.

"He's right in there," said the woman in white. The door was open and I could see him from the hallway. Yet I hesitated. All those years on the inside I'd crafted the perfect speech for him, a definitive address that was supposed to prove that I was stronger than he'd ever expected me to be.

A week in the hospital and four days of talking to the cops. Me, Sala, and our attorney screamed self-defense, but they were itching to hang something on me, especially as I had Raymond's gun and no permit. It was a two- to five-year rap that I was about to take, until I happened to mention what I'd seen in the Old Man's hardware store the night before. My words explained the brick of heroin in the trunk of a car owned by one of the Old Man's companies.

It was poetic justice that I signed an affidavit fingering Alfonse Mitchell as the head of a drug ring and that ratting him out made me a free man. What went around came back around.

I entered the room for the biggest déjà vu of my young life, my torso sore from two gunshots in the same night. He was lying there, a scrawny thing connected to all kinds of tubes for food and waste and to check his pulse. His eyes were on the tiny television before him. Judge Mathis presided over the day's case.

I cleared my throat, and his head swiveled toward me. His eyes bulged and his nostrils flared, and he started to reach for the orange button to signal the nurse. But he stopped himself.

"I ain't mad at you for sendin' me to jail," I said. "Because I set myself up when I let you hook me in. I ain't mad at you for doin' what you did in the street. Because that's the way you get down.

"But you tried to kill my daughter. You punched my girl in the gut, and you tried to kill my child, probably just because it was mine. And I should snap your neck for that shit. But I'm not that man anymore. I still got my life and my health, and I got enough money to hold me for a long time. And I'm gonna live. No matter what you do, I'm still gonna live."

His eyes narrowed as he thought about my words and what they meant. He tried to prop himself up, but he didn't have the strength. It was the end of his road, and we both knew it. A single finger motioned me toward him. And I came. I even leaned over to make sure that I heard him.

"Fuck you, little nigga," he wheezed. I already had two bodies to answer for on Judgment Day. And I could've made it a third. But he wasn't worth it.

"Fuck you, too," I whispered, backing away.

But when I turned to leave, I saw that I wasn't alone anymore.

The Old Man couldn't believe what he saw as Ben left the room and Salamanca came toward him with the child that looked like the both of them. He knew who that little girl was, though he didn't want to believe it. His only daughter had cut off all her pretty "good" hair. Now she looked like a bald space child or some dyke with no makeup and big titties.

"Hi, Daddy," Sala began. "It took us a little while to get here. Cuz we had to clean up all that mess out at your house. But it's done with now."

The Pennsylvania and Maryland cops had been in and out all week, both informing him that they had enough to serve warrants and that he didn't have a chance of living another month outside of the hospital as a free man. And he'd told them to go fuck themselves, too. Because this was it, what was standing right before him. These two were all that he'd been holding on for. God had been more than good to him.

"I've spent seven whole years running from you. At first I ran because you hit me when I had your grandchild in my belly. And I ran because of what you did to Ben. And because you sent people after me. And because you might have sent some people after Ben in jail. But that was all shit I might've been able to forgive.

"But then I went to the house in Detroit. And I saw the way you left things. And it was like you left it that way because you wanted me to grow up and see what kind of a monster you were. You just packed up, rolled out, and fed me lies until I learned how to swallow them, even when I might've been old enough to understand it."

Sasha took backward steps until she was practically behind her mother, frightened by what she saw. But it wasn't the tubes or the liquid shit in the bag on the Old Man's hip. She was afraid because she'd seen the true face of Alfonse Mitchell, the one he'd kept hidden from the world for so long. Salamanca looked down and saw her daughter's fear but tugged her forward anyway.

"This is your grandfather, baby. Say hello."

"Hi," Sasha said nervously. "Nice to meet you." Salamanca smiled, so proud of her little one that it made her eyes water.

"This is what you tried to kill, Daddy. Isn't she beautiful?"

The Old Man didn't answer. But he did feel the trembling inside him, and he felt the piercing pressure against his tear ducts, the emotion coming forth from the stone that was his heart.

Salamanca saw the tears and let her own go as the little girl put her head to her mama's hip. Her speech wasn't coming out as bold and strong as she'd imagined. But she forced out the last of what she remembered as she, like her husband before her, turned away, pulling the child to follow with her.

"Good-bye, Daddy," she said. Her clogged feet clacked out of the room and around the bend, leaving Alfonse Mitchell's tears to fall where no one could see them.

The Old Man turned back to Judge Mathis, who was on to his next case. He was trying to pretend as if the chain reaction had not already begun deep within him. It had started from his feet: that cold numbness he'd heard described in his father's final moments on that country road, that final pulse that shut everything down once and for all.

Then he saw himself as a little boy running through a field of tobacco. Then he was stealing that watch from the five-and-dime. Then came his first fuck, his first kiss, and all the other shit he was supposed to see at the end. But the last frames were of his little girl exiting her mother's womb, his seed coming into full bloom.

He knew it wasn't going to be as pretty where he was headed. So he tried to savor as much of it as he could. But it all went by too quickly. The final light dimmed even quicker. Then there was nothing for him to do but breathe his last breath.

My name is *Sasha Salamanca Baker, and I just turned seven on March 7. I've lived in a lot of different places and around a lot of different people. So I never got used to things being the same, or to seeing the same people for that long, particularly when it came to friends at the schools I went to. And my mommy worked a lot, too. So I didn't get to see her as much as I would have wanted.*

But there was one thing my mommy always told me back then. She always said that one day me and her and my daddy were all going to be together. She said that the day was going to come when I would meet him after his long time away and he would tell me how much he loved me and how much he missed me. And I always believed her when she said that. Because my mommy didn't have any reason to lie. And Daddy didn't have any reason not to love me. And I loved both of them soooooooo much, even when I only saw Daddy in pictures and talked to him on the phone.

But that was all before the fifth grade. Because in the fifth grade we bought a house and got two cars and I started going to a new school. And we all had dinner together almost every night. And they took turns tucking me in and reading me bedtime stories. Harry Potter is my favorite. But I read his books by myself.

So now we live in this nice house and everything is good. Grandma and Uncle Henry and Mr. Carl come by for dinner sometimes. And they play games with me and tell me stories about how it was back in the old neighborhood where Mommy and Daddy grew up. And life is really really great.

But today is a really really really special day because Daddy is keeping a promise he made to my uncle Stevie, who lives in California. Today, they are singing the songs they made together at Constitution Hall in downtown. And from what Daddy says, they haven't done that in a long, long time. And Daddy and Uncle Stevie sure can sing better than anyone I've ever heard in the whole wide world. They've done thirteen songs so far tonight. I counted them myself.

And now the audience is clapping and cheering. And Mommy is crying a little bit and putting her hand on her belly, which seems to get bigger almost every day. We're at the back of the stage, and we can see all of the people moving in the crowd. There have to be like millions of them out there, moving and swaying like they're one big animal, or a bunch of those little dominoes that make shapes when they fall down.

Daddy calls me to come out and I run out on the stage and say hi into the microphone and everybody out there makes all these mushy "Awww" noises. And Mommy comes out, too, and Daddy points to her belly, and the crowd claps and makes mushy noises again. And then Daddy kisses Mommy really long with his tongue. And Mommy kisses him back. And then they both kiss me and hold me between them in front of all of those people.

And then Daddy starts to sing again while Uncle Stevie plays the piano. And it feels like a really old dream coming true, a dream so old that it might've been from even before I was born. But it still feels good, to them, to me, and to all of the people out there listening. But those people don't know what I know. They don't know that Daddy's love and his music are the same thing. And that without one they could never ever have the other.

ABOUT THE AUTHOR

Kenji Jasper is a regular
contributor to National Public
Radio and author of the novels
Dark and *Dakota Grand*. His
journalism has appeared in *Essence*,
Vibe, XXL, and on Africana.com.
A native of Washington, D.C., and
a graduate of Morehouse College,
he now lives in Brooklyn, New York.